a novel

Lovers and Spies

Eugenia Lovett West

Published 2026

ISBN: 979-8-218-44695-6

The Main Characters

The Loring Family

Louisa Loring, eighteen years old when the story begins
Eben Loring, Louisa's father, a lawyer
Susannah Loring, Louisa's mother (who died not long before the story begins)
Will Loring, Louisa's young brother
Jessie, the Lorings' servant
Nat Haddam, Eben's legal assistant
Peggy Shippen, Louisa's close friend

The Morris Family

Mary Morris, *Cousin Molly*, Louisa's mother's cousin
Robert Morris, Cousin Molly's husband

Other Important Characters

Captain Andrew Warren, undercover spy in Washington's Intelligence Service
Major Benjamin Tallmadge, Captain Warren's superior officer in Washington's Intelligence Service
Sarah Colborne, undercover spy in Washington's Intelligence Service, heiress of her aunt Mrs. Sage
Josiah Cox, the apothecary
Finder, British spy

PART ONE

★★★

CHAPTER ONE

July 16, 1778 *Philadelphia*

The once beautiful city lay in ruins. Nearly a month ago, the British army decamped to New York leaving Philadelphia in a state of utter devastation. Fine old trees in the squares felled for firewood. Buildings along the wide streets vandalized, some burned to the ground. In the searing heat of a July afternoon, the stench of refuse and rotting bodies was poisoning the air.

The three people in a hired chaise stared out in mounting horror. As they jolted and bounced over broken cobblestones, Louisa Loring held a handkerchief over her little brother's face. "The smell—so bad. Try not to breathe through your nose."

Her father's hands tightened on the reins. His mouth was set in a hard line. "Scoundrels, ruffians," Eben Loring said through gritted teeth. "The last of the British soldiers must have done this as they left."

Five-year-old Will pushed away the handkerchief. "Our house—" he gulped. "We're back, and we have no house."

Louisa put an arm around his shoulders. "Wait. It may still be there," she said, trying to keep her voice steady.

The thin horse wheezed heavily as they reached Market Street. The shops here had been spared, though most were closed and shuttered. The Court House remained, as did the Indian King Tavern on the corner of

Third Street. Mangy dogs hunted for scraps in gutters. A few shabbily dressed people were out on the once-crowded walkways, those that had stayed through the occupation.

As the chaise turned onto Fourth Street, Louisa shut her eyes. Lately she had neglected her prayers—so much hard work and so little time while they were away in exile—but a merciful God may have forgiven her and spared their home.

The horse slowed and started down the hill. She opened her eyes and let out her breath. God *was* merciful. The large brick house, set well back from the street, was still standing. The panes in the tall windows were shattered, the fan light over the front door was broken, glass littered the steps, but the walls and roof were in place.

The three sat motionless, then her father spoke, "Damaged, but it may be habitable." He got out, tied the horse to a hitching post, then turned and took Will's hand. "Come along, son."

Will shrank back and shook his head. After six long days on the stage from Massachusetts, he was tired and dirty, near collapse. Afraid of what he might see inside.

"Sit here and talk to the horse. He'll like that," Louisa said, then jumped out and followed her father to the front door. It was broken, but at last it creaked open and they stepped over shards of glass. The stifling air in the hall was thick with dust and smelled of rotting food. The wood floor, once bright with polish, was scarred and muddy.

She ran to the front parlor. The upholstery on the two sofas had been slashed into ragged strips. The blue brocade curtains lay crumpled in piles. She stood still, struggling with a piercing surge of grief. She could picture her mother, who had died so recently, sitting at the harpsichord, graceful and smiling as they sang their favorite songs.

A rat emerged from a heap of torn curtains and looked at her with daring little eyes. "No. Oh no," she whispered and ran back to the hall. Her father was coming from the rear of the house.

"Filthy. Unlivable. Everything must be cleaned or replaced." He rubbed his forehead. "Thank God your mother was spared this."

"Thank God," she repeated, echoing their shared anguish over the loss of lovely Susannah. "Filth, rats—it *is* unlivable—but where can we go?"

"Back to the inn where we hired the chaise. It will cost dearly but we have no choice."

"No choice?" She stared at him with mounting dismay. The inn was crowded with other people just off the stage.

"Please, Father, not that noisy inn. Will needs good food and a quiet place to sleep. There *must* be a better way. We have friends—neighbors—what about the Morrises? Cousin Molly is kind and she loved Mamma. They were very close. She'd take us in, I'm sure she would, and it would be so much better for Will."

He was silent, a thin, tired man who had endured so much. After a moment he spoke. "Very well. For Will's sake, we'll go to the Morrises though it may cause serious trouble for me."

Louisa swallowed. The dust was making it hard to breathe. "Trouble? For you?"

He coughed, then cleared his throat. "Louisa, you've proved that at seventeen—no, eighteen—you are intelligent and capable. You worked your fingers to the bone in Braintree. Cared for your mother and Will. I should have warned you that here we are facing new difficulties. Ones that could become dangerous."

"Dangerous? Why? There's no fighting here."

"No, but I'm told the city is deeply divided between loyalists and patriots, that the radicals on both sides are taking extreme measures and spies are everywhere. War provokes violence. Men wrongly accused of treason are being tried and hung."

Treason. Men tried and hung. Grim words, but her father was a cautious lawyer, not given to exaggeration. "That's hard," she said, "but I still don't see why going to the Morrises means trouble for you."

Her father coughed again—the smell was overwhelming. He touched his throat. "Louisa, you must try to understand, I'm known as a patriot, but your mother and her cousin Mary Morris belong to an important loyalist family. Mary's husband Robert Morris made a fortune in shipping. He's one of the richest men in the colonies. I don't know his views, but when I try to start another practice and earn a living, I must be seen as a lawyer who takes no sides in politics That means I must not become beholden to Robert Morris in any way—"

"Lulu, *Lulu,* where are you?" A high-pitched wail from the street.

"I must go," she said, then picked up her skirt and hurried to the chaise. Climbed in and put her arms around him. "It's all right, it's all right," she said, holding him close. "We're going to spend the night at the Morrises. You remember them. You used to play with Robby and the dogs."

"Robby, dogs," he choked and stopped crying,

She rocked him, aware of her promise to their dying mother. The Lorings had escaped to a derelict farm in Braintree, but the harsh northern winter had been too much for delicate Susannah. A slight chill had turned into an inflammation of the lungs. As she lay consumed by fever, she had taken Louisa's hand. "My beautiful shy daughter … it will be hard for you, very hard … but you must take my place … look after your father and little Will."

"I promise, Mamma," she had whispered.

Now, as she rocked her little brother, the troubles that lay ahead loomed. An unlivable house. A wrecked city. The danger to those who were called traitors—a terrifying situation—-but at this moment there was one overriding worry. She must hope and pray that the rich Morrises would give refuge to the sad and needy Loring family.

★ ★ ★

CHAPTER TWO

July 16, 1778 *The same day*

The Morris estate, known as The Hills, was five miles away from the city. The brick and marble house was large, and there were barns, outbuildings, and greenhouses. Extensive grounds had been planted in the finest English style with meandering walks, vistas, and a little pond. Visiting foreign dignitaries could see that elegance had arrived in this part of the colonies.

As the chaise drew up to the front door, a black servant came out to hold the horse. A small boy skipped around the corner, bouncing a ball, then dashed into the house calling "Mamma. Mamma, you have visitors."

A minute later, Mary Morris, known as Molly, appeared. She looked at the shabby chaise, shaded her eyes, then hurried forward. "Can it be—mercy on us, it is—it *is* the Lorings."

Louisa jumped down and ran to meet her. "Cousin Molly—we've been on the stage from Massachusetts for days … we're dirty … soldiers … the house is filthy … we can't stay there, so we came … we came …"

"My dear child." Molly Morris's arms went around her, holding her close. "You're back and you're safe. That's all that matters." She turned. "Eben, you are very welcome. Come in out of the heat. Hero will take care of the horse and bring your trunks." She paused. "First, cool drinks, and after days on the road no doubt you'll want to wash and feel clean again."

In moments, the household was galvanized into action. Louisa and Will followed Cousin Molly to a large bedchamber where maids were setting out tin tubs, pitchers of warm water, and towels.

Will was stumbling, clinging tightly to her skirt. "He's very tired," Louisa said. "I'll wash him before he falls asleep. It was so noisy at the inns. None of us had much rest."

"Poor little one. I'll keep the other children away, but Robby will be so pleased to see him again." She looked at the watch fastened by a ribbon to her waist. "It's three o'clock. There are no other guests and while it's so hot we don't dine until four. After your bath, if you want to come down, you'll find me on the front porch. Delsey is very good with children. She would stay with Will and fetch you if he wakes and wants you."

It was like stepping into another world. Louisa swallowed. She had hoped for kindness, but had not expected such a warm welcome.

Quickly, she checked Will's hair for lice and washed his little body. "Nice Delsey will look after you while I have my bath," she told him. Smiling young Delsey appeared. "You the handsomest boy," she crooned. "You come with me while your mumma washes. Come, and I give you milk and a slice of sweet cake." She held out her hand. He took it and allowed her to take him to the adjoining room.

As Louisa shed her clothes, she looked around feeling dazed. Ten days ago she had slept in a large cupboard. Hung her clothes on pegs. Here there was a dressing table with a tilted mirror. The china on the washstand was painted with pink roses. She had never been aware of the Morrises' great wealth. This was just a place to go to with her mother for tea, sometimes unwillingly. Lying back in the water, the deep feeling of relief was almost overwhelming. Now, for a short time, she would be safe with Cousin Molly.

After a while the water grew cool. She sat up and scrubbed until her skin was raw. Her thick dark hair was wet, but it would soon dry in this heat. The clothes in the hide trunk were crumpled, her best calico dress was faded and outgrown, but she buttoned it over a clean petticoat and went to check on Will. He was fast asleep on the big bed with a small brown and white spaniel curled up beside him.

Delsey was sitting on a chair nearby, humming and fanning herself. "He ate his cake and milk," she whispered. "I'll not leave him, not for a moment."

"Thank you, Delsey. If he wants me, I'll be on the porch with Mrs. Morris," she said softly and tiptoed out.

The wide staircase led down to a vast hall that extended from the front door to the sweep of lawns at the back. The long porch on one side of the house had a fine view of the river and the big harbor crowded with ships.

Cousin Molly was sitting at one end holding a tambour with embroidery. A tall woman with sharp features, she was not beautiful but she had presence and was a leading figure in Philadelphia society while capably managing a large household.

She saw Louisa and waved. "There you are, looking very clean and fresh," she said. "Come and sit down. How is little Will?"

"Asleep. Delsey is with him." She sat down and smoothed her skirt. "I'm trying to remember your children's names. First Thomas, then William, Hetty and Robby."

"And now there's Charles. He's nearly a year old." She put the tambour down. "My dear, we need to talk. There's so much I want to know. We left the city before you and I didn't find out about Susannah until we got back. I was undone. She was my favorite cousin. What happened? Start at the beginning. Did you have to leave Philadelphia in a hurry?"

Louisa took a deep breath. "A great hurry, with only a few clothes. Just as the British were about to march into the city, my father was warned that he might be arrested because his cousins, John and Samuel Adams, are big names in the cause for independence. Mistress Abigail, John Adams's wife, found us a small farm near Braintree. The old lady who lived there had died and left a few furnishings. Four rooms with tiny little windows."

"Not very nice. What about neighbors? People who could help?"

"No close neighbors. It was nothing like life here. People were—well, not as friendly. The loyalists there were forced to leave."

Cousin Molly sighed. "War causes such losses. Such divisions among families. I know of several where fathers and sons have fallen out over politics and don't speak. It's causing much anguish. But who helped you with the work?"

"No one. Instead of practicing law, my father chopped wood to keep the fires going. It was cold. That's what Mamma minded most. She went out one day to collect eggs from the chickens and caught a chill. It turned into an inflammation in her lungs. We—a doctor came—Mistress Adams came—we did all we could. She was buried in the Adams graveyard." She swallowed and stopped. It still hurt to talk about Mamma.

Cousin Molly sighed again. "Terrible for you. Terrible. Susannah had such charm but she was never strong. And to be far away in a strange place—that must have made it even harder."

"Yes. I … I think my father blames himself. Mamma was the glue that held us together. She played games. She could make my father laugh. He tries not to show it, but he misses her dreadfully."

"Poor man. So intelligent, but he needed her

gaiety to temper his seriousness. I remember when he arrived in Philadelphia to present a legal case. How he married Susannah and stayed. You were born, and there was excitement when Will came along. How has this loss affected him?"

"Badly. He used to be so bouncy. Now he has spells of crying and asking for Mamma. I tell him she's in heaven with the angels, but he wants her *here.* I promised Mamma to look after him and I have—I will—but to come back and find the house in such a state—"

"My dear child." Molly reached out and touched Louisa's hand. "You've had to carry a heavy burden, far too heavy, but take heart. We'll have a little service in Christ Church for Susannah. I'll order the mourning rings. And don't fret about the house. When you're rested, we'll go with servants and see what needs to be done. The children will love having Will here, and Delsey can be trusted to look after him. Of course you'll stay with us until the house is habitable."

Louisa bent her head, not sure what to say. To stay here—a way to clean the house—the offer was an answer to prayer, but it might not be acceptable to her father. "Cousin Molly," she began. "You are so kind, so very kind, but I'm afraid—that is, we mustn't impose—"

"Nonsense. We're related, and I loved your mother." She gave Louisa an assessing look. "Gracious me, you've grown several inches and you're turning into a beauty like Susannah. You have her bright blue eyes and that lovely dark hair. Taller, but just as slim. Your friends will be glad to see you."

Louisa shook her head. "I was always very shy but I had two good friends, Abigail Chester and Sally Toland. We did everything together until their families had to leave for New York with the British."

"Well, I'm sure you will make new ones."

The sunlight had moved to the end of the porch. Birds were calling from the maple trees, exchanging news in a chorus of chirps and warbles. For a moment both were silent, then Cousin Molly looked at her watch. "It's getting on and I must see if my husband is back from town. We'll gather in the drawing room at four, then dine."

"I'll go up and unpack, not that there's much," Louisa said and stood up.

"You'll need new clothes—I'll see to that. No, don't shake your head. You deserve them after all you've been through, and no more talk about imposing. It's what your mother would want, and finding ways to help will give me great pleasure.

★★★

CHAPTER THREE

July 16, 1778 *Later that day*

Promptly at four, Louisa left her room and went down to the large drawing room. But as she reached the door she hesitated, fighting a wave of shyness. The sudden arrival of his wife's needy relatives might not please successful Robert Morris. She could only hope that Cousin Molly had paved their way.

For a moment she stood still, noticing changes. The sofas, upholstered in elegant crimson brocade, had been moved and there was a new turkey carpet in front of the marble fireplace. Taking notice of details was a habit that began when she was small and needed to amuse herself during long sermons in Christ Church. Her mother used to tease her. "What color hat was Mrs. Cadwalader wearing today?" Louisa was still apt to say little until she had observed.

Cousin Molly glanced around and saw her standing there. "Louisa. Come in," she called. No retreat. She took a deep breath and walked forward.

Robert Morris was a large man with an open ruddy face, a genial host who loved company. His fleet of trading ships sailed the oceans, but nothing in his manner or dress indicated his importance and wealth.

She needn't have worried about their reception. He came forward and took her hand. "Welcome, young lady. Delighted you've come to us. We'll do all we can to make you comfortable."

"Indeed we will," his wife said. "Now let's go in and eat." She took his arm. Cousin Molly was considerably younger than her husband but Louisa had the sense that this relationship was unusually close.

In the high-ceilinged dining room, French wallpaper depicted bucolic scenes by a river. Robert Morris took his place at the head of the table and began to carve a chicken. Two servants in white gloves placed platters of vegetables on the starched white cloth. Louisa blinked. After months of scanty food, the lavish display was startling.

"It must have been a shock to find the city so desecrated," Cousin Molly said to Eben Loring, now washed and wearing his best coat. "As for that terrible smell—the redcoats dug a large pit by the State House. They threw in dead horses and relieved themselves on the State House floor. As soon as he arrived, General Benedict Arnold, our new military governor, ordered his troops to start cleaning, but people became ill. Even Dr. Rush had a fever. That's why we keep the children up here."

Eben frowned. "General Arnold. How was he received?"

"Oh, very well. He arrived from Valley Forge in a fine coach with a band playing, bells ringing, and crowds cheering. He's taken over the Penn house on Market Street where the British generals had their headquarters. Now everyone is waiting to see how he will govern."

"Is that a concern?"

Robert Morris laid down his fork. "I was told on good authority that General Washington made this an interim appointment. He values Arnold highly and wants to give his wounded leg a chance to heal before returning him to the field." He paused. "The man displayed courage at Valcour Island and at the battle of Saratoga, but to maintain order in Philadelphia he will have to show a different kind of leadership. Time will tell if Washington has made a wise decision."

His wife rolled her eyes. "Well, I pray that Arnold will succeed and there will be no fighting here. Believe me, we are tired of rushing away in fear of our lives."

Eben took a sip of wine. "If I remember, you left long before we did. You must have had a reason."

"We did," Robert said. "After we lost the battle at the Brandywine, it was likely that the British would take the city. My wife and the children—little Thomas had a boil on his leg—were loaded into a caravan of wagons and eventually ended up in our place near Mannheim."

Molly laughed. "That place—it's like something out of a Gothic novel. Baron Stiegel, a German, made a fortune in an iron works. Before losing it, he built a mansion. He called it The Castle and filled it with tapestries. There's even a chapel. God forbid we have to live there again, but we keep it open just in case. The future is still so uncertain."

Two main courses were followed by a whipped syllabub, tarts, and jellies. Cousin Molly turned to Louisa's father. "Once you're settled, Eben, do you plan to practice law again?"

"I do, though it may be hard to start over."

Robert Morris nodded. "I'm afraid you're right. I should warn you, the situation here grows worse by the day. Food is scarce and prices are rising. The delegates to Congress are squabbling and trying to keep the power in their own colonies." He paused. "By the by, there's an empty space in one of my Front Street buildings. Small, but suitable for an office if you care to take it."

Louisa held her breath, but her father's answer was civil enough, "A kind offer, sir, but I need to look around." He took another sip of wine. "If I may ask, how is the war affecting your business?"

"Now that the river is open for commerce, my ships can sail again. There'll be losses to privateers and the British and, of course, storms, but that's to be expeced. No, the real danger to me comes from the deep political divisions in the city, the fighting between patriots and loyalists. I'm not a confirmed loyalist, but certain radical patriots would like to ruin me. On the other hand, they know that when Washington was short of gun powder, my ships went to foreign ports to trade goods for weapons. I also provided financial assistance. For the moment, I'm not their target but that could change at any time."

"In what way, sir?"

"The fact is, we are facing serious internal violence. Established structures of law and order have not been replaced. The city is full of double agents. Infiltrators. Clever spies, and both political sides are using scurrilous methods to get the advantage, stopping at nothing. Innocent blood will be shed. Frankly, it's hard to know who among our friends can be trusted."

Eben frowned. "Grim words, sir. What do you consider the greatest threat?"

"The greatest threat? There are so many." The ruddy color in his face darkened. "We fought well at Monmouth but it ended in a draw and our troops are greatly outnumbered, The French need more proof that we are capable of winning a battle before making a larger commitment. Money is needed to pay the military and our currency is rapidly losing value." He hit the table with his fist. "I tell you, the next few months will be crucial. Let's not delude ourselves. We are in grave danger of losing the war and any hope of independence."

For a moment no one spoke. Then Molly raised her hand. "Have we quite finished eating? Robert, perhaps Eben would like a glass of port. Louisa and I will retire to the porch for a breath of fresh air but we need a thunderstorm, not just a faint breeze that only teases."

Her husband straightened. The color in his face subsided. "Quite right. My apologies, ladies." He turned to Louisa's father. "It's still very warm. Will you have a glass of port? Or would you prefer to stroll down to the pond? I want to check on the greenhouses. A considerable amount of damage was done and we're in the process of rebuilding."

"I'd prefer a stroll, sir."

"An excellent idea," Molly said. She rose from the table. Louisa followed slowly. As they reached the porch, Molly looked at her. "Louisa, I'm afraid the talk of war has upset you. My husband is deeply worried, he feels his responsibilities keenly, but he seldom expresses his views in public."

Louisa hesitated. "I—I'm not upset. It's just that having been away in exile so long—I feel so utterly *unprepared*."

Cousin Molly went to the railing. She stared out at the large warship that was moving toward the middle of the harbor. Then she turned.

"My dear, I wasn't prepared for war, but it happened. Bad things happen. We can't see ahead—and maybe that's just as well. As for the future, I can only say this. You and I—we must try to live one day at a time—and we must never, *ever* give up hope."

★★★

CHAPTER FOUR

July 17, 1778 *Yorktown, New Jersey*

The reduced Continental Army had left the town of Monmouth, the site of the major battle, and was marching slowly north. Today it was in Yorktown, New Jersey, camped near the home of patriot Samuel Delevan. The vast fields were lined with canvas tents.

At three o'clock, Captain Andrew Warren stood in the small hall at Washington's temporary headquarters. He was waiting to meet with his superior, Major Benjamin Tallmadge, the head of Washington's intelligence service. Before being given new orders, he must convince Tallmadge that he had served his time living an undercover life as a spy. Make him see that he was determined to be back with his former regiment, the Massachusetts First.

As he waited, he summed up what he knew about Tallmadge. A Yale graduate, in 1776 Tallmadge had enlisted in Connecticut's Second Regiment of Light Dragoons. He took part in the battle for New York and later joined Washington in Valley Forge. His energy and abilities were outstanding, and Washington soon promoted him to the rank of major with a key position on his staff.

Andrew Warren's transfer to intelligence had come after the battle at the Brandywine River was lost due to lack of advance information about the fateful early morning surprise attack. With no previous training, he was recruited because of his looks. Average height, dark hair, gray eyes, no remarkable features. Last winter he had prowled around Philadelphia disguised as a woman or a peddler or a waiter. He had established a network of patriots to pass him information; he collected it during the night, and at dawn snatched a few hours of sleep in a damp cellar.

Now, at last, he had a chance to change that sordid life. He waited, tamping down mounting impatience. The Delevan house seemed inadequate for the number of aides coming and going, and a strong smell of cooking wafted from the kitchen. Finally a door opened and Tallmadge appeared, a tall, well-built man in his mid-twenties, with courtly manners and a keen, decisive mind.

"My apologies for the wait, Captain," he said, then led the way to a front parlor with a view of the narrow dirt road. "Take a seat. We have a lot of ground to cover. To start, Washington has new orders for you. Last winter you did valuable work in Philadelphia and he wants you to repeat the performance in New York."

Andrew took a deep breath. He must stand firm, not give an inch. "With respect, Major, I joined the army to fight, not be a spy. I want to rejoin my old regiment. Take part in the next battle when it comes."

"I see." Tallmadge got up and went to the window, stood there for a moment, then turned. "I respect your feelings. Like you, I prefer to be fighting, but to defeat the enemy we must expand our intelligence. Washington learned its value during the French and Indian Wars. Now he's using invisible inks, code names and numbers, and writing reports designed to spread misinformation. Your work is essential to this effort."

Andrew shook his head. "Not essential. There's nothing in New York that can't be done by someone better qualified."

Tallmadge came back to his chair, sat down, and

looked at him. "Captain Warren, understand this. The work you do is difficult. Few can do it, that's why Washington wants you in New York. It's likely that General Sir Henry Clinton will try to gain possession of the Hudson River, and we need your boots on the ground there. It's crucial to know in advance what Clinton is planning. Outwit and stop him."

Andrew was silent. The hope of returning to his regiment was fading fast.

Tallmadge cleared his throat. "Another concern—one that involves you—is the need to prevent more plots against Washington. The old saying that no one is indispensable doesn't apply to him. He has made mistakes, but no one else has his ability to observe, learn the facts, then take action. Assassination is a constant threat—as you well know."

"But if I'm in New York—"

"You played a part in the Valley Forge incident. At Monmouth you uncovered the double agent, ex-Captain Jamieson, who came close to killing Washington. You found out that Jamieson ordered his rogue servant to murder British Captain Colborne during the battle. As I understand it, that was for a personal reason, but Jamieson and that servant are still at large, a constant threat. They may be hiding in or near New York. To find them is another priority."

Again, Andrew was silent.

Tallmadge straightened. He gave Andrew a wry smile. "I realize this comes as a blow, but good intelligence remains our best weapon. And theirs. No doubt there are British spies in Philadelphia sending information back to headquarters in New York. We must do better."

Andrew clamped his lips together. This was a bitter pill to swallow, but further argument was useless—and his feelings were of no account in a war. The General must be protected and orders were orders, especially when they came from the commander-in-chief. He would have to obey them or resign.

"About New York," he said curtly. "Is there a plan in place?"

"Developing. We have contacts in the city and an expanding network to watch activities on Long Island. Locate the British outposts and see who is manning them."

"How does this network operate?"

"Trusted men go back and forth to the city. Some are farmers selling produce, some have business interests. Your main task will be to infiltrate Clinton's headquarters—" he stopped as the door opened and an orderly looked in. "Your meeting with the General, Major."

Tallmadge got to his feet. "Duty calls. Warren, your willingness to serve as before is noted and appreciated. Come back in an hour and we'll work out more details," he said and left.

Slowly, Andrew stood up and went to the window. Once again he was sentenced to live in such secrecy that even his family had no idea where he was.

"Bloody hell," he muttered. The army was a great leveler. Few knew his family was one of the oldest and richest in Boston, or that his father was a confirmed loyalist. Growing up, he was a spoiled only son, living in utmost comfort, adored by his parents and two sisters. Women chased after him, and many nights were spent drinking and playing daring pranks with his friends.

In June of 1775, he was a student at Harvard College, skimming through philosophy, logic, and history classes. The brilliant patriot Joseph Warren saw promise in his young cousin and became his mentor, encouraging him to apply himself to his studies. The relationship ended when, at the battle of Breed's Hill, Cousin Joseph died fighting with a bayonet so that others could escape. The next day Andrew joined the Massachusetts First. He had expected to fight, not live like an underground animal, but Tallmadge had delivered the bad news with exceptional kindness.

There was time to have a closer look at the camp before another session with Tallmadge. Turning away from the window, he picked up his hat and went out. As he neared the hundreds of tents, a bugle sounded. Smoke rose from fires where food was being cooked. Many layers of organization were needed to look after troops who would soon be marching again. From General Washington down to the lowliest foot soldier, every man had a duty to perform.

A private going toward headquarters saluted and passed by. He returned the salute and kept walking. No doubt Washington's generals would present him with proposals, but history showed that too often plans were only as good as the paper on which they were written. Events took on a life of their own. One adjutant might bring news of the enemy's position. Another would arrive with a different story.

Squaring his shoulders, he went on, a small cog in this large wheel. The stakes were high. His yet unknown enemies lurked in the shadows, infiltrating silently, aiming to kill. To survive, he had no choice but to sharpen his wits. Go forward with the part he had been ordered to play.

The same day New York City

The big harbor was filled with British warships and big victuallers bringing food for troops recently arrived after a long march from Monmouth. General Sir Henry Clinton, commander of the British forces, had established himself at Number One Broadway, an impressive mansion built with an eye to the Grecian style.

It was late in the afternoon when a young man left a meeting at Clinton's headquarters. His height was slightly less than average, his hair was light brown, his eyes hazel, his features even. Not handsome, but highly presentable. He walked slowly toward the Grand Battery, deep in thought.

The orders he had just received were life changing. Clinton had been persuaded to re-establish espionage operations in Philadelphia with a new set of double agents. Therefore, wasting no time, this young man was to move to Philadelphia. Infiltrate Congress and obtain military plans. Find those who were vulnerable to blackmail. Spread misinformation. Cause deep divisions. Discover who could be lured from the cause of independence and turned into a traitor. From now on the code name *Finder* would be used for all communications.

The mission held promise, but making money was his top priority. He had accepted the position after negotiations ensuring that he would be paid well in gold, with a substantial reward if successful. In the past, he had seen how the rich lived, and he was determined to move into that world. Establish himself as an equal and sit at their tables.

There were reasons for this obsession. His life had begun in the back streets of Bristol, England. His indigent father was dead, his mother had been a maid in the house of a wealthy trader who saw that the boy was intelligent and apprenticed him to an accountant in London. Ten years ago he had sailed for New York, hoping to make a fortune in the colonies. Former British governor William Tryon had hired him to do accounting, but the job soon involved more than working with numbers. He became adept at handling Tryon's extended espionage. In fact, it was high praise from Tryon to Clinton that had landed him this assignment.

As he passed the Grand Battery, he considered his next step. Once in Philadelphia, he must find work with a highly placed official. Being invited to social events was key, and luckily he had developed engaging manners and was a good dancer. Easy enough to mix with the colonial elite while gathering information and spreading scurrilous lies.

But there was one complication. Last winter a strong patriot network had inflicted serious harm on British occupation forces. In retaliation, and to prevent further damage, he was to find and exterminate the entire group.

He had voiced concern, saying that this was not his area of expertise, but his objection was overruled. Instead, he was given a letter of introduction to a bookseller named Strant, a man with extensive contacts on both sides. For a price, Strant would, no doubt, be able to find him hirelings to do the dirty work. He'd had to comply, but until now he had always managed to separate himself from actual killing and violence. Still, there might not be many victims in this network—and the process of extermination might not take long.

The sun had moved to the west, and a chilly breeze was whipping up the waves in the harbor. Thrusting his hands into his pockets, he turned toward his favorite tavern on Vesey Street. To celebrate, he would treat himself to a bottle of good wine and a platter of roasted beef. A new game was about to begin, one that he was well able to play—and to win.

★★★

CHAPTER FIVE

July 17, 1778 *Philadelphia*

The debilitating heat wave continued, and early morning dew on the grass was no substitute for a long soaking rain. At noon, the day after the Lorings arrival, Louisa and Cousin Molly and two servants from The Hills set out for the house on Fourth Street, prepared to begin the heavy work of making the house habitable.

Eben Loring followed in the hired chaise. To Louisa's great relief, he had decided that since Robert Morris was not involved, he would not object to Cousin Molly's help, not when there was no reasonable alternative. He would return the horse and chaise to Mr. Beale's inn, then begin the search for office space.

A thorough inspection of the house showed that the main damage was in the kitchen and scullery areas. Windows were opened to let out the dust and the smell. Cubba began to sweep glass from the front steps. Her daughter, Mercy, went to scrub down the privy in the back yard.

"It's lucky we brought the big carriage," Cousin Molly said to Louisa. "I should go and try to replace those filthy pots and pans. As for the front rooms, they'll need new draperies and upholstery. General Arnold closed shops so merchants could make an inventory of goods, but Plunkett Fleeson is advertising materials. Will you stay or come with me?"

"I think I should stay and keep working." She hesitated. "Whatever it costs, my father will pay."

"Don't worry. I'll keep a list."

As the carriage rolled away, Louisa took a deep breath and went into the dining room. Everywhere she looked, there were reminders of Mamma. Broken cups in her favorite tea set. The chair seat covers she had made with such skill ripped into pieces. It was as if the house had been wounded and was begging for help. The wanton destruction was hard enough to bear, but there was another task that must be faced before her father returned. One that would require every ounce of courage.

She was wiping down the long table when Cubba put her head around the door. "Missie Shippen, she here to see you."

Louisa dropped the cloth. "Oh, *no.* At the door?"

"She in the hall and she bringing flowers."

Louisa put a hand to her forehead. "Tell her I can't—no, wait, I'll have to come." Seeing Peggy Shippen again was the last thing she needed, but the Shippens lived next door. Although he was formerly a judge in the vice-admiralty court, cautious Edward Shippen had played it safe and taken his family away before the British arrived.

With a wrench, she pulled off the apron that covered a shabby homespun dress. As small children, she and Peggy played together, but soon had different sets of friends, different sewing and dancing classes. In the past, Peggy had always made her feel shy and insignificant. She most certainly did *not* want to see her now.

Peggy was standing in the hall, holding a bunch of flowers in one hand and a pot of jam in the other. She was a classic beauty, a small, fine-boned girl with large gray eyes and a mass of fair hair that curled naturally, the envy of her friends. Her pale blue muslin dress had a lace frill around the neck and she was wearing a fashionable skimmer hat.

"I've brought roses from our garden and home-made jam," she said, "And I was very sorry to hear about your mother. She was so pretty and she always had a kind word for me."

"I—thank you." She hesitated. "This house—so filthy—we're just starting to clean it."

"Well, at least you're back from exile and so are we." Peggy tossed her long curls. "Such a misery. First it was a farm in Amwell, that's in Jersey, then a relative's place on the Schuykill River. Just as dull and dreary. My father is a frightful worrier, but when he heard the British and the loyalists had become friends he decided it was safe to come back. Thank goodness, because you wouldn't believe the fun we had here last winter."

Louisa stared. "Fun? You had fun with the *British*?"

"Their general, Sir William Howe, liked to entertain and his officers knew precisely how to enjoy winter quarters. A dashing lot, some of them had titles. There were balls every Thursday night at the City Tavern. Musicales, theatricals, skating on the river. One of them, Captain Andre, had a name for our set. He called us The Little Society of Third Street. We were all in tears when they left—" she stopped as Mercy appeared, twisting her apron.

"What is it, Mercy?" Louisa asked.

"There's rats in the scullery, missie. Big ones."

"I'll come," she said, wanting to hear no more about entertainments with dashing British officers. Reaching out, she took the flowers and the strawberry jam. "Will's favorite. Please thank your mother for me."

"She said to ask for anything you need. She'll come to call soon." Peggy glanced around. "The officers billeted here were nice enough. It was their batmen and grooms that did this as they left. Went rampaging through the city." She paused. "I saw Mrs. Morris's big carriage. Are you staying with her?"

"For a few days. At The Hills."

"The Hills? I've never been there but I hear it's very grand. You're lucky to have her for a cousin."

"Yes, I am."

"Very lucky. Well, I mustn't keep you from the rats in the scullery. Don't work yourself to the bone." With a wave, she turned and walked lightly to the door. Louisa could guess what she was feeling. Duty carried out, flowers and jam delivered. Peggy would never choose to befriend a girl wearing homespun, but a cousin of the Morrises couldn't be entirely ignored.

Louisa watched her go with mixed feelings. By now she knew that there were several sides to volatile Peggy, a girl who liked to dance, but also to study articles in the *Pennsylvania Gazette* and talk politics. There were three older sisters and a feckless brother, but Peggy was clearly the judge's favorite child. She was clever and well-read, but when crossed she would fly into hysterics and take to her bed for days. A creature of many moods.

The house was growing hot and her father would soon be back. She put the flowers and jam on the floor, summoned up courage, then ran up the stairs.

The front bedchamber was large, with a four-poster bed hung with crewel curtains. Tall windows looked out on the street. Aside from a soiled mattress, little damage had been done here. But last September, as they rushed to leave, her mother's finest clothes had been locked into a small storage space behind the chimney.

It took a moment to find the key and open the door. Silk dresses, hats, and dainty petticoats lay crushed together, untouched. She let out her breath and picked up a buckled slipper. The clothes, the scent—she could see her mother twirling in front of the mirror, hear her mother's voice: "One day you'll be wearing shoes like this. Just now you're my shy little duckling, but you're going to be a beauty, my love. Quiet and intelligent like your father, not a flighty chatterbox like me."

"Oh, Mamma. Where are you? We need you so

much." She dropped the slipper and buried her face in a blue silk dress. For months, she had done her best to control her grief. The consuming pain of loss. Now a wave of uncontrollable anger came surging up.

"Why? Why?" she choked, "We were so happy before the war, so very happy." Furiously, she tore at the thin silk, ripping it with her fingers. "You didn't have to die, Mamma … it was those patriots in Boston who started this war … all they cared about was getting their independence … nothing else … it didn't matter to them how many would suffer …"

She dropped the dress and began to beat the wall with her fists. "I hate this war," she gritted. "I hate those patriots. I hate independence. I hate it, hate it, *hate* it—and I always will."

Eben Loring stood on the corner of Walnut Street experiencing acute annoyance. After returning the horse and chaise, he had set out to find a cheap room where he could start his law practice and earn a living. He did not appreciate being approached by a stranger, a small fellow wearing a plain brown coat and hat who was asking him to join a patriotic network of informers. It was time to put an end to this unwelcome encounter.

"I don't know you," he said firmly. "What's more, I have no interest whatsoever in what you propose." He turned and began to walk away.

The man fell into step beside him. "Hear me out, sir. You recently returned from exile in Braintree. Your kinsman Sam Adams is a delegate to Congress from Massachusetts. You are close to John Adams, though he's away on a diplomatic mission in France. Therefore you have strong ties to the Sons of Liberty."

Eben drew in his breath. The man knew too much about him. "No," he said sharply. "I have no intention of involving myself with you," and he walked on.

The man kept pace. "Sir, this is no crackpot scheme. The British and wealthy loyalists here are financing double agents, spies, and informers. Patriots must join together and expose them or we may lose the war."

Eben frowned. Along with grim predictions about the war, Robert Morris had warned him about spies and undercover agents. He did not expect to meet one openly on Walnut Street.

"I have business to attend to," he snapped. "If you're asking me to become a spy you're wasting my time—and yours."

"Informer, not spy, sir, and you are in a unique position to provide information. You have ties to leading patriots. Your late wife came from the loyalist faction. You know these people. You have a foot in both camps and that makes you a valuable asset."

A band of ragged soldiers led by a drummer boy marched by, giving him a chance to collect himself. As the noise abated, he took a deep breath. "You've made it your business to investigate me. I know nothing about you. I bid you good day." Again, he began to walk away. And once again the man followed.

"I appreciate your caution, sir," he said in a low voice. "Here are the facts. I taught mathematics at a school here. My younger brother was killed in the Paoli massacre along with many others who gave their lives for freedom. Since then, my mission in life has been to work for a great cause, the chance for independence."

By now they had passed Fifth Street and were reaching the dignified State House, an enduring symbol in the midst of devastation. The putrid smell of dead animals dumped into the cellar lingered, but a number of men were at work on the torn grounds. With a fierce outpouring of determination, the city was being restored.

The small man coughed and spoke again. "This building still stands but it could be destroyed and the delegates who come here hung for treason." He paused. "Ask yourself this, Mr. Loring. What future do you want? Freedom from tyranny or one ruled by officials in London?"

Eben hesitated. He had no wish to prolong the encounter, but this dedicated man deserved the courtesy of an answer. He drew himself up. "Sir, I respect your work for the cause of independence, but I'm here to practice law. It would be against my principles to play one side against the other or to make use of my connections."

The man shook his head. "Fine words, sir, but I believe that before long you will see reason and join us. All I ask is that you keep your ears open. When you hear anything of interest, place the message in the hollow of the hitching post in front of Carpenter's Hall. A courier will pick the message up and takes it to General Washington's headquarters. If you do this after dark, there's little risk. We use code names. Mine is *Teacher*. Yours, for instance, would be *Legal*."

Eben stiffened. A new recruit with the code name Legal. From past experience, he knew that given the slightest encouragement, this type of zealot was apt to leap to conclusions, often the wrong ones. The small man seemed determined to bring in more recruits—and given an inch would take a mile. This must be stopped at once. He turned and looked him in the eye.

"Sir, I listened to your case and I gave you a civil answer. Understand this. I made no commitment. None whatsoever. Never try to contact me again." He turned on his heel and marched toward George Street. The man didn't follow.

The sun was hot. He lifted his wide-brimmed hat and wiped sweat from his face. He had resolved to be free of politics, to walk a fine line of disengagement, but he was born in New England with patriot roots. His cousin, John Adams, had supported him after his parents died of smallpox. Paid his tuition at Harvard College and taught him law. John Adams was owed.

At the corner of Market Street, he slowed. With hindsight, he should have ignored the persistent man from the start. Walked away without a word. Never have given him a chance to enlist him. In their blindness, zealots could cause great harm. Now he could only hope he had not made a serious mistake—with unforeseen consequences.

Wiping his face again, he tried to see ahead. He could stay neutral during the war, but if the British were defeated, he would stand firm with the patriots and help to form a new country. Will was too young to take part, but Louisa was capable and intelligent. No doubt she would be eager to join the struggle to ensure independence. In the meantime, he must do his best to carry on without his precious Susannah.

He loosened his neckcloth, struck once again by a pain that was almost physical. Pain mixed with guilt. If he had not been advised to leave the city, she might be with him today. Laughing with him. Listening to his complaints about a difficult client. Singing and playing the harpsichord. Under the surface charm and gaiety, she had embraced her family with constant caring love.

But looking back was useless and only led to more pain. He straightened, adjusted his neckcloth, then started down the long hill to face a damaged house and his two motherless children.

★★★

CHAPTER SIX

July 27, 1778

Philadelphia was experiencing a whirlwind of recovery, though nothing could replace the old trees. Available rooms were filled with delegates to the Second Congressional Congress. Shops had reopened and were doing a brisk business in spite of high prices. The smell was abating, though streets were still piled with refuse.

Many foreigners were arriving in the city. On July 12, crowds had turned out in force to celebrate the long-awaited arrival of the French. Cheers resounded as twelve battle ships, flanked by smaller frigates, came sailing up the river and entered the harbor. The first ambassador from France, Comte Conrad Alexandre Gerard, was welcomed with an impressive parade. Seated in wealthy Congressman John Hancock's elegant canary-yellow coach, he received salvos from cannon and salutes from lines of soldiers. With great fanfare, the coach made its way to the mansion once occupied by General Sir William Howe and where General Benedict Arnold now lived.

The Loring family had returned to their home, but now there was a helping hand, a black servant named Jessie. Tall, of uncertain age, with a soft voice and a calm face, she soon became a mainstay. Louisa had been trained to do housewifely tasks like waxing furniture and polishing silver, but Jessie had taken on the harder tasks. Even more essential, she had earned Will's trust by letting him stir the batter for cornbread and by crooning songs to him. He no longer cried for Mamma.

Last week General Arnold had issued invitations to a large ball to be held at the City Tavern. "It's time you appeared in society," Cousin Molly said to Louisa. "I think you should start by coming with us to this event. No need to feel shy, I'll keep you under my wing. What's more, I'll order my dressmaker to make you a truly fine costume. You'll outshine every girl in the room." The dressmaker had obliged and created an elegant blue silk gown with a low-cut bodice, puffed sleeves, and a modified hoop skirt. An elaborate flower and pearl arrangement would hold up Louisa's mass of long unpowdered dark curls.

It was her first big party, and as she dressed it was hard not to let apprehension overcome excitement—and fear that she would become tongue-tied, too shy to speak.

Jessie, hovering nearby, drew in her breath. "You very beautiful, missie. Will, look at your sister." Will gazed, wordless, his finger in his mouth.

"I know. It's hard to believe it's really me," Louisa said, leaning over to give him a kiss. "Say your prayers and mind you're fast asleep when I get home. Goodness, I must go down. The Morrises are calling for me and it wouldn't do to keep them waiting."

The big Morris coach was drawn by four matched gray horses. The driver and footman in red and gold livery sat on the high perch. The footman opened the door and pulled out the step. As she climbed in and took a seat beside Cousin Molly, Robert Morris smiled approvingly.

"I don't doubt you'll turn heads tonight, Louisa. Quite an event, though the glorious July Fourth celebration was impressive. Eighty diners, an orchestra, toasts, and cannon fire. I'm told General Washington gave the troops double rations of rum because they fought well at Monmouth."

Molly Morris shook her head. "And *I* was told that after that dinner a certain woman was identified as a British collaborator. A crowd followed her in the street, jeering and beating drums. Not a pleasing sight." She paused. "As for our host General Arnold. I gather he's living very high on Market Street. Ten servants. Sentries standing at attention with shouldered arms. The best of wine and food when he entertains. Heaven only knows what *this* evening will bring."

The City Tavern, situated on the corner of Walnut and Second Streets, was a tall building topped by a pedestal. Founded by fifty-three leading citizens, it was one of the finest taverns in the colonies, much favored by the British officers during the occupation. At their Thursday night balls, loyalist daughters had flirted with officers resplendent in scarlet uniforms as their mammas looked on, hoping for a possible marriage. Tonight, months later, many of the same families would be back there again.

Louisa stayed close to Cousin Molly as they went up the stairs to the Long Room, the site of large parties. As they walked in, her eyes widened. Dozens of wax candles in ornate sconces lined the walls and shone down from crystal chandeliers. Ladies were decked out in imported silks and brocades, towering ostrich feather headdresses, high-heeled jeweled slippers and wide hoop skirts, shipped over by indispensable family agents in London. But several were wearing homespun and cobbled shoes, as if to make a statement. Louisa retreated behind Cousin Molly wishing she could just stand there, observe, and not be seen.

An officer wearing a Continental Army uniform came toward them, a tall man with a thin face and lively dark eyes. He made a small bow. "The Morrises. A great pleasure."

Robert Morris returned the bow. "Good evening, Major. I believe you've met my wife, but allow me to present her cousin, Miss Louisa Loring, lately returned from exile in Massachusetts." He turned to Louisa. "This is Major David Franks, senior aide to General Arnold."

Louisa curtsied. "How do you do?" she managed to whisper.

He smiled down at her. "Servant, Miss Loring." He hesitated. "The musicians are about to start the first dance. A gavotte. Will you do me the honor?"

She looked at Cousin Molly. "But I don't—" she stammered.

"Miss Loring would be delighted," Cousin Molly said firmly.

She swallowed. Her feet felt frozen to the floor. There had been years of dancing classes, but only with a dancing master. Impossible to remember all the complicated steps of a gavotte.

"Miss Loring?" He offered his arm. The musicians picked up their instruments. As the music began, she and Major Franks joined the set that was forming. There were a few seconds of sheer terror, but as the dance progressed, she began to feel easier with the steps—and there was no need to speak.

The gavotte ended and the major bowed. "A pleasure, Miss Loring. You dance extremely well. But before I return you to your cousin, shall I introduce you to General Arnold?"

She nodded and gave him a small smile; he was a perceptive man who had gone out of his way to be kind, even if it was just to gain favor with the Morrises.

The General was holding court at one end of the room, sitting in a carved chair and resting his injured right leg on a fancy stool. He had dark hair, light blue eyes, and a hawkish nose. Tight-fitting breeches showed his muscular figure to advantage. Several guests were vying for the attention of the famous hero, but they moved aside as she and Major Franks came up.

"General," he said. "May I present Miss Loring, a cousin of the Morrises? She has recently returned from exile."

Louisa curtsied. The General gave her an assessing—and appreciative—look. "You may indeed. I have great admiration for Robert Morris. I trust you are enjoying the dancing," he said, then turned and gave an order to a waiter.

Major Franks took her arm. "Now to find your cousin in the crush." He paused and looked down at her. "Miss Loring, I must go about my duties, but I hope you'll allow me to pay you a morning call."

He wanted to call? On *her*? She struggled to find words. "Sir, I'm not—that is, we're not—the house—the soldiers—" she stopped as a young officer came up to them and bowed.

"Lieutenant Mercer at your service, ma'am. May I have the pleasure of the next dance?"

Major Franks laughed. "No need to find your cousin, Miss Loring. I predict you'll be engaged for many hours."

The next dance was a polka, and after that a minuet, followed by a spirited country dance. Partners appeared. She accepted them, trying to hide her surprise. Being seen with Major Franks must be the reason for this attention, but it didn't matter. She *did* know the steps. The music, the sensation of moving in a pattern—she felt heady with elation. She *loved* to dance.

As another polka ended, her partner, a young captain, bowed, "The room has become very warm. Would you care for a glass of punch?"

"Thank you, I would," she said, fanning herself and speaking above a whisper.

A number of girls and their partners had gathered around the large punch bowl. Peggy Shippen's best friend, Becky Franks, was among them. She looked Louisa up and down.

"Well. If it isn't little Louisa Loring, grown up and dressed to the nines. I saw you dancing with my cousin

David. Beware. He's clever and he knows how to butter his bread on both sides."

Louisa, taken aback, said nothing. She looked around and saw that Peggy Shippen was walking toward them. Becky rolled her eyes. "Here she comes after making eyes at General Arnold for over twenty minutes. Always looking for a chance to put herself forward. Tell us, Peggy. Has he asked you to ride out in his big carriage? Or maybe dine with him at his house?"

Startled, Louisa held her breath. Peggy and Becky used to be best friends, always together. What would happen now? Peggy tossed her head. "Don't be ridiculous, my dear. We talked about the battle at Monmouth, how General Lee was sent to the rear in disgrace and General Washington had to gallop to the front and rally the troops."

"That was all?"

"Sorry to disappoint, but that was all." Peggy turned. "Louisa, I hardly recognized you. A pretty dress and you dance so well. No wonder you had so many partners." She tapped Louisa's hand lightly with her fan. "Mr. Strant has the latest periodicals at his bookshop. Several of us meet there most mornings. You might like to join us one of these days."

An invitation to join these popular girls? She was too amazed to answer, but Robert Morris was making his way through the crowd. "Good evening, young ladies. Louisa, I've come to fetch you. People are starting to leave and we must get back to The Hills."

Cousin Molly was waiting in the coach. She shifted to make room for Louisa. As they moved off, she let out a sigh. "Well, that's over, everyone looking around to see who wasn't there and who was. I was quite surprised to see Joseph Reed and his sour little English wife. They live next door to General Arnold but are not invited to his parties. I hear he resents any slights to her—and he never seems comfortable in his own skin."

Her husband coughed. "Don't underestimate the man, Molly. As a delegate from Pennsylvania and leader of the radical Whig party, Reed has achieved considerable power. What's more, he's determined to persecute those he feels might still be loyal to the king."

"So I'm to mind how I speak of him. Very well." She turned to Louisa. "Did you enjoy yourself?"

"Oh, I did. That is, after we came in and I didn't know what to say to Major Franks."

"All you needed was a little push. You were a notable success, my dear. Notable. Looking lovely and dancing with such grace. I predict that from now on your shyness will give way to confidence."

They were passing St. Joseph's Church. At this hour, the street was quiet except for the clomping of the horses' hooves. She sat back and closed her eyes. So much had happened in such a short time. The kindness of Major Franks which led to more dancing. Peggy's invitation to join her tight little circle. She opened her eyes and took a deep breath.

"Cousin Molly, I know very well that any success I had was because of you—the dress you had made for me and because I came with you and Cousin Robert. I'm sure that's why Major Franks asked me for the first dance."

Cousin Molly reached over and patted her hand. "I don't think Major Franks would have paid such attention to a homely girl. Did you meet again later?"

"No, but he asked if he could call."

"Goodness. We must be sure the new curtains for the parlor are hung soon. Robert," she turned to her husband. "What do you know about Major Franks?"

"Major Franks? A good deal. I made it my business to find out about him."

"Well?"

"His family is a highly respected Jewish merchant family. Franks joined up with General Arnold in Quebec three years ago and saw action at Saratoga. He likes the ladies, but at age thirty-eight he's still not married. He's fluent in French and Spanish and is extremely able. I gather the General makes use of him in many ways. Will that do you?"

"For the moment," his wife answered. "Louisa, after tonight I think there will be a flock of those morning callers. Your father had better be prepared and have some good Madeira wine on hand. It will be like your mother all over again. Her parent's parlor used to be filled with suitors, but in the end your father won the prize." She hesitated. "I hope there was no difficulty about my giving you the dress and taking you with us tonight. I know how independent he is."

"He didn't object. I believe he thinks it's what Mamma would have wanted for me."

"He's right. She would be proud of you." She sighed again. "A long night, but at least people refrained from airing their views about the war and hidden spies. Or did I just not hear them. What about you, Robert?"

"No one talked openly, my dear, but the fear remains."

The coach had turned the corner and weas going down the hill. "Moses will see you to the door," Robert Morris said as they reached the Loring house. "Please give your father my regards."

"I will, sir. And thank you again for taking me with you tonight." She gathered her wide skirts and stepped out.

The air was still very warm. As she reached the door, it opened. Her father stood there, holding a lantern. "I've been working in the dining room but I heard the coach. Come in," he said and led the way down the hall.

She followed him and sat down. "It's late. Did Will go to sleep without a fuss?"

"He did. Jessie's very good with him. I went up and heard his prayers."

The long table was covered with papers. He pushed them aside. "Did you enjoy yourself? Was there dancing?"

"Oh, I did," she said, aware that he was attempting to show interest. "There was dancing and I met General Arnold." She reached up, pulled off the pearl headdress, and shook her hair loose.

"What did you think of him?"

She sat back, pleased that he wanted her opinion. "To be honest, I thought he acted like a man trying to impress. He had his injured leg on an embroidered cushion and a very fancy cane. Cousin Molly says he lives in grand style with a houseful of servants."

"Not appropriate for a man who came to govern with an even hand. Was there talk of politics?"

"Just on the way back. Cousin Molly said she was glad people hadn't pushed their views on the war and spies. Cousin Robert said no one had talked openly, but the fear was there."

"He's right. No one is safe." His voice was strained.

She glanced at him, surprised at his vehemence. There were new lines in his thin face and threads of gray in the brown hair. Making a living was difficult, but she was relieved that he had managed to distance himself from both loyalists and rabid patriots. No need to tell him how much she hated them. It might be childish of her, but the feeling was still strong.

The house was silent. She yawned and pushed back her skirt—the heavy silk felt hot and cumbersome around her legs. He leaned forward and handed her the lantern. "You should go up. When I finish, I'll use a candle."

"All right. I will." Slowly, she got to her feet and picked up the lantern. Tomorrow she would polish the table with her mother's special wax. Play ball with Will and start giving him lessons. The ball was over. It was as if a fairy godmother had waved a magic wand and changed her into a different girl, but the past few hours were fading away—and it would be wrong, very wrong, to let one small success go to her head.

Alone in the dark dining room, Eben picked up a paper, then put it aside and thought about Louisa. It was startling to see her dressed in fine silk and looking so much like Susannah. He must accept the fact that her life was going to change. There would be more parties, a busy social life. She deserved enjoyment, it's what Susannah would want for her, but it saddened him that they saw less and less of each other.

Making a living was now a serious problem. In these uncertain times and as currency lost value, people avoided hiring lawyers. His new office was located above a shop on Market Street. The rent was high, but location was key. A narrow staircase led up to a small room with barely enough space for two desks. He had given the smaller one to a young apprentice named Nat Haddam.

Several weeks ago Haddam's burly red-faced father had come with an unusual proposal. He was a farmer, but he wanted his son to better himself and become a lawyer. The boy was bright and he'd had good schooling. He could live at home and Loring would be paid a weekly fee. For Eben, this money would help to pay the high rent. They had settled on a three month trial.

So far, the trial was working well. Nat Haddam was a quick learner and had a real interest in the law. A good-looking young man of twenty-two years, he was tall, with thick brown hair, an open expression, and pleasing manners. At Monmouth, he had been shot in the right leg. The wound had healed, but a slight limp would prevent him from seeing action again.

The candle was flickering, almost out. It was late, after midnight. He gathered the papers together and placed them in a leather bag; somehow he must find more ways to pay bills and put food on the table. He rubbed his eyes and picked up the candle. Exhaustion was not an option. He would go up to his room and sleep for a few hours before facing another day.

★★★

CHAPTER SEVEN

August 1, 1778 New York

Nearly two weeks had passed since Captain Andrew Warren had received his new orders from Major Tallmadge. Now back in New York, he was working around the clock to form a new network. His headquarters was the cellar of an abandoned warehouse on the harbor. A dank, rat-infested place, but recruits could reach it either by land or by water. To have a place to go for a few hours of sleep, he was renting an attic room over Rivington's Coffee House, favored by the high-living British officers. James Rivington, the King's printer, was a good fellow who appreciated fine wine and could tell an entertaining story. The officers would find it hard to believe that Rivington was an active and staunch supporter of American intelligence.

Following Tallmadge's instructions, Andrew had contacted the ring of spies operating out of Long Island. Their mission was to take information from the city and row it across Long Island Sound to Connecticut where it would be picked up and rushed to George Washington's headquarters. It was hazardous work, dependent on the evasive cunning and courage of a few daring patriots.

A double agent named Hercules Mulligan was also proving to be an asset. A tailor by trade, Mulligan made clothes for British dignitaries, charming them with his smooth Irish tongue. Alexander Hamilton had recommended him, and he reported directly to Tallmadge.

But Andrew's most valuable find was Jason Brown, a British footman who had sailed from England with General Clinton. Jason soon decided that his future lay in this big new country. As a reward for keeping his ears open at Clinton's headquarters, he would receive land at the end of the war and Andrew was paying him well.

Last week Jason reported that Clinton had given a big reception at Number One Broadway. When bringing wine, he had listened at the door and learned that a Captain John Andre had applied to be one of Clinton's aides.

This was not good news for Andrew. Last winter, while working as a waiter at the City Tavern in Philadelphia, he had observed Andre and his fellow officers. Andre seemed more ambitious than the others. At parties, he would often join the senior officers, It made sense that he would attach himself to Clinton and rejoin his tight little group of friends. But having clever Andre at headquarters could be a serious risk to his own undercover operations.

It was likely that soon the depressed Clinton would pull himself together and take action, possibly march toward the Hudson River. At their last meeting, Tallmadge had asked Andrew to give him advance warning of Clinton's movements. Therefore Andrew was training his recruits to be alert to unusual work in the gun shops and around the harbor. Failure to anticipate a troop movement would be a devastating blow to a decimated and struggling army.

By now he was working around the clock. So far there had been no signs of activity, but there was always the fear that he hadn't done enough. Reliable information was still the chief weapon in this precarious war, but too many people were influenced by misinformation. It was a tool used to good advantage by those intent on creating chaos, one that was extremely difficult to identify and suppress.

Same day Philadelphia

The young man with the code name Finder was now in Philadelphia. As he became familiar with the city, he liked the well laid-out squares. The wide streets and fine brick buildings. In spite of the destruction, it far surpassed the hodgepodge of narrow streets in New York.

To get a sense of the current situation, he had spent several days sitting in various coffee houses and taverns listening to the talk. He had learned that there was a wide gap between the rich and the poor. Continental currency was now almost worthless. Dissension prevailed. In fact, he could report back to British headquarters that it would be difficult for the rebellious colonies to unite, win the war, and establish independence.

After gathering information about several highly placed individuals, he was being interviewed for an accounting job. In the meantime, he was able to start the task of infiltrating Congress and finding vulnerable delegates. Use the *Packet* and other papers to spread lies and misinformation. But while waiting, he must deal with the thoroughly distasteful part of his operation. Today he would go to the bookseller named Strant, the contact who could help him eliminate this tiresome patriot network,

Along with the letter of introduction, headquarters had provided him with information. The shop owned by respected Ludwig Strant was merely a front for a far more lucrative enterprise. An immigrant from Germany, Strant had arrived penniless and done well. He claimed to have no politics, but he had developed connections on all sides. Information was sold discreetly to those who could pay.

The shop was located on Decatur Street. It was late in the morning when he went in and purchased a book on local history. Noted that the steady flow of customers made this an ideal place to conduct an undercover business.

Strant was a small man with plain features and shrewd gray eyes. He greeted and treated each customer—old and young—with admirable courtesy and attention. Finder waited until the shop was quiet, then murmured that he had come from British headquarters in New York and would like a word in private.

"This way if you please, sir," Strant said, and led him to a small back room. Motioned him to a seat and folded his hands. "Now. How may I serve you?"

"My request is—shall we say—unusual.' He handed over the letter, then went on to explain that he wished to hire a man who had successfully performed tasks of a criminal nature.

Strant tapped his fingers on the scarred wood desk. "Before we go on, you should know my terms. I buy and sell information. I am paid in gold for each transaction. Is that acceptable?"

"It is."

Strant thought for a moment, then sat back. "As you say, it's an unusual request, but a man named Ralph Pottle worked for last winter's British network here. I happen to know that he committed a number of crimes including violence and murder. He was never caught, and he still lives at the Bunch of Grapes Tavern near Front Street where he uses the name Paul Brown."

Finder nodded. "Bunch of Grapes Tavern. Ralph Pottle, alias Paul Brown."

"Just so. The fee for this information will be five gold sovereigns."

With reluctance, Finder paid—Strant must be making a fortune. Back on the street, he gave way to serious misgivings. He knew his limitations, that he could never bring himself to commit physical violence or to kill. But hiring a murderer could lead to trouble. He would talk to Ralph Pottle, alias Brown, but make no commitment.

That evening when it was dark, he made his way to the Bunch of Grapes Tavern, a run-down place that appeared to be favored by sailors and dock workers. Went in and demanded to see the manager. After receiving a generous tip, the surly man allowed that a Paul Brown lived here, and Brown was summoned from his room in the cellar.

Finder motioned him to the front door where they could talk without being overheard. Ralph Pottle wore a hat pulled low over his face. One shoulder was slightly higher than the other. An unsavory fellow, but he was willing to eliminate people if he was paid in gold. He could also round up a ragtag lot of British deserters to watch and follow suspects until their routines were known. At that point, he would go in and take them down.

Finder listened and considered. Time was passing. Unless he went back to Strant, he had no viable alternative. "You're hired," he said sharply, "but I'm not coming here again." He handed Pottle two gold sovereigns. "An advance so you can begin work. Report to me at the meat stall in the Farmers Market on Wednesday. Ten o'clock. Understood?"

Pottle grunted agreement. Finder turned quickly, pushed the door open, and hurried back to the busy street. He still had acute misgivings about Pottle, but orders from headquarters had been carried out and it might not be long before he could free himself from this repellent hireling.

Thrusting his hands into his pockets, he headed toward the City Tavern. In the Coffee Room, after ordering a rum and whisky, he would try to join the group of Congressmen who lived there. In the course of conversation, he could insert a highly inflammable but credible lie. Spreading misinformation was a devastating weapon. Now was the time to use this skill, and apply it where it could do the most harm.

★★★

CHAPTER EIGHT

August 6, 1778 *Philadelphia*

The morning was fine and sunny. A welcome breeze had dispelled the stifling blanket of heat. Humming under her breath, Louisa set out to meet Peggy Shippen and Becky Franks at Mr. Strant's bookshop. She was wearing a yellow muslin dress with a blue sash, one of the new dresses that hung in her wardrobe thanks to Cousin Molly. It was less than two weeks since her first ball, but like a butterfly emerging from a cocoon, her entire life was changing. Her fashionable new clothes and notable success at parties had led to acceptance from the elitist girls. Now she was included in their tight little group.

The streets were dirty and Louisa went carefully in her high clogs, holding her green parasol high. All was well at home. Will was putting on weight—an appealing child with yellow curls and a wide grin. Jessie had a grown son in Baltimore and knew how to manage little boys, giving Louisa time to be with her new friends.

After passing the crowded markets, she turned left into Decatur Street. In the old days, she often went with her mother, an avid reader, to Mr. Strant's. His new shop was next to the printer John Dunlop, but much remained the same. The periodicals, the latest newspapers, the array of tempting novels. It was a place that served a need and gave great pleasure.

The door was open. She went in and was greeted by Mr. Strant. "Good day, Miss Loring. A fine one. How may I serve you?" he asked with a smile.

"I've come to return the poems of John Donne," she began, then stopped as Peggy Shippen and Becky Franks emerged from behind the table of periodicals.

"Just in time," Peggy said to her. "We're off on a mission and you must come with us."

"Oh? What kind of mission?" she asked. It was flattering to be included.

"A call on Sarah Champion. She lives in that big house on Third Street. She's in mourning for her aunt—why she doesn't go to parties."

"But she doesn't know me."

"That's right, I forgot. You left before she came to town almost a year ago. Never mind. Just come. You'd be doing a good deed."

As they went back to the street, the girls put up their parasols and began to walk in single file. "I'll tell you about Sarah," Peggy said over her shoulder to Louisa. "It's the most amazing story. Last fall she arrived from a village in Connecticut where her father is the pastor. So countrified, dressed in homespun. Her aunt, Mrs. Sage, bought her the finest clothes, had her taught how to dance, and when the British officers arrived—"

"She became the leading belle and put this one's nose out of joint," Becky broke in.

Peggy tossed her head. "That's true, but I forgive her because she never puts on airs and she's so much fun. And now, would you believe, Mrs. Sage has left her a fortune. An enormous amount of money. I know because my father is her trustee. She's told him she wants to sell her house here and move to Sageton, her big estate. Madness, sheer madness, to leave and bury herself in the country. We are determined to make her change her mind."

Louisa listened with growing interest in a village girl who had become a leading belle and was now an heiress. She vaguely remembered her mother talking about Mrs. Sage, a formidable dowager of great wealth.

The impressive Sage house was four stories high, with tall windows and an ornate fanlight. Becky seized the brass knocker and banged loudly. After a moment, the door was opened by an elderly butler wearing gold and green livery.

"Good morning, Cato," Peggy said. "We're here to see your mistress."

"Yes'm," the old man said dolefully as he bowed them into the wide hall. "She and Lorelia, they out back sorting silver. Please to step this way and I tell her you here."

"Cato looks unhappy, he doesn't like change," Becky observed as he shambled away.

Louisa followed the other two into the elegant front parlor. The chairs and sofas were covered with gold damask. Large mirrors reflected fine furniture and a crystal chandelier. The room was even grander than those at The Hills, but it had an air of never being used.

"Of course he doesn't," Peggy said. "Nor do we, which is why we will not, *not* let Sarah go off to that godforsaken place. Get ready. Here she is."

The girl coming through the door was wearing an apron over a plain black dress. "What a nice surprise," she said warmly. "I wasn't expecting you, but now I have an excuse to leave my work. Sorry to be untidy," and she brushed back a lock of auburn hair.

Louisa studied her, trying not to stare. Sarah Champion was not a classic beauty, her mouth was too wide, but her hazel eyes were large and she had an enviable figure.

"Never mind tidy," Peggy said, blowing a kiss, "but that's a horrid black dress. How long are you planning to stay in mourning?"

"A few more weeks, at least. Shall I ask Cato to bring lemonade? It's still very hot."

"Thank you, but we can't stay long," Peggy said as they sat down. "Sarah, this is Louisa Loring who lives next door. Her family went into exile, to a small village in Massachusetts. That was before you came, why you haven't met."

Sarah smiled. "Louisa Loring. What a pretty name. I'm delighted to meet you." She paused. "So, ladies, tell me the news. Are you dancing the nights away?"

Peggy laughed. "Indeed we are. The French ambassador is still the big name in town—it's a competition to see who can give the most lavish entertainments. Our slippers are in tatters. and some of us are practicing our French. My father is moaning that new clothes for three daughters will ruin him."

"Poor man. I feel for him."

"We pay no attention. Sarah, I'm sure General Arnold would be happy to receive you at small gatherings, even in your gloomy blacks."

"Oh, you know I couldn't. Not observing proper mourning would raise too many eyebrows."

"Stuff and nonsense." Peggy leaned forward. "Dearest Sarah, we've come, bending low on our pretty little knees, to beg you not to sell this house. I mean, think of all the parties we can have in the white ballroom. We won't ask any of the Whig girls, though. You should see the looks they give us. We'd be tarred and feathered and run out of town if they had their way. What's even worse, the new officers are a paltry lot compared to the British."

"True," Becky said, pulling a long face. "When I think of the fun we had—admit it, Sarah, aren't you missing Charles?" She turned to Louisa. "Captain Colborne was Sarah's escort last winter. He was so handsome and good-natured and they were always together. In your shoes, Sarah, I'd still be drenched in tears."

Sarah smiled, but Louisa noticed that her hands moved to clutch the arms of the chair. "Well, thankfully

I'm not—that is, not drenched in tears. No time. Since Aunt died, you can't believe how much I've had to do, all the arrangements for her funeral, even though it was a small one because so many friends had to leave with the British for New York." She turned to Louisa. "When you returned from exile, did you find your house much damaged? Have you found coming back very difficult?" She was talking very fast, as if to end the talk about British officers.

Louisa looked down at the carpet. "Well, yes. Quite difficult," she said, keeping her voice steady.

Becky spoke up. "Sarah, Louisa's mother died last winter while they were away. It was very sad. Now Louisa has to manage the house for her father and look after her little brother."

Sarah reached out and touched Louisa's hand. "What a dreadful loss. I'm so sorry. How old is your brother?"

"He's five."

"And now you look after him." She hesitated. "I know these New England villages. I was raised in one. Perhaps you'll come and have tea with me and tell me about your time there." There was real sympathy in her voice.

Louisa nodded. "Thank you. I should like that."

Peggy began to tap her foot. "Enough about villages. Sarah, I warn you, we're not giving up on you, not for one moment, but now I must be off. My father is waiting to discuss the latest *Gazette* with me."

Becky rolled her eyes. "Such an avid little student. Who are you trying to impress?"

"No one, but I like to talk about the news, not just cut my friends to pieces."

Sarah laughed. "Peace, you two. We all know that Peggy reads a great deal and has a very sharp mind. Anyhow, it was good to see you and to meet Louisa."

"Well, we'll be back," Becky said, getting to her

feet. "We don't want you to be a recluse in the wilderness, though in a way that would be to our advantage. You took the shine out of us last winter."

"I did no such thing," Sarah retorted as they went into the hall. "You two were always steps ahead of me." They reached the door and she opened it. "Enjoy yourselves," she called as they went out.

A large carriage came down Third Street, raising a choking cloud of dust. Louisa lagged behind, staring at Becky's dark hair and Peggy's fair curls. An adroit, competitive pair, but Sarah Champion was different. Sympathetic and thoughtful. Perhaps over tea she would learn more about Sarah's unusual life—and there must have been a reason why she had not wanted to talk about British officers and her escort Captain Colborne.

Peggy tilted the parasol to shield her face and turned. "Well, what did you make of Sarah? She certainly liked *you.* I notice that *we* weren't asked to come back and have tea."

Louisa hesitated, not wanting to add to Peggy's annoyance. "I think she was just being kind."

Becky looked at Peggy. "Louisa's right. Much as I like to rip people up, I have to admit that Sarah *is* kind. She always encouraged shy Constance Brown to play the harpsichord at our musicales."

"Well, that's true. And when my father refused to let his daughters take part in the Mischianza tournament, she came over and cried with us. Very well, but I don't think we changed her mind about selling the house. Where are you going now, Becky?"

"Not to improve my mind and talk about politics. No, I'm off to read the Bible to my dotty old grandmother. Will I see you tonight at Mrs. Allen's card party?"

"No. Far too boring."

"So for once we'll be spared the sight of you glued to General Arnold's side. Much too obvious, my dear," she added and began to walk toward Chestnut Street.

Peggy shrugged and shook her head. “Pay no attention to Becky. She and the other girls are jealous because General Arnold favors me. In fact, he tells me that he’s planning to give another *very* big ball, one to impress the French. See that you’re wearing a new dress and brush up on your French. *Au revoir*, *mademoiselle*,” she said and turned toward her house.

Louisa walked on. So the General was going to give another ball. Surely Major Franks would be back for that. According to Becky, the Major was away on family business. By now she had met any number of men, but he was the one she wanted to see again.

The street was quiet and she had almost reached her house when she heard heavy steps behind her. A hand seized her arm. She whirled around. The man wore a dirty wool cap and his breath was foul with drink. “You be a rich little whore,” he snarled. “Paradin’ around in yer fancy clothes while the likes of us starve. Your money or I’ll cut your throat and throw you in the creek.”

“No,” she gasped and tried to free herself.

“A pox on you.” He seized her satchel, wrenching it from her arm, and staggered off down the deserted street.

Her legs were shaking as she ran to her house. Flung the front door open, locked it, rushed to a window in the parlor, and stared out. He had gone. No one was in sight.

She straightened and took a deep breath. The hatred in that man’s eyes—but he hadn’t hurt her. Useless to notify the authorities, and telling her father would only lead to more of his lectures. He must begin to accept the fact that her life had changed. After last winter’s hardships she deserved to have a bit of harmless pleasure in the company of her new friends.

★★★

CHAPTER NINE

August 11, 1778

At seven in the morning, there was light outside but the house was still quiet. Eben liked to be up before the others, with time to think about mounting problems. One was headstrong Louisa. She was still attentive to Will, playing games and teaching him his letters, but she was spending far too much time with those frivolous loyalist girls. Susannah would have known how to handle this. He had made several attempts to advise restraint and had only made matters worse. He was gradually losing touch with his daughter.

Another matter of deep concern was the need to earn more money. He had made a decision that was giving him great pain. There was only one person he felt he could approach for help and that was his influential second cousin Congressman Samuel Adams. He had never been close to Cousin Samuel, a fiery leader in the cause for independence, but Adams was family. When they met last week, Adams had hired him to study the slowly evolving Articles of Confederation. It was a humiliating reversal of his determination to stay neutral. At some point he would have to tell Louisa why he had changed his mind—just not yet.

As he finished dressing, he was surprised to hear a knock on the door. He opened it. Jessie was standing there. She looked worried.

"I beg pardon, sir, but Jem, the boy who does the heavy digging in the garden—he's in the kitchen. His mammy sent him. Their master died last night and—and there was something bad about the way it happened. Sir, she begs you to go with Jem to where they live in Elfreth's Alley."

Eben frowned. He knew the black community helped each other, but this request was unusual. "Jessie," he said, "there's a law. When a person dies, officials must be notified."

Jessie shook her head. "I know that, sir, but she's afraid. Very afraid. I know Mandy and she has good sense. Before the war you helped people like us in trouble. Why she's asking for you now."

He hesitated, but only for a moment. He had come to respect Jessie's judgment, and it was true that he had assisted black people in the past.

"Very well, Jessie. I'll go. Tell the boy to wait."

At this hour there were few people on the streets as he followed Jem, a strong-looking boy of about twelve.

Elfreth's Alley was a block of modest houses built closely together. The third front door on the left was painted green. As they came up, it opened as if someone had been watching for them. The woman who stood there was heavier and younger than Jessie. Her skin was a lighter color. She opened the door wider to let him in.

"I'm much obliged, sir. Much obliged," she said softly.

Eben cleared his throat. The situation must be resolved quickly, but he had learned to start slowly. "Your name is Mandy. Is that right?"

"Yes, sir. That's right."

"And your master is dead. What was his name?"

"Merrill. Jonathan Merrill. He was a good master. We been here since Jem was born." The soft voice wavered.

"I can understand why you're upset, Mandy," he said, "but there's a law. Officials must be notified. Why did you send for me?"

She swallowed. "You'd best come upstairs, sir, and see for yourself. Jem, you go feed the chickens."

He followed her up steep stairs to a small bedroom, simple and clean. A sampler on the wall depicted a sundial with the inscription "Count Life by Sunny Hours." A man wearing a white night cap lay on the narrow bed under a crumpled quilt. His open eyes had the unmistakable fixed look of death.

Eben bent down, then straightened as if struck by a cattle prod. Looked again. There was no mistake. This was the man who had stopped him on the street. The persistent zealot who had tried to recruit him into working for independence using the code name Legal.

For a moment he stood motionless, startled and appalled. He wanted nothing to do with the man, alive or dead. All the same, he must steady himself and hear Mandy's story.

She was standing by the door. He turned. "Your master may have died in his sleep," he began. "Was he ill?"

"No, sir. He wasn't ill."

"Was there anyone else in the house? A wife? Children?"

"No one, sir. The mistress, she in Baltimore with the daughter and a new baby. Me and Jem, we live at the back of the yard."

"So your master was alone in the house when he died."

"Yes, sir." Mandy plucked at her apron. She was doing her best to hide distress. He must proceed carefully and not show his mounting concern.

"You seem like a sensible woman. Jessie said the same," he went on. "But you sent for me because you felt there was something amiss about your master's death. What was it that upset you?"

She folded her arms and spoke in a halting voice. "It's—it was like this, sir. Soon as I set foot in the house I knew something was wrong—

"Yes?"

"There was dirt from the garden under the parlor window, like someone had climbed through it with muddy shoes."

"You don't lock the windows?"

"Not all of them. Not when it's this warm."

"What time did you come in?"

"About six, sir. The master, he eats early, then he goes up to his room to write. When he didn't come down for his coffee and bread, I knocked on the door."

"And?"

She hesitated, then the words came pouring out. "He was lying there and I see he'd passed. Then I look down and I see the dirt—just there, sir, by the bed, those little bits of dirt. That's when I knew someone came in and did something bad to my master."

"I see." He stared at the dirt. It would have been dark, late at night or before dawn. An intruder would have carried a small lantern, but he might not have looked down and seen his tracks. A serious mistake, but more evidence was needed.

Mandy was silent, waiting. Avoiding the dirt, he went to the window, looked out, and tried to apply logic. The small man who called himself Teacher had worked undercover to recruit patriots. He must have done something that attracted attention from an unknown enemy—but there had to be a compelling reason for someone to break in and kill him. Easy enough to smother a sleeping man with hands or a pillow. There was no sign of a struggle.

He straightened and turned. "You were right to

send for me, Mandy," he said evenly. "I'll do what I can, but on one condition. No one must know I was here."

"Yessir. You can trust me and Jem to say nothing."

"Very well." He paused. "Where does your master keep his papers?"

"In the big desk, sir. Over there against the wall."

"I want to look at them. Then I'll come down and we can begin to make the necessary arrangements."

"Yes, sir." She pulled the quilt up over the staring eyes and left.

He went to the desk, pulled up a chair and sat down. Took off his hat and dropped it on the floor. Masses of papers lay on top of the desk and in drawers. He began to sift through them. Household expenses, long sums of shillings and pence. Letters from a cousin, from a daughter. Essays and graphs from his work as a mathematics teacher. Many aspects of Teacher's life were written down, but there was nothing at all about his major interest—his consuming recruiting activities.

He paused, then went through the papers again. What was he missing? A small notebook lay in a corner. He opened it. The first page listed three local addresses, but the rest of the pages had been ripped out, leaving rough edges.

Sweat broke out on his forehead. If the torn pages had a list of names, even in code, and if the list was in the wrong hands, then everyone on it was in danger.

He sat back and wiped his face. This was damning evidence, and the situation called for a clear head. He needed help. Washington's intelligence should be informed. Teacher had mentioned a drop box for couriers near Carpenter's Hall. He could go there after dark, but to be of any assistance headquarters must have a way to reach him. They needed a contact, one who could be trusted.

After a moment he came up with one name. Cox the apothecary cared for his family for years. He might act as a contact.

Nothing more could be done here. He stood up, seized his hat, and hurried from the suffocating room and the dead body on the bed. The body of a dedicated man who still was causing great harm. Mandy met him at the foot of the stairs. "I'm finished up there," he said. "Now we must make a plan. Except for his wife and daughter, did your master have relatives in the city?"

"No, sir. His brother was killed in the battle at Paoli while the soldiers were sleeping."

"What about a doctor?"

"There's one who comes for the mistress. Doctor Twifoot, but the master, he only uses—used—the apothecary."

He frowned, turning this over in his mind. Cox never left his shop. It would have to be fussy old Twifoot. "Right," he said firmly. "Here's what you must do. After I leave, clean up the dirt, then send Jem to fetch Doctor Twifoot. He'll notify the officials and see that word goes to your mistress."

"Yes, sir, I can do that."

He glanced at her. Black servants were adept at tight-lipped silences and blank faces, but she ought to be warned.

"This is hard for you, Mandy, and you've done well. Very well," he began. "I don't want to alarm you, but be careful, you and Jem. All you know is that your master died in his sleep. You found him this morning and you sent your son to fetch Doctor Twifoot."

She pulled at her apron, and raised her head. "We'll be careful, my boy and I. We thank you, sir, we surely thank you for helping us."

He nodded and put on his hat. She mustn't sense his growing fear. "As I say, there may be trouble. Remember, I was never here." He paused. "Whoever killed your master could be watching to see who comes in and out. I should leave by the back door."

"This way, sir," she said, and led him to the rear of the small house.

All was quiet except for the sound of hens clucking in the yard. He walked quickly to the street, then paused. It was a short distance to Drinkers Alley, then he would make his way to the office by a roundabout route. No, first he should go home. Pick up some papers and eat enough to get him through the day.

As he turned the corner onto Fourth Street, he slowed and adjusted his neckcloth. After all, there might not have been any list on those ripped out pages—or the list might not have contained the proposed code word Legal. On the other hand, the worst might happen, leaving his children orphans. Nothing was certain, and uncertainty was harder to bear than knowing the truth.

Bracing himself, he took a deep breath. Will was too young to sense trouble, but Louisa, even in her high flying state, was observant. From now on he must be outwardly calm. Show a composed face to his family and friends—and pray that God would be merciful and give him a reprieve.

On the following day, the Farmers Market was crowded with shoppers. Ladies pinched cabbages and smelled butter. Vendors of used clothes and cooking utensils shouted their wares.

Two men came up to each other at the meat stall. Both were wearing sober dark coats and vests, not likely to attract attention. Standing side by side, they faced the stall and appeared to be studying the display of beef and poultry.

"It's done," the shorter one muttered. "I took him down and found a list of names. You owe me." He reached into a pocket and pulled out a paper.

Finder frowned. "Any trouble?" he asked, barely moving his lips.

"None."

"You're sure?"

"Certain."

"Very well. Next week. Here. Same time." Hands moved quickly. A folded paper and a small bag of coins were exchanged. Finder turned and strolled away, moving at a leisurely pace.

There was no one in sight on Seventh Street. He took out the paper, glanced at it, and put it back in his pocket. Pottle had not disappointed. Obtaining this list was an important first step, and the names were in obvious code, easy to translate into actual people: Sawbones, a doctor. Legal, a lawyer. A foolish mistake on the part of the dead victim.

As he reached Chestnut Street, he walked faster. By using his accounting skills along with excellent recommendations, he now had a job with a highly respected trader and was creating a new persona for himself. With this connection, he hoped to receive invitations to social events, the best way to infiltrate and make influential friends.

He was also deeper into spreading misinformation. At the moment, he was advancing the resentment of the poor toward the wealthy elite, and there was the possibility that Benedict Arnold would continue to live beyond his means. Find himself in debt and be a promising candidate for turning.

At the end of Chestnut Street, he slowed his pace and allowed himself a brief moment of satisfaction. A promising start, but the need to make a fortune was key. In order to receive more gold, he must invent diverse ways to impress headquarters with his outstanding ability. It made little difference to him which side won. His aim now was to raise the level of uncertainty and fear.

★★★

CHAPTER TEN

August 13, 1778

Once again the fashionable City Tavern blazed with light. General Arnold had made sure that no expense was spared in his effort to show the foreign dignitaries that Philadelphia was their equal in elegance. All his wishes had been carried out, even to the tallest of available wax candles.

Tonight the dignitaries were resplendent in full dress uniforms—the lively Spanish envoy, Juan de Miralles, the affable French ambassador Comte Conrad Alexandre Gerard, and the newly appointed Consul to France, an Englishman named John Holker.

Rising to the occasion, the ladies had outdone themselves in their determination not to appear provincial. Their new gowns were made of imported silks and satins. Fanciful headdresses towered above powdered wigs.

Louisa arrived with the Morrises. At her first ball, she had trembled with fright, afraid to speak. Now she was able to laugh and talk and was ready to dance for hours. And her first partner was the one she had most hoped to see—Major David Franks.

Her heart did a little leap as he smiled down at her. "Apologies that I haven't paid you a morning call. I was away on business, and lately it's been work around the clock preparing for tonight."

"I understand. Getting ready for all this must have been extremely taxing."

"It was." He looked around. "Miss Loring, I would far rather talk than dance. If you have no objection, I suggest we remove ourselves to those chairs in the corner."

Her breath caught in her throat. "N—no. I don't object."

"Excellent. I'll fetch us some punch."

She nodded, acutely aware of Major Frank's hand on her arm, then sat down. This was far more than the former kindness he had shown to a shy young girl. It was an attention that would certainly be noticed

He returned with the glasses, then seated himself, stretching his long legs. "To your very good health," he said, raising his glass. "Tell me what you've been doing since we last met."

She hesitated, took a sip of punch, and smiled. "I won't bore you with details about running a household or trying to teach my little brother his letters. Sadly, no dark secrets, no daring adventures."

"Well, I hear you and my cousin Becky meet almost every day at Mr. Strant's. Are you a great reader? Novels? Poetry?"

"A little of both. No sermons and heavy classics. I left school when we went into exile and there was no time for books."

"I think I know why. Becky told me that you had an extremely hard winter. My most sincere condolences on the loss of your mother. A trite expression, but this isn't the time or place to say more." He paused as if to change the subject. "How wise of you not to wear a collection of exotic feathers on your head or powder your hair."

"Not wise. Just easier, and I don't want to tower over my partner like that lady over there."

"A monstrosity, but perhaps she wants to pretend that she's part of the French court—and that General Arnold is the king."

She laughed. "The French ambassador is a master of diplomacy, but I sometimes wonder what he really thinks of us."

"Or what he writes in his secret reports."

For a few moments they discussed the problems facing the foreign dignitaries, and exchanged views on a wide range of topics. When the music stopped he shook his head. "The gavotte has ended and I see Captain Crawley approaching, determined to partner you in the next dance. And I must get back to my duties."

"Of course."

"Miss Loring." He leaned forward and touched her hand lightly. "I enjoyed this chance to talk. You have a good mind—and I look forward to our next meeting." As Captain Crawley reached them, he stood up, bowed, and walked away.

Fortunately, the next dance was an uncomplicated reel. Her feet moved mechanically but her head was spinning like one of Will's tops. Major Franks had singled her out for attention. He had shown real sensitivity about her mother. They had laughed together like old friends—and he said she had a good mind.

As the musicians paused for a break, there was a rush to the withdrawing room set aside for ladies. Headdresses were adjusted and torn flounces repaired. One girl had taken off her high heels and was tending to a blister on her toe. Peggy Shippen was there, smoothing the lace on her bodice. She turned to Louisa.

"A great success, though it's a pity General Arnold can't dance. I saw you sitting off to one side with Major Franks. He looked very taken with you. Quite a conquest, my dear."

"Hardly a conquest. We just talked for a few moments."

Peggy laughed. "I say it's a conquest. I think I must arrange a way for the two of you to meet less formally. Yes, it's exactly what I'll do." She looked down and pulled at her lace. "That's better. By the way, you won't be going to take tea with Sarah Champion."

"Oh? Why not?"

"She's had very bad news—maybe a death in her family—and she was extremely upset. In a terrible state. She told my father she was going back to her home in Connecticut and he must sell the big house as soon as possible. Such a shame, after all our efforts." She picked up her fan. "Heavens, it's getting on. The General will be wondering where I am."

Louisa watched her go. Would Peggy actually arrange for meetings with Major Franks? And it was sad that Sarah had experienced a loss and left town. She had hoped they might become friends.

After giving the flowers in her hair a final twist, she returned to the Long Room, but now the evening was dull and unexciting. After a polka with Captain Livermore, she was partnered in a waltz by Mason Ross, an aide to Mr. Volker. Then came a country dance with Lieutenant Barlow. All were pleasant and asked if they might call, but compared to Major Franks they seemed so uninteresting and so *young.*

It was nearly midnight when the ball ended. She was collected by the Morrises and their big coach moved forward from the waiting line of vehicles and sedan chairs. The footman let down the step and helped the ladies maneuver their wide skirts through the door.

As they went down the street, Cousin Molly patted Louisa's hand. "Once again, my dear, you were a great success. In fact, several ladies remarked on how much you take after your mother, that you're just as pretty. She loved to dance and she always had the most partners." She turned to her husband. "What did you think of the evening? You disappeared for a long time."

"I'm not a dancer, as you know—"

"Indeed I do."

"So I conducted a bit of business in the Bar Room. Diplomacy and trade are linked together. On the one hand, many of these envoys are given diplomatic status from their rulers. On the other, they hope to make profitable trading deals."

"Is that a good thing?"

"We shall see. When our crafty delegate in Paris, Benjamin Franklin, obtained support from France, he made sure that we could trade with other countries. A good prospect for me, but there's no way to gloss over our increasingly worthless currency and mounting debts." He paused. "As for tonight, General Arnold put on quite a show. I wonder if he can afford it, though he's made money on a number of transactions, not strictly illegal, but sailing very close to the wind."

"I'm not surprised," his wife said. "Except for his success in the military, he's nothing but a jumped-up apothecary from Connecticut. Aside from his shady finances, he and little Peggy Shippen are making quite a spectacle of themselves. She never leaves his side, makes eyes at him, and laughs at everything he says. So difficult for the Shippens—the town is filled with wagging tongues, all eager to create scandal. Louisa, the two of you are such friends. Perhaps you could drop a word of warning in her ear."

Louisa shifted on the seat. Warning the willful Peggy about her behavior would either provoke laughter or flaming wrath. And being the target of gossipy old tabbies would never bother Peggy in the least.

"I could try," she said, "but I don't think she would listen to me."

"No, probably not, and that kind of advice is never well received. Well, no matter. Tell me about your partners. Were there any favorites?"

"No favorites." If Cousin Molly had noticed her

sitting alone with Major Franks, there might be a similar warning about unseemly behavior. To change the subject, she turned to Robert Morris. "Cousin Robert, even though the French hate the British, why are they joining the fight for our independence?"

"A good question, young lady. They need to keep a strong presence in this continent, though they find it difficult to deal with our foot-dragging Congress. Our best hope is that the king will decide the war is too costly and send no more troops to Clinton." He paused. "Speaking of Congress, I was interested to hear that your father is now working for Samuel Adams. Not long ago he seemed determined to take no side."

Louisa stiffened. She clutched the edge of the leather seat. Could this be true? Could her father have abandoned his beliefs and gone over to zealot Cousin Samuel? It was hard to believe, but Cousin Robert would know.

She swallowed. "He may have mentioned it," she said quickly, wanting to conceal her shock. "When he finally comes home he's very tired. We don't talk about politics."

On Walnut Street they passed a watchman swinging his stick. Cousin Molly sighed. "Another late night and so much to do at home. We've hired a new tutor for the boys and I'm not sure he'll last. At least there's no big function tomorrow night. I won't have to lace myself into tight stays or put on a heavy headdress."

Louisa was silent, still trying to hide her dismay.

The coach had turned down Fourth Street and was reaching the Loring house. Louisa cleared her throat. "Thank you both, thank you so much for tonight. I had—a lovely time."

"A pleasure, my dear," Cousin Molly said. "Sleep well."

She got out and the footman lit her way down the path. But as they reached the door she took a deep breath. Her father—the alliance with Samuel Adams—why had he said nothing to *her*? It was hard that she had to hear it from Cousin Robert.

She was relieved when it was Jessie who opened the door and let her in. "The master was tired," she said. "He went up a while ago. You'll be wanting your bed. Here's a candle for you."

"Oh, Jessie, I'm sorry to keep you up so late. I'll see you in the morning."

Back in the familiar room, she shook her hair loose, pulled off the heavy dress and laid it on a chair. Put on her cotton cap and nightgown and slipped under the light covers.

But she was far from ready to sleep. Placing her hands behind her head, she thought about Major Franks. Why was she so attracted to this man, far more than to any other she had met? She could list the reasons. His intelligence, his sensitive perception about Mamma, the way they had laughed and talked. And there was the look of his long muscular legs under the tight white breeches. The way his neck fitted his shoulders. The touch of his hand on hers.

Restlessly, she turned on the pillows. An experienced older man must have had many women in his life. What could he see in an untried young girl? She must read more classics. Improve her French. Bone up on politics. If Peggy arranged for meetings, there would be a chance to find out about his likes, his dislikes, his plans for the future. Would he leave the military and be a successful trader? It was astonishing to realize how intensely she wanted to see him again. It was as if her senses and heart were opening to a new world of feelings.

With a sigh, she blew out the candle and closed her eyes. So much to ponder, so much was uncertain, but all she could do now was try to be patient and wait.

★★★

CHAPTER ELEVEN

August 18, 1778 *New York City*

On this hot and humid afternoon, Rivington's Coffee House was filled with thirsty British officers. For Andrew, this place had proved useful; he often put on a waiter's coat and handed around ale and wine while listening and collecting information.

The talk today had centered on the chances of seducing several loyalist ladies. At four o'clock, he finished his shift, headed for the kitchen, picked up a meat pie, and stepped outside. A farmer with a wagon filled with vegetables was pulling into the busy yard. The driver was part of the Long Island network that operated in and out of the city. Messages from Tallmadge to Andrew would be inserted into the wall behind a stack of water bottles. As the wagon stopped, the farmer saw Andrew and nodded.

It was nearly five o'clock when the yard finally emptied and it was safe to extract a paper. The message was brief.

Visit your ailing cousin soonest. Bring ten shillings.

Brief, but clear. He was to report to Tallmadge as soon as possible, using the words *ten shillings* as a password to get through sentries and patrols.

"Bloody hell," he said under his breath. Tore up the paper and thrust it into a bucket of swill. He had planned to meet a new recruit tonight. Instead, as soon as it was dark, he must go to the nearest livery stable, hire a sturdy horse, and ride to White Plains in Westchester. Take back roads and hope to avoid an enemy patrol or a band of Skinners or Cowboys, rival marauders who cavorted around the countryside robbing and kidnapping for ransom. Wearing a farmer's wool cap and work clothes would make him a less tempting target, but lone travelers were always vulnerable.

There were no attackers on the road that night. He arrived at the camp a little after midnight, gave the password, and was escorted to a billet occupied by a Captain Dewing. His tired horse was stabled, and the sleepy captain gave him food and a bed.

The following morning Andrew made his way to headquarters, a house on loan from patriot Jacob Purdy. It was small, with clapboards painted red. Lines of tents filled hay fields that bordered the wide Hudson River.

Tallmadge greeted him warmly as they met in the hall. He glanced at Andrew's shabby clothes and smiled. "No self-respecting highwayman would bother to stop you. No difficulty with the sentries?"

"They were alerted and a soldier took me to my billet. I came as quickly as I could after getting your message."

"Right. There are meetings taking place in every room. We'll have to talk outside."

A pair of long boards had been made into a bench and placed under a maple tree. As they sat down, Tallmadge reached into his pocket, pulled out a paper, and handed it to Andrew. "The reason I sent for you. Placed in a drop box in Philadelphia and picked up by one of our couriers."

The note was brief:

Teacher found dead at his home. Evidence of foul play. List of contacts may have been taken. Awaiting instructions. Use apothecary. Legal.

Andrew read it twice and hit his knee. "Hell and damnation. This is bad news."

"In what way?"

"Last June when I left with our troops, this fellow, code name Teacher, was the only recruit free to move around the city. Intelligent, motivated, but he may not have had the right instincts for undercover work. Made a mistake and been outed. If he wrote out a list of names, even in code, and it was stolen, then the rest of my old network is compromised."

Tallmadge grimaced. "Teacher was sending information to headquarters, but nothing of any importance. What's to be done?"

"This Legal risked going to a drop box to send this message and ask for help. It would be hard to spare the time, but I should get down there. Locate him through Cox the apothecary who helped us last winter. Hear Legal's story. If necessary, organize protection."

"Anything I can do?"

"There's another problem. This will cost and I'm running out of money."

Tallmadge shook his head. "Understood, but getting money from Congress is like squeezing blood from a stone. Washington is using Alexander Hamilton to write his begging letters—Hamilton has a better way with words. Do you know him?"

"We met briefly at Valley Forge last winter."

"Very competent, with a first-class brain." He glanced at his watch. "Hamilton and Tench Tilghman are having a meeting in the dining room. It might convince them to provide money if you give them a persuasive account of your valuable work."

Andrew nodded. "Worth a try."

In the small dining room, the two men were sitting at a table covered with a green cloth and littered with papers. Washington's senior aide, Tench Tilghman, was the tall, older man. Hamilton was slighter with reddish hair. They glanced up. Tilghman stared, then raised his hand.

"Bless me if it isn't Captain Warren." He turned to Hamilton. "If you remember, this chap who looks like a feckless farmer did fine undercover work for us last winter in Philadelphia. Good to see you again, Warren. What brings you here today?"

Tallmadge answered for him. "Captain Warren is running another intelligence operation in New York and he's here to make a report. I felt he should give you important information on the situation there."

Canvas camp chairs were pulled up. Andrew cleared his throat. It was important to present these men with a brief but clear summation of his efforts and why money was needed. Choosing his words with care, he went through his activities, ending with the rumor that General Clinton was losing sleep for fear that London would bypass him and send troops to defend the West Indies.

Hamilton frowned. "He has reason to be worried. At the moment the French fleet is in Boston, getting repairs after the storm prevented the attack near Newport, but Versailles may order the less than impressive Admiral D'Estaing to go south. That means the British will have to support their lucrative sugar-producing interests there. Not a good prospect for Sir Henry."

For a moment no one spoke, Andrew glanced around the table. These were able, dedicated men who, in the words of the Declaration of Independence, had pledged their lives, their fortunes, and their sacred honor to take part in the fight known as the Great Experiment. Men who would be hung for treason if the war went the wrong way.

Tallmadge pushed back his chair and stood up. "Thank you, gentlemen. We'll leave you to get on with your business, but I trust you can find a way to provide Captain Warren with the money he needs. Good information in advance is crucial if Clinton tries to take the river."

"Difficult, but we'll do our best," Tilghman said. "Good luck to you, Captain."

"Thank you, Colonel." He bowed and followed Tallmadge back to the narrow board bench. During the short meeting, the weather had changed. A breeze was turning leaves inside out. Dark clouds were gathering in the east.

Tallmadge narrowed his eyes. "You made a good case, Warren, and while you talked I was working out a plan for Philadelphia. Consider this. Go there in your captain's uniform. No disguises. For cover, I could give you false orders asking you to find an important deserter and bring him back to headquarters. Provide you with papers that should take care of questions from officials."

Andrew shifted on the hard seat. "A manageable plan, but I could be up against significant adversaries. Loyalist, British, or both. It might take time and resources to find a killer."

"It might, so the sooner you start the better. While you're there, sound out feelings about General Arnold. His orders from Washington were to preserve tranquility in the city and give security to individuals of every class and description. Instead we hear about questionable financial dealings and outright corruption. A lavish life style. An affair with a much younger loyalist girl. Demands for pay he feels he's owed. Washington is not pleased—" he broke off as an orderly hurried toward them. "Major, a courier has come with messages. Urgent, he says."

"Five minutes, tell him."

The wind was growing stronger, the clouds heavier. Tallmadge stood up. "There's a storm brewing. Go back to Captain Dewing's. I'll send an orderly with the papers and as much money as I can muster." He hesitated. "One last word. We're stretched very thin, and few have your ability. Be careful, my friend. Be very careful." He touched Andrew on the shoulder and walked quickly toward the house.

Andrew watched him go. Tallmadge was only a little older, but their relationship was based on trust and respect. Rank was observed. They never spoke of personal matters, but in another setting they could easily be close and valued friends. Praise from Tallmadge made his work bearable.

All the same, nothing could change the fact that by giving responsibility to Teacher he had blundered badly. With luck, a thorough search might turn up the missing list of recruits in Teacher's house. If not, it meant he must find a way to prevent the rest of his brave recruits from being targeted and killed. Like Teacher.

Same day Philadelphia

It was mid-morning when Finder left his employer's office on Second Street and set out for the City Tavern to study the notices of stocks and shipping cargos. The Tavern catered to customers with various needs. A subscription room contained magazines and newspapers. The Coffee Room was popular for drinks and transacting business, and the spacious Long Room upstairs was used for large functions.

Part of Finder's accounting job was to study the latest notices. He was now a trusted aide rather than a mere bookkeeper and that had opened a number of doors. He had been to several parties and no doubt would be asked to more. A good dancer with excellent manners, he was well on the road to being accepted by society and developing useful contacts.

No hardship. He liked the way these people lived, in comfort and some elegance. In fact, it was becoming harder to balance work with an increasingly demanding social life. Fortunately, he only needed a few hours of sleep.

Today, while walking, he reviewed his situation. Gold was coming on schedule from New York, though he detested having to deal with Pottle—a chain was only as strong as its weakest link. Still, Pottle had obtained a crucial list and was working on the next victim. There were many bakers in the city, but Pottle had narrowed the field to the one on Spruce Street. A flag with thirteen stars hung in the window. The baker's routine had been established and Pottle was preparing to go in and make the kill.

In the meantime, as he ferreted out potential turncoats, his main target continued to be Benedict Arnold. In some ways, he could identify with Arnold—both of them were driven by ambition to become rich and accepted by society. But Arnold had arrived as a hero and then succumbed to greed. Now he was vulnerable, deeply in debt, and feeling undervalued. Recently a message had come from headquarters in New York linking Arnold to a man named Joseph Stainsbury. Ten years ago, Stainsbury had left London for Philadelphia and opened a shop that sold fine china. Affable and gifted, he wrote verses and had decorated General Arnold's dining room. Moreover, Stainsbury appeared to be an informer, playing both sides. Not long ago he had carried a message from discontented Arnold to Captain John Andre in New York. An interesting development, one that required close attention.

Now, as he reached the front door of the City Tavern, he came face to face with Mr. Cadwalader, an elderly gentleman and retired general.

"Good day, sir," he said with a bow that acknowledged the other's rank and age.

"And a good day to you, sir," Mr. Cadwalader replied with a courteous nod.

Several of his new acquaintances were sitting in the Coffee Room. They waved an invitation to join their table. He smiled, crossed the room, and sat down. "Good morning," he said, "but it may turn out to be rather a bad one. I've just heard a very disturbing story ..."

★★★

CHAPTER TWELVE

August 28, 1778 *Philadelphia*

It was the day of the Morris's big entertainment at The Hills and Molly's fervent prayers had been answered. The weather was sunny, not too hot, and there was a slight breeze. All morning, a stream of coaches and carriages had rolled up to the front door. The guests were greeted in the hall by their host and hostess and invited to stroll through the English-style gardens filled with bright flowers. Artfully planned vistas led to leisurely walks in the fresh, clean air, a welcome change from the pervasive stench in the city.

For Louisa this was a command performance; Cousin Molly had made it clear that she would be in need of her pretty young face. Dressed in a favorite yellow muslin with a blue sash, she was doing her duty and escorting an elderly Frenchman around the gardens, but her mind was on David Franks. Where was he now? Last week they had gone to a boxing match with Peggy and General Arnold. They had attended a rowing race on the river, several other open air functions, and there had been a number of drives out into the country, sitting in the General's big coach.

She had never imagined that she could feel so happy. Her feet didn't seem to touch the ground as she went about her tasks, humming and going over their conversations. Was it love, this compulsion to be with him? Becoming breathless when he touched her hand? Did she want to spend the rest of her life with him? She jumped as the little Frenchman spoke to her.

"Mees Loring, do you agree?" he asked, pointing to a bed of dark red roses.

"Do I—yes, I do," she said quickly, but as they moved on her thoughts returned to David Franks. She could see him coming toward her, smiling, dark eyes pleased. At night, lying in bed, she tried to see ahead. He enjoyed her company, the laughter and their conversations. but what were his intentions? Did *he* want a future with *her*?

By now Peggy and General Arnold were a seriously courting couple. It was flattering to be Peggy's confidante, but she was well aware that she was being used. Peggy was rash, but not rash enough to be seen alone with General Arnold. Louisa lived next door, easy to reach, and she was not a gossip. Still, the using went both ways. The outings with David depended on maintaining close ties with volatile Peggy.

The Frenchman was chattering on about the exquisite color of the roses. With admirable patience, she led the garrulous little guest toward a greenhouse and managed to say a few words in halting French.

Promptly at three o'clock, the doors to the large dining room opened. The porcelain platters on the long table were filled with a lavish selection of turtle, duck, ham, chicken, and beef, along with tarts, custards, jellies, fools, trifles, and syllabubs, to be topped off with raisins, almonds, pears and peaches. Robert Morris, a generous host, had provided fine imported wines along with rum and punch. As course followed course, toasts were made and applauded. Important deals were initiated, friendships cultivated, and disagreements shelved for the moment.

It was late in the afternoon when the visitors

finally departed with a chorus of thanks. As the last carriage left, Molly Morris took a deep breath and turned to Louisa.

"I've been gracious for hours on end and I'm exhausted. We should go and revive ourselves on the porch while the servants clear up."

The long porch overlooking the river was peaceful in the fading afternoon sunlight and the pleasant breeze. Molly collapsed into a chair. Carefully, she removed the turban that matched her gown of imported lavender silk and laid it on the floor.

"A great deal of work," she said, "but I think it was a success."

"Oh, it was, it really was—and I can't believe how much some of them ate."

"You were a great help with the gentlemen *and* the few ladies. You even spoke a little French." She reached out and patted Louisa's hand. "Goodness, how you've changed in just three months, but perhaps you were never shy. Maybe it was just that your mamma did all the talking. You didn't have a chance to get in a word."

Louisa laughed. "Today wasn't hard. At dinner I sat next to John Holker. He told me that he and Cousin Robert do business together."

"They do. Holker's English father is a well-known trader based in France. His son came here last summer and now the ambassador has made him the Consul for the French in Philadelphia. A promising young man, received everywhere." She paused. "Did you meet Juan de Miralles? Robert has traded with him for years, but Juan also has a commission from the king of Spain to make an alliance with us. He must be nearly sixty, so urbane, and such colorful costumes. Clever as a bagful of monkeys, too. We were so pleased when he decided to come from Cuba and settle in a house on Third Street."

"Next to the Sage house. Peggy Shippen took me to meet the owner, Sarah Champion. She told us that she was going to sell the house and live in the country." No need to mention the fact that Sarah had left town suddenly and in great distress.

"So I've heard. Such a shame, no one can understand why she would part with that lovely house. Her aunt, the formidable Elizabeth Sage, would be turning in her grave."

The sun was moving toward the river. Molly shifted in her chair and glanced at Louisa. "I feel as if I've seen almost nothing of you lately, so busy getting ready for today."

"I understand. So much to do."

"But I hear that that there's a great deal of gossip about Peggy Shippen's unsuitable affair with General Arnold. How much it worries the Shippens."

Louisa said nothing. There was always talk about Peggy and the General.

Cousin Molly paused as if searching for words. "I also hear that you're often seen out and about with those two and Arnold's aide Major Franks." She leaned forward. "My dear, I'm quite concerned because this is attracting unwelcome attention to you. Not just with the usual gossips, but with your mother's friends and with people whose opinions matter. I don't like to interfere, but I think you must give up these outings. At least for a while."

Louisa's head went back as if Cousin Molly had slapped her. "I don't understand," she stammered. "Why is it wrong to be seen with the General, a military hero? Peggy is my closest friend. What excuse could I give her? Besides, Major Franks has been very kind—" her voice faltered as color rose from her neck into her face.

Cousin Molly folded her hands. "Louisa, I'm sorry to upset you, but it's important, very important, for a girl to maintain an unblemished reputation. I feel I should warn you if you are in danger of losing yours." She shook her head. "As for Major Franks, he's older, experienced, and far too attached to a tarnished general—"

Louisa clutched at the arms of her chair as anger surged. "But that's not *fair*," she blurted. "You don't *know* him."

Cousin Molly looked startled. She hesitated. "That may be true, Louisa, but I feel responsible—and I care very much for you."

For a moment they sat without speaking. Louisa bit her lip. To quarrel with Cousin Molly was unthinkable, but this was *her* life—and she was not going to give up seeing David Franks. She took a deep breath. "I beg your pardon," she said unevenly. "I know you only want the best for me."

Cousin Molly nodded. "I do, which is why I think you must accept my advice. That's all, and we'll talk no more about this." She picked up the discarded turban and got to her feet. "The children. We haven't seen them all day. We should go and hear their stories. Your Will has become quite a little chatterbox."

But as she led the way upstairs, Molly Morris was filled with dismay. It was obvious that Louisa was more involved with Peggy Shippen and General Arnold than she would admit. And that tell-tale blush—had this inexperienced young girl fallen in love with a far too clever older man? Was the situation serious?

She tightened her grip on the banister. If the child was heading for trouble then she, Mary Morris, was to blame. Three months ago she had given Louisa new clothes and introduced her to society. It was a duty she owed Susannah, but also to encourage a sense of confidence in a deserving child. There was no way she could have foreseen that Louisa would become such an outstanding success with a promising future—always dependent on choosing the right man.

In the school room, a loud game was underway; she could hear Robby's piping voice above the others. She straightened her shoulders and tried to think ahead.

Her days had become a whirlwind of distractions. Children, entertaining, Robert's political problems—it was all very taxing, but somehow she must find time to discover exactly what was going on in the life of this independent young lady—and do it with the utmost tact and kindness.

It was late afternoon on the following day when the Morris chaise, driven by Hero, pulled up to the Loring's front door. Jessie opened it.

"I saw you coming." She patted Will's head. "Did you have a good time?" she asked Louisa.

"We did, but he's very tired. Hungry and sleepy."

"I'll fix some bread in hot milk and bring it to the dining room. What about you, missie?"

"Chamomile tea for me, if you please. Do I smell beeswax polish?"

"With the boy gone, I had time to do some polishing."

The house always seemed small and cramped after a visit to The Hills. Louisa took off her bonnet, sat down and closed her eyes. Her head ached, a sign of deep distress. During the day, Cousin Molly had been busy with household matters and Louisa had played endless games with the children. The parting was affectionate, but Cousin Molly's warning about future outings kept resonating in her mind. If only people would realize she was old enough to manage her own life. After all, many girls her age were married and had babies. She was *not* going to give up her right to keep seeing David Franks—and telling Peggy she could no longer join their excursions would end in head-tossing and imperious demands for an explanation.

Jessie brought her a cup of tea. She thanked her, took a sip, and was surprised to hear the front door open. There were steps in the hall and her father appeared. He was home far earlier than usual.

"I'm glad to see you back, my boy," he said, sitting down and ruffling Will's yellow curls. "What did you do at The Hills?"

Will took a gulp of milk and launched into a lengthy description of how one of the spaniels had been clawed by a cat. His eyelids began to droop.

Jessie came with more tea and a glass of cider for the master. She lifted Will from the chair and removed him, warding off his protests by telling him he had a new quilt on his bed.

As they left, her father shook his head. "That boy will either be a preacher or a politician. He's never at a loss for words. How did you spend your time?"

"Oh, I helped Cousin Molly with the guests and played games with the children," and she gave him a carefully edited version of the visit.

He listened, then picked up his glass. Studied it and put it back on the table. Looked at her, a grave look.

"Louisa, I came home early because there's something I must say to you."

Ominous words. She sat straight. "What is it, Father?"

He cleared his throat. "Louisa, your driving around town with General Arnold and Peggy Shippen is receiving unwelcome attention. I'm sorry, but this must stop."

She jumped. The cup tilted and tea spilled on the table. First Cousin Molly and now her father—she could hardly believe what she was hearing.

She raised her chin. "Father, I'm eighteen, old enough to choose my friends," she said hotly. "Besides, why shouldn't I go about with them? Peggy lives next door and General Arnold is an important figure in this country."

"No longer an important figure, but one who is in serious danger of being investigated for illegal transactions. And Peggy Shippen is not behaving as she should.

What's more, she appears to be using you to her advantage. Until now, I have never actively interfered with your social life, but in this matter I trust you will obey me."

She twisted her hands together. "Why, Father? Just tell me *why* I must obey you."

He cleared his throat again. " It is important for me that you not attract attention to yourself. These public outings must end. Now."

She sat still, then clutched the arms of the chair. This was intolerable. Her father would never be influenced by gossip, so who was complaining about these outings? It had to be someone who was close to him, someone like Samuel Adams. No doubt going about with loyalist Peggy Shippen was annoying to that fervent patriot. He might feel it was his duty to stop his cousin's daughter from associating with her.

"It's not right," she spluttered. "When we first came back you said you would never take sides. You said it over and over. I know you're working for Cousin Samuel—I had to hear it from Cousin Robert. That was bad enough, but Samuel Adams has no right, none at all, to complain about who I see or how I spend my time."

Her father winced. He shook his head. "Adams has nothing to do with this. I had hoped to remain neutral, but we needed more money. We are at war, and in war hopes and plans change"

"War!" The word exploded from her mouth. She hit the table with her fist. "I hate this war. I hate Cousin Samuel. It's men like him who killed my mother. Yes, killed her. If he hadn't pushed for independence we would never have been forced to go to Braintree. Never left this house and she would be with us today, laughing and making us happy." Her voice broke. She turned and ran from the room.

★★★

CHAPTER THIRTEEN

September 6, 1778

Ten days passed before Andrew Warren was finally able to leave New York for Philadelphia. Travel in the hired chaise was slow; it was late in the evening when he finally arrived at the Indian King Tavern on the corner of Third and Market Streets.

For the first time in years, he slept in a comfortable bed and enjoyed a hearty breakfast of ham, grits, fried eggs, and bread. He chatted for a while with the jovial landlord, then set out wearing his old uniform of blue coat with red facings, white breeches and black boots. Once again he was Captain Warren of the First Massachusetts regiment, and he was carrying official papers allowing him to detain a suspect and arrest him.

As he strolled down Market Street, he decided that his first step must be a call on apothecary Cox, a trusted member of his former network. A man who, last winter, had risked ruin, prison, or worse if caught as an informer.

The shop on Chestnut Street was small. A sign—Josiah Cox Apothecary—hung over the door. Through the large multi-paned window, Andrew Warren could see a customer. He stopped outside and waited.

Like most apothecaries, Cox had served many years of apprenticeship and was entitled to visit the sick, apply leeches, and act as a midwife. But he had chosen to stay in the shop making up remedies, often a last resort when home treatments failed. It was the constant flow of people in and out that made him a treasure trove of information. His soft measured voice inspired confidence—and loosened tongues.

At last an elderly lady tottered out and Andrew walked into the tidy shop. Tiers of mahogany shelves on the back wall held bottles of all sizes with rows of drawers below.

Cox was standing at the counter, pounding a mixture with his mortar and pestle. A thin-faced man on the far side of forty, with graying hair clubbed back. He lived alone. His wife had died years ago, and his one son had moved to Newport, Rhode Island.

He turned and looked at Andrew. "Good day, Captain. How may I serve you?"

"Good day, Josiah," Andrew said. "You often served me in the past, but it was at night and I was wearing a disguise."

Cox stared. Then he smiled. "Well, of all things. I'm glad to see you, Andrew. Very glad indeed. You left in a hurry and I thought we'd never meet again. What brings you here in uniform and in broad daylight, if I may ask?"

"I'm in the same line of work in New York, but I'm here because there's trouble in our old network. It's bad, and to sort it out I need your help."

"Don't like what I'm hearing. Go on."

Andrew leaned forward. "Last June, when I had to follow the redcoats out of the city, there was little time to pick a replacement. Jonathan Merrill was available. I had doubts about him, but he was more than willing to take over. Something went wrong and he was outed. Several weeks ago he was killed at his home in Elfreth's Alley."

"Killed? Are you sure? The notice in the paper said he died of natural causes."

"I'm sure. A man with the code name Legal found

him and put a message for headquarters in a drop box. It said Teacher was the victim of foul play and a list of his recruits may have been taken. Asked for instructions and used the word apothecary as a contact to find him."

"Good God." Cox grimaced. "I haven't been active since you left. Didn't see the need, but I may be on that list."

"I never gave Teacher your name. You may be safe, but others could be victims. I need to find this Legal and hear his story—" he stopped as a heavy plainly dressed man came in. He glanced sharply at Andrew, then turned to the apothecary.

"I'll wait my turn," he said gruffly.

"No need for that, sir. How may I serve you?"

"Something to settle the belly. Not too costly."

"I've not treated you before, but I can recommend a tincture of chalk, sugar, and nutmeg. It works well on acid conditions and I have it in stock." He reached for a bottle on the shelf.

Andrew turned and studied the soaps on display at one end of the counter. That sharp look—the man could be an agent leading a double life. He himself appeared to be nothing more than a captain in the Massachusetts militia.

The customer paid and left, and Andrew took his place. "As I was saying, I need to find Legal, then go with him to Teacher's house. We'll search every nook and cranny on the chance of finding that damned list. If not, we have to assume that those on it will need protection. Drop boxes moved and couriers notified."

"That will be difficult."

"That's why I need your help to find Legal. You know the city. There can't be many lawyers who had dealings with Teacher."

"Hard to say, but I'll start consulting my sources. Tonight, when it's dark, come to the back door, but be careful. Spies are thick on the ground. Where are you staying?"

"Indian King Tavern. An improvement on rat-infested cellars—" he broke off as the door opened and an elegantly dressed woman came in. He picked up a packet of cough drops, put down sixpence, and left.

Squaring his shoulders, he sauntered along Chestnut Street. It was going to be a long day and he might as well get a feel of conditions. He passed Carpenter's Hall, crossed the fetid green waters of Dock Creek, then turned into Third Street. He went by several large houses, but as he reached the one he knew well he slowed his pace and stopped.

Last winter, on his first visit, he had come here disguised as a Quaker woman with a face whitened with flour. The rich Mrs. Sage, known to be a firm loyalist, had written to General Washington offering to send information gleaned from British officers. It was a situation that called for tact and discretion. He was new to intelligence and he had handled it badly. In the end, he had dismissed both Mrs. Sage and her complicit niece Sarah Champion as unfit for undercover work. A serious mistake in judgment.

Since then his relationship with Sarah had been as up and down as a kite in a heavy gust of wind, with predictable results. After she overheard a plot to kill General Washington, he was ordered to take her to Valley Forge for questioning. Another failure. "I hate you, Captain Warren," she stammered as they left. "I hate you. I will never, ever speak to you again." But events had forced them together again.

Now he stood still, staring at the fan light over the front door. The shutters were closed, the house looked deserted, and he knew why. After receiving news that the British officer she had secretly married had died in June during the battle at Monmouth, she had bolted to her family in Myles, Connecticut.

Thrusting his hands into his pockets, he thought

about their latest encounter. Recently, with great reluctance, he had carried out Tallmadge's request and gone to Myles to question her about ex-Captain Jamieson, an officer she had known well in Philadelphia. A ruthless double agent, Jamieson was a hunted man, a threat to Washington. That meeting, too, had ended badly. After learning that her husband had died, not in battle but at the hands of Jamieson's servant, Sarah had vowed to join the search to find Jamieson and his killer servant. The other officers in last winter's tight little group were now in New York and could be questioned for information.

She had confronted him at the family farm and made her intentions clear: "Save your breath, Captain. I am going to New York and there is no way in the world you can stop me."

Now, weeks later, he was facing a difficult predicament. He would have to help her when she finally arrived in New York. The woman was motivated, she could charm the birds off the trees, but she would be putting herself in danger. And if she got into trouble, there was nothing he could do to protect her.

A girl passing by glanced at him and smiled. It was time to block out the unpredictable Sarah Colborne and move on. Walking fast, he headed toward the State House, the College of Pennsylvania, the old Court House. Places he had often passed, disguised in daylight or at night as he slunk about collecting information. By now nearly everything except the ancient trees had been restored, and nothing had diminished the dignity of the symmetrical squares laid out by founder William Penn. Compared to New York or to Boston, this was still the crown jewel of the colonies.

To find out more about the prevailing conditions, he sat quietly in a number of coffee houses and listened. There was talk of rising prices and widespread corruption. A man named Joseph Reed. was determined to punish all citizens who had not declared allegiance to independence. Dozens of innocent victims were being accused of treason. General Arnold was less of a hero and more of a man set on enriching himself. Feelings ranged from discontent and mistrust to downright fear about a precarious war and the uncertain future.

By the end of the afternoon, he had reached a disturbing conclusion. Tallmadge had asked him to report, and he would try to put his gloomy observations into perspective. No battles loomed, but the deep internal divisions in the country were far more of a threat to independence than any attack by the British. The moment was ripe for a power-hungry demagogue to step in and take command of the deteriorating situation.

At last it was beginning to get dark and the lamplighter had started his rounds. Andrew finished another cup of coffee, paid, and went out into the street. Out of habit, he glanced around, then began to move toward Cox's shop. For the moment he must put aside the ongoing threats and concentrate on finding Legal. Determine the extent of the danger to his unsuspecting and vulnerable network.

★★★

CHAPTER FOURTEEN

September 6, 1778 *That evening*

The air in the garden behind the shop was filled with the scent of herbs used for healing: Mint. Yarrow. Rosemary. Andrew opened the gate, went through, and tapped on the rear door.

A bolt was pulled back. Cox opened the door and motioned him into the small windowless room he used for storage.

He shook his head. "Bad news, Andrew, very bad news about baker Caleb Sykes. It looks as if he was on that list of Teacher's recruits."

"I know Caleb. What happened?"

"He was killed at his bakery. A blow to the head. I'm told it was early in the morning when he lights fires in the ovens and no one else is there. The till was smashed and money taken. Carefully planned to look like a robbery. According to my source, no arrests have been made."

"Oh Christ." Andrew hit the wall with his fist. "Christ. Caleb Sykes was a fine man with a family. Young children. If he was on that list, I blame myself. Maybe if I'd come sooner—"

Cox shook his head. "It happened, but blame won't bring Caleb back."

"No." Andrew took a deep breath to steady himself and sat down on a wooden box. "No, it won't. There was a chance Teacher might have hidden the list of names in a safe place. I was going to tear the place apart, but he didn't, so that leaves Legal, Cole the blacksmith, Durrell the innkeeper, Mrs. Meadows who owns a little haberdashery, Terry, a harbormaster, and Lessing who runs the stable off of First Street. I must alert them. Let them know I'll try to lay on protection."

"Yes, but don't go yourself. There could be watchers in any one of those places. I use a young boy to deliver medicines. He's trustworthy and he knows the city. I can send him off with a potion and a message from you."

Andrew nodded and gripped the sides of the box. The full impact of this death was beginning to sink in. Last winter he had gone to Caleb's bakery at night on his rounds and was always given a loaf of freshly baked bread. Caleb was young and strong, with a pretty little wife and three lively children. A patriot who didn't deserve to die because of his beliefs. But to honor and revenge Caleb, he must not let anger override cool judgment.

Cox shook his head again. "A sad business. We'll look after Caleb's wife and children, but now we should move on. You asked me to find a lawyer who uses the code name Legal. I have a source who has the time and ability to do searches. He's come up with a name. Eben Loring, with an office on Market Street. I happen to know him. A good man. I'm sorry he's caught up in this."

"Eben Loring. Market Street. Tell me all you know about him. I should be prepared before I go there tomorrow."

Cox pursed his lips. "Loring is a New Englander, a cousin of Samuel and John Adams, but his wife was a White from a prominent loyalist family here. He had a good practice before going into exile in Massachusetts. His wife died there, a lovely lady. I've taken care of the family for years. It's hard to imagine how he ever got involved with Teacher."

"Does he have children?"

"Two. A son and a daughter. The boy is young, perhaps five or six, but the girl is seventeen or eighteen."

"What do you know about her?"

"I'm told she's very pretty. Her cousin Mrs. Morris, the wife of the rich trader, escorts her to all the grand parties. This comes from ladies who need salves for feet that hurt from dancing in tight slippers with high heels."

"So she goes about in society. Far safer if she was a child still in the school room."

"Why is that?"

"Our opponents take advantage of divisions in families. They'll kidnap a young person in order to wring information out of a parent. Or for ransom money."

"That's stooping very low."

"It's a trick as old as the hills and it works." He tightened his hold on the box. "Josiah, we're up against a vicious lot of British or dedicated loyalists or both. You know the city. What's your thinking?"

Cox frowned. "Only a guess, but I tend toward the loyalists. Many were born in England and still have strong ties to the king. Difficult to find and expose them."

"Very, and here's the situation. I can only stay a few days. To protect the others, I need to organize. Maybe use John Jeffries, the older patriot who organized a group of ex-soldiers last winter. Carried messages and performed smaller tasks. Is he still around?"

"Came into the shop last week."

"It's a lot to ask, but would you be willing to use your sources and work with Jeffries? The situation may turn ugly. I'll know more after I talk with Loring tomorrow."

"We may not be able to prevent another attack, but I'm willing—" he stopped as the shop bell rang loudly. "I lock up after dark, but people still come. Let me know what happens with Loring. After dark tomorrow." He slid the bolt and opened the door. "Keep watching your back, my friend."

It was a pleasant night, warm but not humid. A sliver of new moon was joining the stars, tiny pinpoints of light in the vast sky. Walking at an even pace, listening for footsteps behind him, he headed toward his inn, trying to work out his next moves. History showed that every operation required a leader who could inspire followers. Hannibal had led his army across the perilous Alps. Washington had rallied his retreating troops at the battle of Monmouth. A ruthless and competent leader was leading a successful operation in Philadelphia. To prevent more murders, he must rally his own limited resources. Fight on until this unknown leader was rooted out and defeated. A daunting task and he was stretched too thin.

By now he had reached narrow Elbow Lane. A few more steps took him to the door of the Indian King Tavern. Music and a roar of voices indicated that an entertainment was underway. He braced himself, took a deep breath, and went in, the very picture of a pleasant young officer ready to have a few drinks and join in the fun.

★★★

CHAPTER FIFTEEN

September 7, 1778

For Eben Loring, life was a struggle to present a confident appearance to the world. During sleepless nights, he grappled with a heavy load of problems. One was the fear of an attack. Not in a house filled with people, but it could happen as he walked down a street, the fatal shot or stab in the back that would turn his children into orphans.

As for Louisa, she had apologized for screaming that Sanuel Adams was responsible for her mother's death. Although she felt it was extremely unfair, she would no longer take part in public outings with Peggy Shippen and General Arnold. For Will's sake, the two of them had achieved an uneasy truce.

The days were still hot, but there was a chill in the early morning air. As he went up the stairs leading to his office, he forced himself to focus on the day ahead. Under his tutelage, Nat Haddam now had a good grasp of the law, and being at college with gentlemen had smoothed rough edges. And, through his father, he provided useful news of the violence and unrest in certain parts of the city.

A meeting with Samuel Adams at the State House was scheduled for later this morning, but so far work with Adams had not led to more clients. He sighed, opened the door, and went in. An officer wearing a Continental Army uniform was standing by the window.

Nat came forward. “The captain came in half an hour ago,” he said in a low voice. “He said he needs a lawyer.”

Eben paused, taking stock. A military man in some kind of trouble. An unwelcome interruption, but he must be courteous and ask a few questions.

“Good morning, Captain,” he began. “What can I do for you?”

The captain paused, then glanced at Nat. “If you don’t mind, sir, this is a private matter.”

Eben hesitated. He’d prefer to have Nat stay but wouldn’t insist. “Very well,” he said and turned to Nat. “Please go to the Dunlop the printer. We need more ink and a dozen of his best quill pens.”

Nat nodded, picked up his hat, and left.

Eben went to his desk, then motioned the captain to the spare chair. “Sit down, sir. May I ask why you need a lawyer?”

The captain sat down. He cleared his throat. “I’ll come straight to the point, Mr. Loring. My name is Warren, Andrew Warren, formerly with the First Massachusetts, now attached to General Washington’s intelligence service. I’ve come from his headquarters in White Plains with orders to find the man who uses the code name Legal.”

Eben kept his face expressionless as his mind raced. Was help from headquarters finally here or was this a clever trap? Why had Nat been asked to leave? The situation called for caution and careful handling.

“A code name, you say. Why come to me?”

“Some weeks ago my superior, Major Tallmadge, received a message from a man signing himself Legal. He wrote that an agent in our network here, code name Teacher, was dead. There was evidence of foul play and a list naming his recruits may have been taken. Contact apothecary."

Eben stiffened. This was precisely what he had written, but he needed more proof. It was time to go on the offensive. "An interesting story, Captain, but I fail to see a connection to me."

"Then this should convince you. Two days ago another of Teacher's recruits was brutally killed in his shop. A baker named Caleb Sykes. I'm in Philadelphia to find out who is responsible for these killings and to provide protection for the others on that list. If you are Legal, we need to work together, wasting no time."

Eben rocked back in his chair. He knew that bakery. Killed in his shop—but it might not be connected to that list. He looked at the captain. "There's violence in the city. It may have been a robbery and Sykes resisted."

"No, sir. There's no mistake. You must accept the fact that Sykes was killed because his name was on that list."

Eben grasped the edge of his desk to keep himself from doubling over. The first encounter with Teacher on the street … the sight of him lying dead on the bed … now Sykes the baker … until now he had been able to live with hope. No longer. He let go of the desk, groaned, and covered his face with his hands.

The only sound was a fly buzzing around the room. After a moment the captain spoke. "Sir, by sending that message and alerting us, lives may be saved, including your own. I will do my best to give you and your family protection, but first you must tell me all you know. Leave nothing out, even if it doesn't seem relevant."

It was humiliating to lose control. He lowered his hands and struggled to pull himself together. The captain was here to help and was owed accurate information. He straightened and stared at the dust motes floating in the air. To put his actions into the right sequence required intense concentration.

Slowly, the story unfolded. The summons to Elfreth's Alley. The shock that the dead man was the fellow who had tried to persuade him to join the cause. The fact that during the night an intruder had climbed through an unlocked window and left a trail of dirt leading to the bedroom. Small bits of dirt, hardly noticeable in the dark.

The captain frowned. "He must have used a candle or a small lantern that didn't shed much light. In any case, he left evidence that made an observant servant suspicious enough to send for you." He paused. "About the death. What do you think caused it?"

"There were no signs of a struggle, but my guess is that he was smothered as he slept."

"A classic way to kill without leaving a trace. What then?"

"I looked through every paper in his desk. He was a prodigious note taker but there was nothing about his work for the cause, the main focus of his life. I decided to take action and send that message. You know the rest."

The sound of men shouting in the street came through the open window. The captain stood up. He started to speak, then stopped and began to pace around the small room. When he turned his face was grim.

"There's no getting around the fact that the level of danger to you has been raised. How and where did you meet Teacher?"

He hesitated. This was painful. "I came back from exile determined to take no sides," he said in a low voice. "When Teacher accosted me on the street, I should have walked away but he was persistent. Dedicated. I made no commitment, none whatsoever, but because I was courteous enough to listen and speak to him, he put me on that list."

The shouts on the street became louder. The captain continued to pace, then he sat down. "A few more questions. Who knows about your dealings with Teacher? What about the young man in your office?"

"My apprentice. The boy was wounded at Long

Island. He's able and patriotic but I've told him nothing. Jessie, my servant, knows I went to Teacher's house after he died, but that's all."

"Servants have sharp ears. They know far more than we realize. I gather your wife is dead and you have children."

"Two. My son is five. My daughter is eighteen."

"A young lady. Old enough to be told about your situation and help with the changes that must be made."

He shook his head. "That—well, that may be difficult. Last winter we were exiled in a small farmhouse in Braintree, Massachusetts. Louisa took on hard work and nursed her dying mother. Now she looks after her little brother but—" he stopped.

"Go on."

"We came back at the end of June. My wife's cousin, Mrs. Robert Morris, introduced Louisa to society as her mother would have done, but success has gone to her head." He paused. "The truth is, we've quarreled."

"What about?"

"My daughter is intelligent and observant, but she hates the idea of independence. Blames patriots like Samuel Adams for starting the war—and that going into exile killed her mother. She has very strong feelings—we used to be close. Now we barely speak."

"Regrettable." The captain rubbed at a smear of dirt on his white breeches. "Regrettable because you need support from everyone around you. Your apprentice, your servants, and your daughter—they must be made to understand the danger you are facing." He paused. "I can see that it would be extremely difficult for you to explain what has happened, but there's one solution. It might be easier for them to accept the bad news if it comes from me, not you. If you agree, I could come to your house tonight and talk to them. Is that possible?"

"It may not make an impression on my daughter, but yes, it's possible."

"Give me directions. I'll be there around nine o'clock after it's dark." He frowned. "Before I leave, we should go over the procedures I have in mind. From now on, no walking alone in the streets. You'll need a small vehicle and a driver who lives with you and can act as a bodyguard."

"I have no horse or vehicle. There's a small barn with room for a horse, but a bodyguard—is that necessary?"

The captain stood up. His eyes narrowed. He leaned down and put his hands on the desk. "Loring, for God's sake, accept the changes. There's a ruthless adversary out there. He's already killed twice. We must assume that he's getting ready to kill again."

★★★

CHAPTER SIXTEEN

September 7, 1778 *Later that night*

Louisa stood in front of her wardrobe trying to decide which dress to wear to the much anticipated musicale at the Chew's. Maybe it should be the rose silk, or perhaps the new lilac.

When she heard her father calling from the hall below, she pulled a dressing gown over her petticoat and went to the door.

"Yes, Father?"

"Jessie tells me you're planning to go out. I'm sorry, but I need you here tonight."

She took a deep breath. This could lead to another serious disagreement. "Father, it's a only a musicale at the Chew's. Very sedate, no dancing. Why must I be here?"

"Because a captain from General Washington's headquarters is coming to the house to talk to you—and to Nat and Jessie." He rubbed his hand over his forehead as if it hurt, a growing habit. "He'll arrive around nine. I'll be working in the dining room. When Nat arrives, please send him to me."

"Yes, Father." She closed the door and went to the bed. Sat down and drummed her fingers on the quilt. This was so disappointing. Why on earth would a captain from Washington's headquarters want to talk to them?

A mystery, but her conscience was clear. She had summoned up the courage to tell Peggy she could do no more outings, that they upset her father. There was no falling out. Peggy was annoyed, but Louisa was her friend and confidante. They mustn't quarrel over this.

All the same, she had a sinking feeling that David Franks had lost interest in her. When they happened to meet, he was pleasant but that was all. No plans for another talk. It was as if he had enjoyed the former expeditions and then decided she was too young for further attentions—or a lasting commitment.

She told herself that General Arnold kept him too busy, but had she simply imagined that there was a mutual attraction? She was making an effort to show high spirits at parties. Laughing and paying attention to various officers. It was all very hurtful, but at least she had kept her feelings well hidden from Peggy and the other girls.

Now, with barely contained exasperation, she took off the dressing gown and put on a plain muslin dress and a paisley shawl. Smoothed her hair and went down the stairs.

The parlor was dark. She lit a lamp, sat down, picked up an attempt to embroider a table runner, and waited for Nat Haddam. After meeting him several times here and in the Market Street office, she had quickly dismissed him as a farmer's son, though he seemed well educated and her father depended on him more and more. But before taking him to the dining room, she would try to pry some information out of him.

When she heard a knock on the front door, she went to open it. Nat stood there, hat in hand, tall and presentable. "Good evening, Nat," she said. "Come in."

"Good evening, ma'am." He bowed and stepped into the hall. She took his hat and laid it on the table. "This meeting," she began. "My father says a captain from General Washington's headquarters is coming to talk to us. Do you have any idea why?"

Nat looked uneasy. "The captain walked into the office this morning. He wanted to be alone with your father so I went out. When I got back, he'd left and your father asked me to come here tonight. That's all I know."

"Then I suppose we'll just have to wait. This way." She led him down the hall to the dining room, then went into the kitchen. Will was finishing his bedtime mug of milk. She patted his head and turned to Jessie. "About this captain we're expecting. What did my father say to you?"

"He told me to make sure Will was asleep, then come to the parlor. He didn't say why." Jessie hesitated. "Should I bring in the tea tray?"

"Not unless it's wanted." She leaned down and kissed Will's cheek. "I love you. Sweet dreams and don't forget your prayers."

Back in the parlor, she felt too restless to sew. By now the musicale would be well underway. Which pieces of music would they be playing? Were her friends missing her, wondering where she was? Would the mysterious captain come on foot or in a chaise?

At last footsteps sounded on the path. She hurried to the door and opened it. For some reason, she had expected a heavy, far older man. This one was young. Quite handsome in his military uniform.

"Good evening. Please come in, Captain," she said, hiding her surprise.

He bowed. "Servant, ma'am." He smiled. "You must be Miss Louisa Loring."

"Yes, I am," she said, astonished that he knew her first name.

"Good evening, Captain." Her father emerged from the dining room. "Allow me to introduce my daughter, Miss Louisa Loring. Nat Haddam you met this morning. This way, if you please," and he motioned them into the parlor.

Quickly, the little group arranged themselves. The captain went to stand in front of the fireplace. Her father selected a straight chair. Louisa chose the blue brocade sofa, and Nat seated himself on another straight chair, a little apart from the others.

The door opened and Jessie appeared. The captain nodded to her. "You are?"

"Jessie, sir," she said, placing herself just inside the door.

For a moment the captain was silent, as if collecting his thoughts. Then he cleared his throat. "I'll start by introducing myself. My name is Warren. Captain Andrew Warren, attached to General Washington's intelligence service with headquarters in White Plains, New York. Recently we received word about a suspicious death in Philadelphia and I was given orders to come and investigate. This morning Mr. Loring and I met in his office. We agreed that those close to him should be told about a serious situation, one in which he is involved."

Standing in a parade ground posture, hands behind his back, he began to describe the small network of patriots who, last winter, had risked their lives by sending information to Washington's intelligence.

Louisa folded her hands. If she were at the musicale, she would be sitting with Peggy Chew. According to Becky, last winter Peggy Chew was close to a British officer named John Andre. As he left, he had written her a lovely poem—how long would this tiresome captain drone on about boring recruits with code names?

The captain paused. He crossed his arms over his chest. He seemed to be searching for words.

"There was a reason to explain that network at length," he said slowly. "I'm sorry, very sorry, to have to tell you that Mr. Loring's name may be on a stolen list of recruits. Two of them have already been eliminated. That means he is now in great danger."

No one spoke. It was as if his words had frozen

them into silence. Louisa shook her head. This couldn't be true. Her father had abandoned his principles when he went to work for Samuel Adams, but he was a cautious, sensible lawyer. He would *never* involve himself with spies and code names. She leaned forward.

"Father, I don't believe this. There must be some mistake."

Her father bent his head. He stared at his feet. "The captain is right," he muttered.

Louisa's hands jerked up. "No," she stammered, then dug her fingers into the sofa as a surge of hot anger took hold. How could he have been so *careless*, so utterly *foolish*?

The captain squared his shoulders. "Miss Loring, I know this is hard to accept, but we can't change the facts. Your father needs to be protected. That will be difficult. I'm here tonight to make a plan." He turned to Nat. "I'll start with you, Mr. Haddam. Can you make sure he's never alone in the office?"

"Yes, Captain."

"Jessie, much of the work will fall on you. Mr. Loring must never walk alone in the streets. He'll need a horse and a small vehicle driven by a man to guard him whenever he goes out. I'm told there is a barn with a stall, but is there a place where this man can live?"

Jessie nodded. "There's a room over the stall. I can do it up and feed him in the kitchen."

The tension in the air was palpable. Louisa's breath caught in her throat. Dear Lord, what orders was this officious officer going to give *her*?

The captain hesitated, then walked over to the sofa and sat down, keeping his distance.

"Miss Loring," he said in a low voice. "We live in a dangerous time. Your father was drawn into a troublesome situation and he handled it well. I understand that the two of you have had a serious disagreement, but now he needs your help."

She bit her lip and was silent.

The captain leaned forward. "I'll speak plainly. This is a time when you should all be pulling together. Otherwise the situation worsens. Believe me when I say that discord in a family facing an ordeal can only lead to even more anger and distress."

Discord in a family—she winced as his words struck with painful force. If there was one thing in the world Mamma had hated, it was the slightest dissension in her family. Closing her eyes, she could picture Mamma sitting beside her, reaching for her hand. Telling her that she was behaving badly, that her father was a good man who was doing his best for his family. Telling her that she must put aside petty grievances, show compassion, and make every effort to keep him safe.

She swallowed and opened her eyes. Her father was still staring at the floor. Nat coughed. Jessie plucked at her apron. They seemed to be waiting for a reply. Louisa clenched her fists. Men killed—her father's life in danger—she must summon up the will to do what Mamma wished—and do it now. She straightened and took a deep breath. "Father," she said in a halting voice, "I didn't understand. I'm sorry. I'll do all I can to keep you safe. It's what Mamma would want."

Her father raised his head. He tried to speak, then nodded.

The tension in the room eased. The captain got to his feet and went to stand in front of the fireplace again. "Your help is appreciated, Miss Loring," he said briskly, dispelling emotion. "It's important to give the impression that nothing is wrong in the Loring household. I hear you go to parties. If questions arise, you could say that your father fell and broke his leg in several places. A broken leg that won't heal is a valid enough reason to go about with a gig and driver. Can you manage that?

"Yes."

"Tomorrow a young man named Peter will come

with a horse and a gig—"

"Which I will pay for," her father said quickly.

"Very well." He paused and glanced at the clock. "I believe a workable plan is in place. I'm returning to New York but I can be reached through Cox the apothecary." He paused again and studied their faces. "One last thought. There's no denying that this will be a difficult time. There will be moments of fear but protection for all on the coded list is being organized. Watchers will be in place to look for threats." He glanced at the clock again. "I must leave you to make more calls, but remember this: A major effort is underway to find these scoundrels and put an end to your ordeal." He nodded and made a small bow. "Now I bid you good night."

Her father stood up. "Captain, what you are doing for us is deeply appreciated. Deeply," he added, as they moved toward the door. Nat followed. Jessie had disappeared.

Outside, all was quiet except for the rattle of the watchman's stick as he came down the street. "Ten o'clock on a quiet evening," he called. "Ten o'clock, and all's well."

Alone in the room, Louisa pressed her hands to her head as if to keep it in place. So much had happened in one short hour. So many changes to absorb. The shock of hearing that her father might be killed and why … her anger … then the message from Mamma, still a strong presence in her life.

She let go of her head, stood up, then began to walk around, touching the familiar objects as if to anchor herself. The harpsichord in the corner that Mamma used to play. The polished tea table. The set of embroidered cushions.

But as she walked, questions started to assail her, questions that demanded hard, painful answers. Had she been too quick to dislike Captain Warren? He had shown unexpected consideration—and by using the word discord he had jolted her into forgiveness. Was it wrong to have passed such harsh judgment on her father? On that hot day back in July, clutching Mamma's clothes, grief may have misguided her into laying blame on patriots and independence. Blindly, she had rushed headlong down a slippery path in order to achieve acceptance. Tonight that path had taken an abrupt turn.

After a moment, she walked to the mirror hanging between two long windows. The light from the lamp was dim, but she gazed into it, surprised that her face reflected nothing of the upheaval she was experiencing. Then she took a deep breath. Impossible to see into the future, but one thing was certain. Her life, and the life of those she loved, was about to change in ominous and unpredictable ways.

PART TWO

★ ★ ★

CHAPTER SEVENTEEN

September 27, 1778

The war dragged on with no end in sight, but change was in the air. Nights were cool and early mornings were chilly. The heavy leaves on the trees had turned to vibrant reds and golds and some were beginning to drift down. Change was also taking place in the Loring household. Three weeks had passed since Captain Warren came to the house on Fourth Street and upended their lives. Jessie was handling the added work with her usual calm competence. A patient old horse munched hay in the barn, and Peter, the sturdy young bodyguard, was living in the room over his stall. Until recently, Peter had sailed with a privateer out of New London. A shoulder wound ended his ability to raise heavy canvas, but he was well able to handle the modest little gig.

But the constant fear of an attack lay heavily on everyone's mind. The captain had warned them that enemy watchers were likely to be nearby, that any slip could have deadly consequences.

For Louisa, it was as if a faceless monster lurked in the shadows, waiting to pounce. It was a severe strain to tell believable lies about her father's condition—and she was not a good liar. Will sensed trouble and was growing fractious. She spent time with him, teaching him to read and playing endless games. She even opened the harpsichord and tapped out the songs Mamma used to sing. At night his father read him stories from books of fables and fairy tales. Later they would pray together.

The day began as usual. Shortly after breakfast, Eben and Peter left for the office, and Louisa was startled to see the gig returning and stopping in the driveway. Seconds later the back door opened. Her father stumbled into the kitchen and slumped into a chair. His face was white. Louisa dropped the dish she was wiping. "Father, what—?"

He raised his hand. "Jessie, take Will outside. Now."

"Yes, sir." She moved quickly and took Will's hand. "Come talk to the horse, Will, maybe feed him some grass," she said and hurried him out.

As they left, Peter appeared at the door. He was breathing hard. "Bastards figured out our routine," he muttered to Louisa. "Fellow with a knife jumped at us from the walkway on Second Street. Had my stick handy. Hit him in the face. Might have been more of them so we turned and came back."

Louisa gasped. She braced herself against a chair. "Oh, no," she choked. "Oh, *no*. Father, you must stay here, not go out again—"

"Wait," he said and closed his eyes. He seemed to be collecting himself, then he opened them and looked at her. "Louisa, listen to me. Peter was quick. The attack failed. They won't try again soon. Now fix your mind on that and look after Will—don't let him sense more trouble. By mid-afternoon I'll be back." He stood up and nodded to Peter who followed him through the door.

Slowly, Louisa sat down. Her legs felt weak and her hands were shaking. A man with a knife—it could have gone into her father's body. He could have bled to death in the street—but it hadn't happened. He was going back to the office and she must take care of Will. She rubbed her arms and took deep breaths in an effort to steady herself. But as Will and Jessie returned his thumb was in his mouth. He ran to her and seized her skirt.

"Why did Father come back *now*, Lulu? Why did he send me away?" " She forced her lips into a smile, reached down and stroked his head.

"He came back because he forgot some papers. Important ones. Good gracious, it's time to start your lessons. The ABC book is in that chest in the front parlor. Go fetch it and we'll work on some new letters." His face brightened. He let go of her skirt and ran toward the hall. She shivered and looked at Jessie. "Oh God, Jessie, it's what we feared. A man attacked him with a knife, but Peter was quick and knocked him away. My father said it won't happen again soon and not to frighten Will, but how can we be sure? How *can* we? Oh, what shall we do?"

For a moment Jessie stood still. Then she put a hand on Louisa's shoulder. "This is hard, missie. Very hard, but we just do the best we can. Be brave and not show our fear."

Be brave. Not show fear. Louisa swallowed and got to her feet. "You're right, Jessie," she whispered as Will returned. "Come on, Wills, we'll work in the dining room out of Jessie's way."

Her hands had stopped shaking. They pulled out chairs and sat down at one end of the long table. Louisa opened the worn little book, the one Mamma had used with her. "Where were we yesterday?" she asked him. "Never mind, it doesn't matter. We'll start with the letter D. Now try to find the O and the G. Together they spell the word dog."

"Dog." Will bounced in the chair. He clapped his hands. "Robby has a spaniel called Spot. The Morrises have lots of dogs. Lulu, *that's* what we need. A dog to come and live with us."

She hesitated, then ruffled his curls. "We'll see. Now find the letters."

Will's mouth turned down. "I don't want to do letters," he shouted. "I *want* a *dog*." The lesson ended in tears.

The next few days passed without further incidents and changes were put in place. Apothecary Cox was informed of the attack. There were more watchers and a large tan mongrel was now in residence near the stable. According to Peter, he had a good nature and a very loud bark when strangers appeared. Will named him Brownie and took him plates of scraps; sitting down and talking to Brownie seemed to soothe the little boy. Eben Loring kept his practice going and Peter drove Louisa to several small parties. The need to keep up the pretense with outsiders was stronger than ever and she was filled with despair. Her father had made a mistake, true, but all he did now was go back and forth to his office, no threat to anyone. Who could possibly have a reason to kill him. *Who*? *Why?*

It was early in the morning when Finder left his lodging and headed for his office. He kicked at a stray dog, a sign of his growing frustration with Pottle. When confronted with his lack of action, the man would pull his hat lower, look down, and mumble about the protection for the victims, though he had figured out a sure way to take several of them down. A few heavy verbal lashes had been applied.

His misinformation was doing noteworthy damage, but it was time to move on. Convince his superiors that he had earned promotion. A former associate, Paul Wentworth, was overseeing clandestine operations in Paris. A secretary named Edward Bancroft was leading a double life after infiltrating into Franklin's delegation, also in Paris. Positions that he himself was capable of filling—and with luck there would be no need to deal with scum like Pottle. As for having failed to eliminate the entire patriot network, best to say nothing.

By now he was passing Christ Church. Perhaps he should attend a service there next Sunday. It wouldn't hurt his image to be seen taking communion with the new friends who had invited him into their homes. He liked their children and their dogs. However, it was wrong to be over-confident. Pottle could be caught and interrogated. If his own cover was blown, his escape plan was in place. Still, tomorrow he would change his routine. Walk on different streets and find another lodging. Being outed was not going to happen. To others, perhaps, but not to him.

★★★

CHAPTER EIGHTEEN

October 7, 1778

Louisa found solace in doing hard work in the house. One by one she was cleaning the less used rooms. Today she was wiping down the neglected front parlor when she looked out of the window and saw the Morris carriage stopping in front of the house. "Oh *no*," she said aloud and dropped the wet cloth. For weeks she had been dreading this call. Deceiving her friends was hard enough. Far harder to pull wool over Cousin Molly's sharp eyes. She smoothed her hair, forced her lips into a smile, and went to open the door.

Cousin Molly stood there with a large basket in her hand. "We've all been sick, why I've neglected you for so long. Anyhow, I'm here now with winter vegetables and venison from the country. We've moved down to the Front Street house but we still depend on food from the farm."

"You've all been sick? I'm so sorry—do come in—Jessie will be so pleased—" Louisa babbled. With any luck, Cousin Molly was on a round of errands and wouldn't stay.

"She can pickle some of it. I'll be bringing more," Cousin Molly said as she walked in.

Louisa took the basket. "We—shall we sit in the parlor? I was just cleaning it when I saw the carriage."

"Very well." Cousin Molly seated herself on a sofa

and pulled off her gloves. "Goodness, I feel as if we've quite lost touch. First little Charlie came down with a fever and a cough, then he passed them along to Robby and Thomas and to me. I lay in bed for days, no use to anyone."

"How miserable."

"It was, but enough of my aches and pains. What about you? I trust by now your father's leg has mended."

Louisa swallowed. Her mouth was very dry. "Not quite. It was a bad break and he can't put weight on it. A driver still lives over the barn and takes him back and forth to the office."

"*Still* not healed? What does Dr. Twifoot say?"

"Dr. Twifoot?" She hesitated, "Oh, Doctor *Twifoot.* He came here once when my mother was poorly but my father didn't like him. We depend on Cox the apothecary for whatever is needed."

Cousin Molly nodded. "I have great faith in Cox, but this is very hard for you, all the added care. I'll send Mercy over to give Jessie a hand. She's a good worker and now that we're all well, I can easily spare her."

Louisa swallowed again. To keep up the deceit they had managed to keep outsiders away. Mercy should never set foot in this house. "Thank you—so kind," she said, "but there's no need for Mercy. We're managing very well."

Cousin Molly gave her a searching look. "My dear, you look quite worn out. Are you sure?"

"Very sure."

"Well, I won't press." She sat back, settling herself for a chat. "So. Tell me what you've been doing while I was laid up. Have you been to many parties? Does General Arnold's romance with Peggy Shippen continue?"

"It does." No need to say that she was still Peggy's confidante and that she had read Arnold's passionate letter declaring his love and hopes of marrying her.

"I think Peggy is behaving badly and so do many

others. I must admit I was relieved when you stopped having those outings. Relieved, and glad we didn't fall out over that. What about callers? Anyone of interest?"

"Not really." Louisa twisted her hands. This was not a subject she wanted to discuss. "Tell me," she said quickly. "What about Cousin Robert? Did he escape the illness?"

"He did, thank goodness, but I've never seen him so low. So many troubles, the workhouses are overflowing with needy people. The Overseers of the Poor used to care for indigent women in the Bettering House. No longer, and people are hurting. Yesterday Mrs. Allen was driving herself in her little carriage to visit her sister. A man jumped out and stopped the horse. Said he had lost his job and his children were starving. She handed him all her money. He went off but she was very shaken."

"I can imagine," Louisa said as a shiver went up her spine. She too had been shaken by an attack.

"And now all these dreadful rumors. I don't know whether you've heard, but there may be a new and devastating form of smallpox going around, brought over from Africa. And talk that Washington's officers are deserting him and he's leaving for his home in Virginia. It doesn't seem likely but many people believe it. So worrying, but enough gloom and doom. I'm off to apothecary Cox for a salve. Hetty has a nasty rash on her little bottom."

"Poor Hetty."

"With children, if it isn't one thing, it's another." She looked around. "By the way, where's Will? The house is so quiet except for that barking dog."

"I think he's outside with Jessie."

"Such a beguiling child. Give him a hug from me."

"I will—and thank you again for the food." The ordeal was almost over. She started to get up, but Cousin Molly reached out and took her hand.

"My dear, I hate to fuss but you look so pale. Louisa,

you really do need Mercy. It's no bother and I insist. I'll send her over this afternoon—"

"*No.*" The word erupted like a cannon ball. "I tell you, we don't *need* Mercy. We don't *want* your help—" she choked and bit her lip.

Cousin Molly drew in her breath. "Indeed. Well, it's as clear as the nose on my face that you're in some kind of trouble but I'm not to know what it is." She hesitated. "I'm fond of you, Louisa. I thought we had become close, that you could trust me. It seems I was wrong." She got to her feet. "I won't send Mercy or offer more help, but if you change your mind you have only to ask. I won't call again." She picked up her gloves and walked to the door, head held high.

Seconds later Louisa heard the carriage leave. She sat still, then covered her face with her hands. She owed so much to this kind, generous woman. If only she could have thrown her herself into Cousin Molly's arms and admitted that the broken leg was a sham. It was fear of letting an outsider into the house that made her lose control and blurt out those hurtful words. Words that could never be unsaid.

Pressing her arms across her chest she rocked back and forth. Hot tears streamed down her face. Where was Captain Warren? He was the one person who could stop the killing but he led a dangerous life. He might be wounded or even dead. Losing Cousin Molly, the fear, the feeling of helplessness—It was too much to bear but feet were running down the hall. "Lulu, where are you?" Will's little voice was filled with worry. "You were going to play ball with me. Where are you?"

With an effort, she stopped rocking and lowered her hands. No matter what was to come she must keep her promise to her dying mother.

Hastily, she wiped her eyes and stood up. "I'm here, Willsy. I was cleaning the room and then Cousin Molly came to call. It's all right, my love. It's all right."

★★★

CHAPTER NINETEEN

October 10, 1778

For Eben Loring, life was now centered around the importance of presenting a brave front to his children and the need to keep his office open. His one comfort was to retreat at night to his small upstairs room—he had given the large one to Louisa—too many reminders of Susannah and their happy days before the war. He would open a book and immerse himself in the old classics: Homer's *Iliad* and the writings of Cicero and Seneca, ancient wisdoms that gave perspective. Empires rose and fell, tyrants came and went. The ominous threats to this country would fade into history—and so would his own less significant troubles, but for the sake of his children he tried to be cheerful. Louisa was managing well, but little Will needed assurance that he would always be loved and cared for.

This morning, as usual, he sat with them in the dining room as they ate their porridge. and cornbread.

"It looks as if the good weather is holding," he said to Louisa, laying down his spoon. "What are you and Will doing today?"

"Mrs. Allen has a little grandson visiting. She asked me to bring Will and spend the day with them. Her carriage will take us back and forth."

"Please give her my regards." He got up and gave Will a pat on the head. "You'll have a good time with a new friend. I'll see you later, my boy," he said, picked up his crutches, and went out to the street where Peter was waiting with the little gig.

"A nice morning, Peter. I'll go first to Market Street, then to the City Tavern." Twice a week at eleven o'clock, Sam Adams held a meeting with like-minded delegates at the City Tavern. Eben was there to listen and take notes.

Nat Haddam was already in the office going through papers. By now he was able to handle the less important cases. This gave Eben time to keep up with more demanding work, and he was depending more and more on Nat.

The Coffee Room was always busy at this hour. When Eben limped in on his crutches, the tables were filled and the air was thick with smoke. Adams and two other delegates, Oliver Ellsworth of Connecticut and John Collins of Rhode Island, were already seated. Adams waved him to a chair.

"Sit down, Loring. We've just started." He motioned to a waiter standing nearby. "Another coffee, please." The waiter disappeared. A moment later he was back with a steaming cup of the black brew.

The topic today was the ongoing trial of Silas Deane. "It's causing a serious division among us," Adams said, frowning. "The Lees of Virginia are engaging in a struggle for power, but as Benjamin Franklin once said, 'We must hang together, or most assuredly, we shall all hang separately."

"Hear, hear," Ellsworth murmured. Collins nodded, and the discussion changed to the ever-present problem of finding money to pay the military.

Eben listened carefully and jotted down relevant notes. After a few moments, he picked up his cup and took a sip of cooling coffee. The talk had switched to the failing currency when suddenly, with no warning twinge, he felt a sharp pain deep in his gut. He shifted on the chair and took a deep breath. Told himself to ignore it. But as the pain grew more intense, he began to lose concentration. Sweat broke out on his scalp and began to run down his neck. The faces around him blurred. A single thought hammered in his head: Get out. Get out.

"Not well. Excuse me," he muttered and reached for his crutches. With a fierce application of will, he managed to lurch through the room, down the hall, and out to the street.

His horse was tied to a hitching post nearby. Peter was sitting in the gig. Clenching his teeth to hold back a groan, Eben raised his hand.

"Peter," he managed to whisper. Peter looked around, jumped out of the gig, and ran to him.

"What is it, sir?"

"Pain. Bad. Home."

Moving fast, Peter put an arm around his shoulders and lifted him into the gig. He lay back during the short ride, feeling as if a red-hot poker had been thrust into his belly. Tried not to cry out as Peter carried him into the house and propped him on a chair in the hall.

"Jessie, where are you? Come quick," Peter shouted. "The master's took bad."

In a moment she was there. "What's this? What happened?"

"Don't know. I took him to the City Tavern. He was fine when he went in, then he came out like this. In pain, can't hardly say a word."

Jessie bent down. "Where is the pain, sir?" He pointed to his stomach. She straightened and looked at Peter. "Whatever it is, we have to get him upstairs."

Together they were able to carry him up to his room and lay him on his bed. Jessie took off his shoes and covered him with a quilt. Through his agony he could hear her talking to Peter. "He needs something to ease him, but Cox can't leave his shop. Go fast as you can to Dr. Twifoot's house on Second Street. If he's out, fetch him from wherever he is and bring him here. Don't take no for an answer." She touched a clenched hand. "Icy cold. Shock. I'll fetch more blankets, try to warm him. At least Missie and Will are away for the afternoon."

The door clicked shut. By now the torture was consuming. He lay motionless as fear took possession of his mind. What in the name of God was happening to him? Would he die? At least he was in his home, in his bed, not causing a scene in the public coffee room.

Closing his eyes, he let the waves of agony wash over him. Drifted in and out of consciousness until voices sounded in the room. Jessie spoke in his ear. "Sir, can you hear me? Dr. Twifoot is here to see you."

He opened his eyes. Old Dr. Twifoot was standing at the end of the bed. He put down his bag and folded his hands over a little paunch.

"Mr. Loring, I believe. I had the pleasure of attending your dear wife before you left for the north. A sad loss." He moved closer. "Now, sir. Your servants tell me you are unwell. Pray show me the location of the problem."

With an effort, he raised his hand and pointed to his belly.

"Ah." The doctor pulled back the blankets. He pressed down, causing a spasm of excruciating pain. "There is swelling," he pronounced. Taking a wrist, he felt for a pulse. "Weak, and also chills." He adjusted his white wig, thought for a moment, then cleared his throat.

"Quite so. My initial assessment informs me that the heart may not be affected. Rather, this trouble appears to be in the digestive system." He turned to Jessie who was standing by the door. "I assume you are the cook. What did your master eat and drink this morning?"

"His usual coffee and porridge, sir. A piece of cornbread."

"No ham that could have spoiled?"

"No, sir. Nothing like that. He was well when he

left the house."

"Ah. Hmm." He took a turn around the room, then came back to the bed. Frowned and made a tent of his fingers. "Now for my final diagnosis. In my opinion, sir, you have ingested a substance that has caused an acute assault upon the digestive system. I will administer a strong dose of laudanum which will alleviate the pain. I will call again this evening to continue the drug but I fear your condition is serious, sir. Very serious indeed."

By mid-afternoon Nat had finished work on the cases assigned to him. Now he sat at his small table with mounting concern. Mr. Loring should have returned from the City Tavern hours ago. He would never leave for the day without giving instructions. When heavy feet came pounding up the stairs, he got to his feet.

It was Peter. "Bad news, Nat," he said, panting. "Mr. Loring was took sick at the Tavern. A wicked sharp pain in the belly. I got him home but Jesus, Nat, he's very bad. It looks like he might die."

Nat stared. "Die? That can't be—he was well when he left for that meeting. There was nothing wrong with him then."

"I fetched the doctor, a fussy old crock who drugged him to the eyeballs, but Jessie says there's something on his mind. He wants to see you."

"Me? Why does he want to see *me*?"

"She just said to fetch you and be quick about it. There may not be much time."

"Good God. I'll lock up and come." He thrust papers into a drawer, snatched up his hat and followed Peter down to the gig. Drugged, maybe dying? This was hard to believe—but sending for him might have something to do with his will.

When they reached the house, he jumped out and

ran to the back door. Jessie opened it. The black face was calm, but her voice was shaky. "It's not good, Nat. The doctor gave him laudanum. He slept a little, but then he woke and whispered he wanted to see you."

"You don't know why?"

"No, but be prepared for the worst."

The room was very warm, the fire was blazing, and the smell of sickness was strong, the stench of a body losing control. He let out his breath and walked to the bed. Eben Loring lay still under heavy blankets. His eyes were closed.

Jessie adjusted a cover. "Mr. Loring, sir. Nat's here," she said loudly.

The eyes remained closed. Nat's stomach lurched. Only a few hours ago this stricken man was sitting at his desk reading the latest *Packet*. He had gone over Nat's notes and shown him a precedent in the Talbot case.

He swallowed hard and leaned down. "It's Nat, sir. Nat Haddam. I hear you wanted to see me."

Mr. Loring's eyes opened. He stared blindly at the ceiling, as if unable to focus, then the bluish lips formed four words. "Coffee. Poison. Tell Cox." His eyes closed.

Nat straightened and reached for the back of a chair to steady himself. This was not about a will. The meaning was clear. Mr. Loring wanted Cox to know he had been poisoned by coffee at the City Tavern.

The heat and smell were sickening. He stumbled into the hall and leaned against the wall. Nothing had prepared him for this blow, but he must carry out Mr. Loring's wishes. The situation was far beyond his experience but being in the military had instilled discipline. He must pull himself together and take charge. Go down and give the others the terrible news.

Peter and Jessie were sitting at the kitchen table. "Did he say anything?" Peter asked.

There was no way to soften the blow. "Four words. That's all. Just four words. Coffee. Poison. Tell Cox."

Peter and Jessie sat still, as stunned as if he had come at them with an axe. Then Peter hit the table with his fist. "Poison? Holy Jesus, I watched to see if we was followed like I always do, but I couldn't go with him into the Tavern."

"Not your fault. Someone must have figured out his routine. Picked the one place where he was vulnerable."

For a moment, no one spoke. At last Jessie cleared her throat. "He's still alive. We must ask the Lord Jesus to take pity on this good man. Have mercy and spare him."

Nat murmured "Amen." Peter raised his head. "Miss Louisa. It'll be some bad shock, seeing as how nothing was wrong when she left."

Jessie folded her hands. "I've seen trouble in my life," she said slowly. "We stay calm and we work together. I'll clean him and keep him warm." She hesitated. "Doctor Twifoot will be back to give Mr. Loring his drug. We must mind what we say to him or a tale about poison will be all over town."

Peter snorted. "Pompous old gasbag, I'll tend the fire. Fetch whatever is needed."

Nat stood up. "I'm off to Cox the apothecary. He'll know about poisons."

"I'll drive you," Peter said.

"It's not that far. Maybe you should stay and guard the house. We don't know who might be out there, waiting for a chance to come in and finish the job. There's so much we don't know. I'll talk to Cox. Then I'll be back."

★ ★ ★

CHAPTER TWENTY

October 10, 1778 *Later that day*

It was after three o'clock by the time Nat reached Cox's shop. He'd had no reason to come here before, too pricey, but he knew the apothecary by sight and reputation.

Cox was attending to several young ladies. Nat waited by the door until they made their purchases and left. Cox put packets on a shelf, then turned. He was a small, fatherly looking man, with graying hair tied back.

"Good day, sir," he said in a courteous voice. "How may I serve you?"

"Mr. Cox, my name is Haddam. Nat Haddam. I'm apprenticed to Mr. Eben Loring. He has an office on Market Street and I study law with him."

"A fine profession. What brings you here, if I may ask?"

Nat braced himself. "Sir, I—I've come with bad news about Mr. Loring."

Cox frowned. "Bad news?"

"It happened this morning." He took a deep breath. Speaking with care, he related the facts. The weekly meetings at the City Tavern. The poison in the coffee. The excruciating pain. Loring's four key words to his apprentice, ending with the instruction to tell Cox. "I think he knows he may die. He wanted to make sure you were given this information."

"I see." Cox's lips tightened. "This is most unfortunate. I'm aware of Mr. Loring's difficult situation. The need to pretend he has a broken leg. There was always the chance of an attack, but no one could anticipate this. I must take a moment to think."

Nat shifted his feet and waited. He had delivered the message and ought to get back.

Cox began to walk back and forth behind the counter, then stopped and cleared his throat. "You say Loring had a meeting twice a week at the City Tavern. Was it always on the same day, at the same time?"

"Yes, sir. That was part of his work with Congressman Samuel Adams."

Cox frowned. He ran his hand over the counter. "Poison is tricky. Finding a willing waiter would take careful planning. No doubt Loring was meant to die on the spot, presumably from a heart attack, leaving no evidence. The dose in his coffee may not have been strong enough, or he swallowed very little. In any case, the attempt failed. He was able to get up and walk away.

To determine what was in that coffee we would have locate that waiter, but I'm afraid that's impossible."

"No doubt the waiter was only a tool following orders but it's likely he's left the tavern. It's also likely he may be killed for failing. I'll let Captain Warren know, but I'm afraid it's a case of too little too late to get useful information." He shook his head again. "it's a tragic situation for Loring and his children."

Nat stared out at the street. It *was* a tragic situation—and the apothecary was right. If they waited for the captain, it would be too late to expose whoever was behind the dastardly attack.

The sign above the door flapped in a sudden gust of wind. Nat thrust his hands into his pockets. Mr. Loring had spent countless hours teaching him law. Encouraging him. Trusting him with cases. If he did nothing to help his mentor now, he would have it on his conscience for the rest of his life.

He took his hands out of his pockets and drew himself up. "Sir, there's this. I owe a great deal to Mr. Loring. To help him, I'm willing to go to that kitchen early tomorrow morning. Ask a few questions. I'm a farmer's son. I can dress and talk like one though I might come away with nothing."

Cox picked up a packet of cough drops and put it down. Again, he appeared to be thinking. After a moment, he turned and studied Nat. "This is an unexpected offer, young man. Quite unexpected. Chancy, but you appear to have a good head on your shoulders. As they say, nothing ventured, nothing gained. A warning, though, before we continue. Spies and informers are everywhere. No doubt some have been planted in the City Tavern, even in the kitchen. If you go in and ask questions you may be putting yourself at risk."

"In what way?"

"That's hard to anticipate, but here's my advice. Once you leave, try to act as if you could be followed. Stop at corners. Look around as if you're not sure which way to go. Watch for the same face, maybe wearing different clothes. Then lose yourself in a crowd if possible. Are you sure you want to proceed with this?"

"I'm sure."

"Well, whatever happens you'll have repaid your debt to Mr. Loring. About tomorrow, go before they start serving. I want a report, but come through the garden after dark and knock on the back door. Safer for both of us."

"Understood."

"Now for a potion to take back with you," He pulled a bottle from the shelf. "A mixture of charcoal and herbs. It may not wash out the poison but it can't harm. Above all, don't let Dr. Twifoot bleed him. It's his remedy for every ill. Miss Loring can spread the word that her father now has a severe case of dyspepsia, much like the ones that attack General Arnold."

"Thank you. I'll tell her, sir."

The afternoon was growing damp and cold. As he headed toward Fourth Street, he felt as if familiar ground was shifting under his feet. The impact of what had happened so suddenly was beginning to take hold. Peter's shocking news … the sight of Mr. Loring lying in bed, poisoned and suffering … anger … and now the sense that he had been handed daunting responsibility and must keep a cool head.

The back door was locked. He rapped on it, bracing himself for what might have happened while he was gone. The bolt slid back and Jessie let him in.

"He's the same," she said in a low voice. "Missie and Master Will came home a while ago. They're in the dining room. Missie is very shook up. You'd best go in."

"I will, but first—" he reached into his pocket and pulled out the bottle Cox had given him. "Cox says this can't do any harm, but on no account let Dr. Twifoot bleed him."

"No fear of that. Except for the drug, he'd never set foot in this house again."

Louisa was sitting on a chair, holding tightly to Will. The boy looked at Nat and put a finger to his lips. "My father's sick," he whispered. "You mustn't make a noise."

"I know." He ruffled Will's hair. "I know, and I'm sorry," he said and sat down."

Louisa raised her head. Her face was very white. "Will, here's Jessie. She has a treat for you—"

"A treat? What kind of treat?" He jumped down and went with Jessie to the kitchen.

Louisa put her elbows on the table. She pressed her fingers to her head. "We came back from Mrs. Allen's," she whispered. "I went up … I couldn't believe … he was well this morning and now he's going to die … first my mother, now my father …" her voice broke. She covered her face with both hands and put her head down on the table. Her whole body was shaking.

Nat sat still, not knowing what to say. If Miss Loring was his little sister, he could hug her and stroke her hair. But even in this agonizing moment, he must keep his distance. Show proper respect—but something must be done. He grasped the edge of the table and took a deep breath.

"Miss Loring," he began haltingly, feeling his way. "Your father is a brave man and he's going to fight to live. This is a terrible blow, but while there's life there's hope. We must hold onto that hope and not give in. Do everything we can to give him the best possible care. I think—I believe—this is what he would expect from us." He let go of the table and sat back.

A log sputtered in the fire. He waited, afraid to say more, but slowly her body stopped shaking. Her hands were still pressed to her face, but he could see that she was struggling for control. After another long moment, she lifted her head. Pulled out a handkerchief and wiped her swollen eyes.

"It was seeing him lying there, so—so *changed.* I—I still can't—but yes, we must give him every care—not give in—that's what he needs, what he would want from us—" she was talking very fast.

He winced. Talking fast was a sign of delayed shock. He'd seen it in the army. He leaned forward and spoke softly. "You're right. It's what he would want from you."

She swallowed and was silent. After a moment she straightened and pushed back her hair. "Yes. He would—Jessie and I can do it."

He frowned. This was more than he had hoped for, but it wasn't right. "Miss Loring," he said in the same soft voice, "I understand how you feel, but nursing is constant hard work."

She shook her head. "I took care of my mother

until she died. Dr. Twifoot will want to send a nurse, but we can't risk having an outsider in the house, one who might gossip."

"No. But all the same—"

"Wait. Let me think." She pushed back her hair again. "Will—he mustn't see his father. Peter can go with a note to my cousin Mrs. Morris. My father's leg is worse, he's in great pain, and I would like to send Will for a visit. She's kind and Will loves being with her children."

He listened, trying not to show surprise. One evening, many weeks ago, he had taken papers to the house. Miss Loring had come down the stairs, about to leave for a ball, dressed in a blue silk gown with flowers in her hair. She had looked like a princess in his little sister's picture book. He would never have guessed that she had this much resilience. The ability to rally and make decisions—but she had support. Jessie was a pillar of strength. Peter was reliable. Now all they could do was see if Mr. Loring would make it through the night.

The room was growing cold. The fire was almost out. He got up, added logs until the flames flared up, then turned. "Miss Loring, is there anything more I can do for you? If not, I'll leave and go home. Peter will come for me if I'm needed at any hour."

She stared as if seeing him for the first time. "I can't think of anything—but where do you live?"

"On Cuthbert Street. With my family. I'll let myself out." He picked up his hat and coat and left, closing the door behind him. Unless Loring died, he had to be up early, ready to go to the kitchen at the City Tavern.

Peter was waiting in the hall. "How is she now?" he asked.

"Better. Able to look ahead and make plans. Fetch me if I'm needed during the night. You know where I live. I'll be back tomorrow morning, but if nothing has happened. I should check the office."

"Aye, right. Me and Jessie, we'll do what we can

but it sure looks bad."

Outside the wind was rising, rattling the chimney pots. He pulled his new coat tighter, a replacement for one that was worn and shabby; a high-priced clothier had traded it for venison and prime beef.

It was a twenty-minute walk to Cuthbert Street. His house was small and shabby compared to the Loring's, but years ago when he won a scholarship to college, he vowed that he would never apologize for his humble background. He respected his hardworking father, he loved his little sister, and he was grateful for his mother's undemanding care. No matter how late he came home, there was always a hot meal, a warm welcome, and interest and pride in his work.

Wincing, he slowed the pace. The wound in his leg from the battle at Monmouth had healed, but it still throbbed when he walked too much, and it had been a long day, starting with Peter's appearance at the office—and that was another problem. If Loring lived, it might be a long time before he was able to work and earn. Money was needed. The office must be kept open for clients.

As he reached the corner of Sixth Street, he stopped and looked around. Like many in the city, he was aware of the dark world of espionage but he never expected to be part of it. His wish to help the afflicted Loring family was stronger than ever, but once again he had the feeling that he was walking blindly on unfamiliar ground. This was a situation that required the expertise of a man like Captain Warren and one fact was dauntingly clear: His own lack of experience would be severely tested when he walked into that kitchen tomorrow.

★★★

CHAPTER TWENTY-ONE

October 11, 1778

It was just after seven in the morning when Nat left the house wearing one of his father's brown smocks and a blue wool cap. In case a bribe was needed, three pieces of silver from his own savings were tucked into a back pocket.

There were few people on the streets. He walked quickly, fighting a recurring wave of apprehension. He knew how to talk like a lowly servant boy, but did he have the wits to ask the right questions? Whatever happened, he must not let his anger show.

The City Tavern's large kitchen was hot. Strong smells of baking bread and roasting meat filled the air. A heavy man wearing a white apron and a tall cook's hat came toward him, holding a tray. "What's wanted?" he asked gruffly.

Nat pulled off his cap. "Sir, happens me master sent me to find the waiter what took coffee to Congressman Adams's table yesterday morning. In the Coffee Room, it was."

The man raised thick eyebrows. "You want to find a waiter yesterday morning in the Coffee Room? Not a chance. Off with you, boy."

Nat wiped his nose. "Happens he's owed money. Me orders is to find him and give him the money what's owed him."

A young fellow was standing at a table nearby, kneading dough. He began to laugh. “Money owed? Then it’s me you want.”

An older man was cutting vegetables. He waved his knife in the air. “None of your sauce, Pat. It was Dan and now he’s gone.”

Nat scratched his head. “Gone? Gone where? Got to find him or the master will give me what for.”

The young fellow rubbed his floury hands on a cloth. “Master beats you, does he? Tell you this. Dan wasn’t a bad bloke. Down on his luck, but he knew how to wait, why he was hired when we was shorthanded. Could be he lives down in those shacks by the wharves. Bunch of Brits like him deserted when the redcoats left and now—”

“That’ll do, Pat,” the cook said sharply. “Get back to work and you be off, boy. You’re wasting our time.”

Nat scuffed his feet, put on his cap, and hurried back to the street. For a moment he stood against the wall, thinking. He now had a name and a location, but it would be weeks before Captain Warren arrived and could take action.

People passed by. Nat pulled himself away from the wall. According to Cox, the waiter might be killed because Mr. Loring didn’t die on the spot. Therefore a decision must be made. He could go home and change his clothes—or he could go to the shacks. Maybe get a step closer to finding the scoundrels behind the attack. Deserters living rough wouldn’t welcome a stranger asking questions. It would be far more hazardous than walking into the City Tavern kitchen, but he had faced the enemy at Monmouth and overcome fear. “In for a penny, in for a pound,” his father often said. For Mr. Loring it was worth taking the risk—and no one else could do it.

The port on the Delaware River was the busiest in the colonies. French warships rode peacefully at anchor, ships of all sizes plied the choppy waves. Many were owned by traders and were being refitted before sailing out to distant lands. But constant dangers lurked on the high seas: Battles were waged between rival countries. Privateers attacked without warning to steal valuable cargoes.

He had seldom been in this part of the city. Going slowly down Water Street, he passed wharfs with names like Wales and Attwood. On and on, but just beyond Plumsteads he saw a large warehouse. Below it, almost hidden from sight, lay a huddle of small shacks.

A worn path led him down from the street to a trampled open space. The derelict structures had been built from rotting boards with tar paper roofs and no windows. The place seemed deserted.

"Ho there. Is anyone about?" he shouted.

Silence. He tried again. "Is anyone here?"

No answer, but there was a muffled sound in the nearest shack. Bracing himself for trouble, he walked forward and knocked on the flimsy door. Waited a few seconds, then opened it a few inches and peered in. A man lay cowering on a straw pallet. "Don't kill me," he whimpered, covering his belly with one hand. "For God's sake, don't kill me."

Nat opened the door wider and went in. A bottle of whisky lay on the dirt floor beside the pallet. The smell of filth was sickening. If this terrified man was Dan the waiter, he presented no threat.

"It's all right," he said quickly. "I'm nowt but a stable boy. I won't hurt you."

The man raised his head. He stared at Nat with bloodshot eyes. "Who are you? Get out," he said in a slurred voice, then fell back on the pallet.

Nat stood still, thinking fast. A frightened drunk, barely able to speak. How to get information out of him? His best chance would be to treat him like a child. Speak slowly, using simple words.

"You are Dan the waiter," he began. "I won't hurt

you. A bad person told you to put poison in a cup of coffee. Give me his name and I'll give you this." He reached into his pocket and held up a piece of silver.

The man stared. The sight of money seemed to penetrate his disoriented brain. With an effort, he pulled himself up. Blinked and rubbed his head as if that might help him regain his wits.

Nat averted his eyes and waited. The filth, the smell—it was hard to believe anyone could exist in such squalor. After a moment the man raised himself higher. He coughed violently, and a stream of disconnected words came pouring out of his mouth.

"Not always like this … had schooling … came here on the *Trident* … waiter in the officer's mess … mates and I deserted … no work. Then it happened." He coughed again and stopped.

Nat stiffened, every sense alert. Somehow he must keep the man talking. A few crusts of bread covered with flies lay on a battered crate. He pushed them off and sat down.

"What happened, Dan?" he said softly. "Tell me what happened and you can have the money."

Dan spat. A gob of spittle streaked with blood landed on the pallet. He rubbed his head again, then sat up and leaned forward.

"I'll tell you straight," he said in a stronger voice. "He came here. Said he'd pay us to watch houses. Follow people."

"A man came to you. How long ago was this? Weeks? Months?"

"Weeks, like. It was hot."

"What did he look like?"

"Hat over his face … one shoulder shorter … if we messed up he'd kill us one by one." He spat again. "Has by the balls … we call him Killer Man."

"Did he give you the poison?"

"Little bottle … ten drops … didn't work … now

I have to die." He fell back on the pallet.

A horn tooted on the river. Nat shifted on the crate. His stomach was churning. He had information. He should get out of here, but before Dan collapsed again he had one last chance to learn more.

"Look, Dan. Look at this. Two pieces of silver. Yours if you can tell me more about Killer Man. Anything at all."

Dan groaned. He spat up more blood. "Warm night," he said at last. "Very warm. One of my mates—he's got balls. Followed him. Followed him to a tavern." He stopped.

Nat's eyes narrowed. He forced himself to speak slowly. "What tavern, Dan? What was the name of this tavern?" Dan shook his head. Nat moved closer. He thrust the silver into Dan's face. "Think, Dan. Think hard. Give me the name of that tavern."

Dan stared at the silver then hit his head. "Fruit," he muttered. "Something with fruit." Nat leaned down and shook Dan's shoulder. "Which fruit? Apples? Pears? Grapes?" Dan didn't answer. He gave a racking cough and fell back on the bed. Clutched his belly and closed his eyes.

Nat shuddered, then placed the silver on Dan's hand. "I'm leaving, but listen to me. You can use this to get away. Hide yourself and be safe." Dan didn't open his eyes.

Nat turned. Gulping fresh air, he ran back up the path to Water Street. It was over but as long as he lived he would never forget those wrenching moments with Dan in that foul shack. He had managed to wring important information out of a frightened drunk, but there were dozens of taverns in the city.

At Coome's Alley, he stopped and looked around. No one seemed to be following him. He let out his breath. It was only mid-morning with much left to be done. Cox must have a report, but that would have to wait until it was dark. Rather than go straight to Fourth Street, he would open the office and work for a few hours on the pending cases. Thanks to Mr. Loring, he now had a fair understanding of law and there were books available for reference. If the worst had happened and his good mentor was dead, Peter would come to tell him.

It was after three o'clock when he knocked on the Loring's back door. Jessie let him in. "I went to the office," he said to her. "How is he?"

"No worse, but the doctor has little hope. Master Will is with the Morrises and missie is with her father. Go up and say a few words to him. He's drugged, but he may take in more than we know."

The bedroom was hot, the fire blazing, but there was no longer the stench of sickness. Miss Loring was placing a warming pan under the blankets. She turned when she saw him at the door.

"He made it through the night," she said under her breath. "Come and speak to him. It's hard to know how much he can understand, but it's important to keep trying."

"Jessie said the same." He went to the bed and looked down at the thinning face. Reached out and touched the blanket. "It's Nat, sir. Nat Haddam," he said in a steady voice. "I've come from the office. A client came in. I thought you'd like to know."

Loring's eyes remained shut, but his lips twitched slightly. Miss Loring nodded. "He heard," she whispered.

"I think he did." He glanced at her. She was wearing a white cap and a large white apron. By now he was aware that the deceptively frivolous surface hid a surprisingly strong will. All the same, she looked worn out. There were dark circles under her eyes. "Were you up all night?" he asked.

"Jessie and I take turns. We rub his legs to keep up the circulation and try to give him the potion that Cox sent. Dr. Twifoot has drugs to ease the pain. That may go on for a long time unless—" her voice quavered.

Miss Loring shook her head and touched the altered face. "It's so wrong. He made one little mistake, but he doesn't deserve to suffer like this."

"No, he doesn't." He cleared his throat. "Take heart, Miss Loring," he said, hiding his sadness. "He's still with us and he's getting good care. He may pull through." He hesitated. "Unless I'm needed here tomorrow I'll keep the office open. I think that's what he would want."

She nodded. "You're right. I'm sure that's what he would want.

"I'll be off then, but I'll be back tomorrow, sooner if you need me," he said and turned toward the door. This was not the right moment to tell Miss Loring about Dan, but his success in the shacks had given him enough confidence to take another and far more risky step.

★★★

CHAPTER TWENTY-TWO

October 12, 1778

It was late afternoon. Nat had closed the office early and now he was standing at the rear of the Bunch of Grapes Tavern on Front Street. Last night Cox had narrowed the search to this disreputable place, but when Nat told Cox that he wanted to go there and investigate, a dubious Cox had given him a dire warning. "Far better to wait for Captain Warren. Put yourself in a leader's shoes. By now he knows the attack on Loring failed. He'll want to know if Loring is able to give any information. You're a likely source. Therefore you may be targeted and find yourself in trouble." Nat had assured him that he had no intention of confronting a killer, just wanted to know where to find him. After all, a servant might be bribed to accept a trumped-up story and give him information. They had almost fallen out, but in the end, Cox had reverted to his "Nothing ventured, nothing gained" motto and agreed.

But now as he stood in the fading light, Nat had the sinking feeling that he had been overconfident; that, in the sinister world of espionage, he had taken on far more than he could handle. Perhaps Cox was right, they should wait for Captain Warren, but Cox hadn't seen Mr. Loring lying drugged in his bed. Seen a caring daughter nursing him around the clock. Compelling reasons to risk coming here.

He crossed his arms over his chest and waited, tamping down mounting frustration. Several men had appeared for a quick smoke, but they seemed too high in rank to approach. Cursing under his breath, he was about to leave when a young boy wearing a dirty smock came out. He slouched against a wall and began to chew on a piece of rawhide.

Nat composed himself. He walked toward him as if coming from the street. "Good evening," he said in a pleasant voice. "I work for a lawyer who is looking for a witness who may live here. He wears a hat pulled down over his face and one shoulder is higher than the other. My lawyer will pay well for any information about him." An unconvincing tale, but it would have to do.

The boy straightened and spat out the last of the rawhide. His left eye slid to one side. "Must be our Mr. Brown," he said in a sullen voice. "What's to know about *him*?"

"Is one shoulder a little higher than the other?"

"Yah."

"Is he here now?"

"Nah."

"How long has he lived here? The more you tell me, the more I pay," and he jingled the silver coins in his pocket.

The boy got the message and now the words came fast. "Mebbe a month. Mean. Keeps to himself. The owner here don't like him. Says he's up to no good, but Mr. Brown has money. Hands out big rent for a room in the cellar."

"Does he ever have visitors?"

The boy scratched his head, "Not him—no, wait. One bloke, weeks ago. Mebbe there been others."

"Can you describe the one you saw?" He jingled the coins again.

"Happens I was scrubbing the hall floor when he comes in. Asks for a Mr. Brown. Owner told me to fetch him, then get on with my work. They went to the front door and talked real quiet. Didn't hear nothin', but it struck me as queer, like."

"Why?" The boy was more intelligent than he looked.

"He spoke like a real toff. A young gentleman, like, so what was he doing with our Mr. Brown? Nothing good, but he handed him money."

Nat cleared his throat. "He gave him money? Are you sure?"

"A clinking bag of it. Coins it was, not paper." He scratched his head again. "That's all I know, mister. Where's the pay?"

Nat pulled out two pieces of silver. "Take it. Best to say nothing to Mr. Brown or the owner."

The boy grinned. "No fear." He bit the silver to test it, then ran back to the door.

Nat turned onto Front Street and hurried to join a protective crowd on the walkway. Against all odds, he had managed to get valuable information. The killer lived at that tavern using the name Brown. He was receiving money from a gentleman but there were dozens of them in the city. Any further action would have to wait for Captain Warren. He looked around to make sure no one was following, then joined a group of shoppers—the Lorings depended on him to earn money. An unexpected success, but it was time to stop combining the search and the need to keep the office open. He would wait a few days, then bring the tired Loring household together. Give them the good news—carefully edited—that the waiter who poisoned the coffee had been found and was no longer a threat.

★★★

CHAPTER TWENTY-THREE

October 15, 1778

Louisa had never been so discouraged. Lately there were signs that Eben Loring's condition had stabilized but two nights ago, with no warning, he was in agonizing pain, barely able to breathe. Dr. Twifoot administered a massive dose of morphine and spoke at length to Louisa. "There are four humors in the body, Miss Loring. The sanguine, the choleric, the phlegmatic, and the melancholic. I cannot determine which of these has affected your father, but relapses are inevitable. I've seen it many times. You must prepare yourself for the end."

But her father survived and the household rallied to support him. For Louisa, Jessie's quiet competence was a source of strength and the two had achieved a closeness that was blind to custom and color. Nat's visits to her father, bringing a little money, were deeply appreciated. But today as he came in, he stopped her in the hall.

"I'll go upstairs now, but when I come down, I would like to speak to you and Peter and Jessie. Meet with all of you."

This was surprising but she nodded. "Very well. I'll fetch them. We'll be in the dining room."

A few minutes later, the four were seated at the long polished table. Nat shifted in his chair, then cleared his throat. "I've asked you to come because I think you should hear some good news. The City Tavern waiter who put poison in the coffee has been found. He won't cause more trouble and Cox has notified Captain Warren. In the meantime, we need to carry on as usual. Keep up our guard."

The other three sat motionless. Then Peter hit the table with his fist. "Jesus Christ, let me get my hands on the bloody bastard—"

Louisa pushed back her hair, then held up her hand. "Peter, wait. Nat, this is amazing news. I'm glad—of course I am—but tell us more. Where is the waiter now? Who found him?"

Nat looked uncomfortable. She could see that he was reluctant to go on. "There's not much more to tell except that to catch him it was important to move fast. Cox suggested that I go to the City Tavern kitchen and ask a few questions. A waiter there had left but was living rough in a shack by the river. He was in bad shape, but he told me about a scoundrel who pays British deserters to work for him."

Peter hit the table again, "Blimey, mate, that took some nerve to go there."

"Now Captain Warren can act quickly when he comes. That's it, and now we can get on with our work."

Louisa sat still. Peter was right. It took real nerve for Nat to go to that place, but by now she knew him well enough to realize that he was holding something back. His voice was stilted and he clearly wanted to say nothing else.

She leaned forward. "I agree with Peter," she said. "It was good of you to do it, but there has to be more. I mean, someone higher up must have given that waiter the poison. Planned and given him orders. He may come after us again. She took a deep breath. "Nat, this is very confusing. I can see that you're not giving us the whole story. Please tell us what else has happened. I think we're owed."

For a moment Nat stared down at the floor. Then he raised his head. "If you insist—"

"I do."

"Very well. The man who ordered the poison rents a room in a tavern. What matters is that he had a visitor who gave him money. A well-dressed young gentleman. He may be the brains behind many attacks but it would take a massive search to find him, using resources that we don't have.

No one spoke. Louisa closed her eyes. So much to absorb, but it all came down this: The man behind the poison attack on her father rented a room in a tavern. He could be getting money from a young, well-dressed gentleman. And one of these well-dressed men had ruined their lives and might strike again.

"Miss Louisa," Nat's voice. "I'm sorry if this has upset you."

She opened her eyes. "I'm not upset. I'm angry. Very angry. This gentleman—it's not likely, but he could be someone who mixes with us at our parties. Someone who is plotting attacks while he dances the gavotte. Now that I'm not with my father at night I can go to more parties. I'm a good observer. If I think someone could be a double agent I can ask a few questions, I know it's a small chance, but I have to at least *try*."

Peter opened his mouth, then shut it again. Jessie coughed. Nat leaned forward. "Miss Louisa. I understand your feelings, but you'd be searching for a highly dangerous man. It's doubtful that he goes to your parties but let's say he does. You observe and you ask questions. If he suspects you of suspecting him, it could lead to serious trouble."

"Serious trouble?" She clenched her fists. "I don't care. My mind is made up. I'll do anything—*anything*—to find the man who nearly killed my father. See that he gets what he deserves." She could feel the heat rising into her face.

Nat was silent. He seemed to be thinking. "Consider this, Miss Loring," he said at last. "Looking for that man and asking questions carries risks, but there's a way you could do it without arousing his suspicions."

She gave him a wary look. "Oh? And what do you suggest?

"Turn it around. Concentrate on listening. You have one advantage. The toff—gentleman—doesn't know you're looking for him. So instead of asking questions, watch for someone who asks for information about your father's health, more than just a polite inquiry. Someone who's not close to you and would have no reason to be inquisitive. Listen, and do nothing that would tip him off. Then you can give me his name and I'll pass it along to Cox."

She hesitated, then loosened her hands. "All right. I'll watch and listen. Say nothing."

The tension in the room eased. Peter stood up and muttered that the old horse needed to be fed. "I'll bring tea," Jessie said and they left.

The clock in the front parlor chimed the hour of six. She glanced at Nat, seeing him in a different light. Once he was a mere apprentice wearing shabby clothes. But since the attack he had managed to retain the law practice and much needed money was coming in. To help her father, he had gone to menacing places. With no experience, he had faced hazards with unusual intelligence and ability. He had understood her need to find the deceiver who was leading a double life. Accepted it and presented her with a face-saving solution.

"Nat," she began.

"Yes?"

"For weeks you've kept the practice going and I'm grateful. You took risks for us, though you tried very hard to hide your part."

He frowned. "Not dangerous, but I don't think I should have told you about the well-dressed gentleman—"

"No, don't think that. It means I have a chance to do something for my father." She pulled her shawl closer and looked at him. "Nat, you've done so much for us. I—I don't know how to thank you."

He shifted in his seat. "No need. I owe your father. It may take time to find the person responsible for attacking him, but it will happen. He will be stopped from doing further harm and made to pay."

"Stopped and made to pay, though a king's ransom wouldn't be enough. Now for our tea. I think we deserve it." She turned and picked up the brown teapot that Jessie had placed at the end of the table. Filled two cups, sipped, and made a face. "Rum. Jessie has filled the pot with *rum*." They looked at each other and began to laugh.

Finder stood in the Farmers Market and waited for Ralph Pottle, the twisted criminal who knew too much about him.

At ten o'clock on the dot, Pottle appeared, his hat pulled down over his face as usual. What in hell was the man hiding? A scar that could identify him?

"Go to pots and pans," he snapped and led the way to the booth. Standing at the edge of the crowd, he faced Pottle.

"You're in big trouble," he began. "You've been on the job for weeks and only two on that list are dead. I gave you poison to silence Legal, a key player. He's still alive and may be able to talk. Get rid of the protection around him. No more of your excuses. Finish him and at least two others or when we meet next week there will be no more gold. Do you understand? None. That's all I have to say." He turned on his heel and strode away. Pottle didn't follow.

But as he reached Second Street, he began to have second thoughts. Threats of no pay might precipitate action, but there were problems. Legal could cause trouble but he was well protected. It would be extremely hard to silence him.

A drunk on the corner came staggering toward him. But as he gritted his teeth, dodged, and kept walking, a new plan began to take form. He ought to change direction. Think bigger. A competent leader was the backbone of any operation. Remove the leader and the structure would fall apart. To achieve this would be difficult, it might take time, but it had to be done.

He avoided a beggar with a cup and tried to think ahead. It was important to do well at his job with the trader, continue creating harmful divisions, but he could cut back on his social life. Much as he disliked the thought of involving himself, he must concentrate on finding the mastermind behind Legal and this troublesome network. Use his well-honed skills to ferret him out, then order vicious Pottle to follow and take him down.

★★★

CHAPTER TWENTY-FOUR

November 15, 1778 *Middlebrook, New Jersey*

The long, warm, golden days of autumn were long gone. By mid-November summer was but a memory and people were bracing for the hardships of the long winter months.

Earlier in the fall, General Washington had made a strategic decision. He would divide his army into three sections. One brigade was to stay on the west side of the Hudson River, and another would be posted to Elizabethtown, New Jersey. The main portion of his troops, a little over eight thousand men, would go to Middlebrook, New Jersey, using the Watchung Mountains and Lookout Rock as a barrier against surprise attacks.

For Andrew Warren, Major Tallmadge's request for a meeting meant leaving New York and making the long ride into central New Jersey. But today the weather was milder, the roads were clear, and the sturdy Narragansett mare settled into the steady pace for which the breed was famous. At mid-afternoon he slowed as he reached a side road with distant signs of a recently established camp.

"Almost there," he said to the mare and patted her heaving flank. An unwelcome interruption, but by now he knew the Major would never send for him without good reason.

The mare snorted as a sentry stepped into the road and motioned them to halt. After giving the password and receiving directions, Andrew was allowed to ride on. Nearby, raggedly dressed soldiers were hard at work building log huts from felled trees; it was a skill learned from winters in Morristown and Valley Forge, but he could see that most of the army still lived in lines of canvas tents.

The new headquarters was a large white house. There were no visible Life Guards which meant that Washington was not in residence. After making sure that the mare would be rubbed down and fed, Andrew headed for the front door. It was open and he walked in.

The wide hall smelled strongly of fresh paint. An orderly, a youngster with big ears and pock-marked skin hurried forward.

"Captain Warren from New York," Andrew said. "Major Tallmadge is expecting me."

"Yessir, yessir, he surely is. I'll find him, I'll tell him ye're here," the boy chattered and ran off.

After a short wait, the major appeared. "You made it, Warren. Good to see you," he said warmly. "Any trouble on the way?"

"None, but I should start back as soon as possible."

"Then we won't waste time," Tallmadge said and opened a door. "House belongs to a John Wallace. Recently built, and there's still work to be done before Washington arrives. I came ahead to arrange for security." He turned and spoke to the hovering young orderly. "Jenkins, bring bread, cheese, ale, and any hot food Cookie has on hand."

"Yessir, yes. Right away, sir."

The big front room was sparsely furnished with a round table and two straight chairs. Andrew laid his coat and hat on the bare floor and sat down.

Tallmadge threw a log on the smoldering fire and took the other chair. "To begin, what's happening in

New York? Are you in touch with the Culper outfit on Long Island?"

"Useful information has been exchanged. We think Clinton may make a few skirmishes this winter but his real aim is to take the Hudson River. Separate the north from the south. But lately there are signs that some sort of military operation may be underway. Two large ships entered the harbor and large armaments are being repaired or replaced."

"What about Clinton himself?"

"Sir Henry was always moody, but now he's deeply depressed. Knows how much he's disliked and wants to go home. Worries that the French fleet may stay in the West Indies to protect their rich sugar islands. Blames the Howe brothers for not winning the war. To cheer himself, he organizes fancy entertainments at headquarters and in his borrowed country house. Acts in plays. Fiddles on his violin."

"Meanwhile, who's doing the work?"

"Captain John Andre. He's back from serving with General Grey and he's by far the most intelligent officer on Clinton's staff. Last winter, when I was a waiter at British parties, I had a good chance to observe him."

"What's his background?"

"He comes from a Swiss merchant family with money. Moved with them to England and joined the Royal Welch Fusiliers. Saw service in Germany, was captured in Canada and sent to Pennsylvania. Was exchanged, then bought a commission in the Twenty-Sixth Foot. In 1777 he became an aide to Grey."

"Which means he took part in the Paoli massacre. Our soldiers bayoneted as they slept in their tents."

"No doubt he did, then spent the winter living the high life in Philadelphia. He moves in top social and artistic circles. Speaks four languages, writes verses, paints, but he also does military maps and has European connections. What's more, he's starting to collect and handle intelligence for Clinton."

"A key player. Any more developments?"

"One that's of interest. I told you about the English footman we infiltrated into headquarters. He's made a point of getting to know one of Andre's couriers, a man with no head for hard liquor. While they were drinking knee-to-knee in a sleazy tavern, the courier complained about his monthly trips to Philadelphia, trips that take him at least three days each way, always at the end of the month."

"And?"

"His orders are to leave a large container under a certain bridge a few miles north of the city. Cover it and ride off. But on the last trip he succumbed to curiosity. Opened it and found three bags of gold sovereigns hidden under a layer of Tilson tea caddies—carrying tea makes him a respectable merchant selling goods. We should have watchers at the bridge, ready to follow whoever picks it up, but we don't have that kind of manpower available."

"Unfortunate, because following a money trail often gets good results. Keep me posted." Tallmadge paused as the orderly appeared with a tray of food. Thick bread and cheese, steaming coffee in mugs, and two bowls of cornmeal mush.

The orderly put it on the small table and scratched his head. "Cookie's making stew but it ain't ready yet. Mebbe some of them old apples?"

"No, this will do. Go along now, Jenkins," Tallmadge said dismissively, then motioned Andrew to pull up his chair. "A local boy. His mother is a widow and they need money. Mrs. Washington would soon have him trained, but she's in Mount Vernon where Washington would like to retire with no worse worries than a blight on the tobacco crop. That won't happen. I think we're in serious danger of losing this war—and not in any battle."

"Why do you say that?"

"I say it because Congress seems incapable of action. You saw the men out there, some with no hats, some short of blankets. Officers are leaving because they're not paid. We depend on each state to raise money, and too many delegates are fixed on gaining control and power. Putting their own ambitions before the needs of the country. And we aren't getting much help from the French."

"A bleak outlook. Very bleak indeed. What's to be done?"

"We carry on with the principles laid out in our Declaration of Independence. We don't give up on what some are calling the Great Experiment. We do our best to make the right choices. Ones that can last."

For a moment neither man spoke. The silence was broken by the sound of loud hammering above. Tallmadge finished the mush and wiped his mouth

"Enough on that subject." His lips tightened. "Warren, you've given me useful information, but I asked you to make the journey for another reason."

Andrew waited. At last, an explanation for the inconvenient summons.

"It's this. The General has decided that to get help from Congress he must travel to Philadelphia. Beg and twist arms. He'll go at the end of December which gives us only a short time to prepare. There'll be meetings and parties for weeks. British and loyalist opponents in Philadelphia will see this visit as a rare chance to remove him and end the war."

"No doubt they will."

Tallmadge paused. "I understand the need for this trip but protecting him will be extremely difficult. Even harder if word of the visit leaks and gives the enemy time to plot. News spreads fast and few can be trusted."

"True."

"The situation will require an intensive search to find and deter threats. As I see it, attackers will make use of embedded spies, double agents, or outside forces. We need to have a counter-force on the ground looking for possible suspects, and we need to start now."

"What do you have in mind?"

Tallmadge paused again, then looked at Andrew. "Warren, as you know, every operation needs a designated leader. You've been given difficult assignments in the past and handled them well. You know the city better than anyone else. I would like you to lead this critical search. It would be an official appointment. You will have every assistance."

Andrew stiffened. Lead an intensive search to find and prevent a threat to the General? He opened his mouth to say there must be someone better qualified—then stopped. Tallmadge was right. He knew the city. He would have to comply with this unexpected order.

Tallmadge was waiting for an answer. He clenched his fists and put them on his knees. "A tall order, sir, but I'll do my best. You can be sure of that."

"I am. How soon can you leave New York?"

"I'll have to find someone to replace me."

"Well, as soon as you can. Now for details." Tallmadge drummed with his fingers on the table. "You'll have baggage, so a crew will row you across the river to the Jersey side. We have a safe house in Elizabethtown, run by a Mrs. Comstock—her son was taken prisoner at Monmouth and died. One of my aides will meet you there. He'll have a carriage and you can go on with him to Philadelphia."

"Understood. When is the General expected here?"

"Around the eleventh of December, then we move on. The General and Mrs. Washington will stay with Henry Laurens, the president of Congress. A big landowner in South Carolina. His son John is one of Washington's aides."

"I've met him. A good man."

A crash above made them both jump. Tallmadge grimaced. "They're trying to finish before the General comes. It'll soon be dark. You'd better spend the night here. Have some of Cookie's tolerable stew."

Andrew suppressed a smile. "If I remember, your orders were to leave New York as soon as possible."

"Point made." He hesitated. " One more clarification. Until now we were able to contain the threats. At Valley Forge we uncovered the killer stable boy and ex-captain Jamieson, still in hiding, but in Philadelphia we face countless opportunities to assassinate the General. Public appearances. Servants in various houses. The dangers will be greater and your part will be essential."

Andrew frowned. "Communications were easier when you were in White Plains. A courier should go to Rivington's Coffee-House and ask for Amos. I'll take it from there.

Tallmadge nodded. "Any more questions? If not, I think we've done all we can for now and you should be on your way. I'm off to find some provisions to sustain you on the road." Andrew watched him go, a man carrying a heavy load of responsibilities. As for his own assignment—one thing was clear. He would be taking on a task far more difficult than any he had ever expected to do. A daunting task with overwhelming implications. If he failed to see a threat, if an attack on the General ended in disaster, he would carry a heavy burden of blame for the rest of his life.

Later that night, Finder set out to play whist at the Cadwalader house on Chestnut Street. Once it would have pleased him to be invited to that house and mingle with the establishment, but now all he felt was acute depression. There had been no more killings, Legal was still alive, and his own attempts to find the unknown leader had failed. Late last night he had made a major decision.

It was time, past time, to get rid of Pottle and return to New York. Convince headquarters that he was ready to move upward and onward.

As for taking down a patriot network, best to say nothing. If pressed, he would point out that the British were no longer in Philadelphia. It made no sense to spend more money on a paltry lot who could no longer cause serious trouble.

By now he had reached the corner of Chestnut Street. The large Cadwalader house was in sight and others were arriving. He slowed and adjusted the lace frill at his neck. For the next few hours he must ignore his frustrations. Play well—but make sure to lose a little money.

Several hours later, the gaming at the tables was over and the players were invited to the library for drinks and conversation. As he expected, the talk began with denunciations of the zealot Joseph Reed. But as the wine flowed, a wealthy merchant, Timothy Allen, announced that he had heard from a reliable source that General Washington was coming to Philadelphia in December. It wasn't yet official, but before long, plans for entertaining him would begin, and leading hostesses would be fighting over who had precedence.

For Finder, this was riveting news. As he sipped his drink, his mind was racing. The security around Washington would be extremely tight, but it was a given that in all attempts at protection there was sure to be a flaw. The challenge would be to find the flaw and act on it.

To do away with the irreplaceable general when he came in December—the thought was so intriguing that he had to steady the hand holding the wine glass. The risks would be great, but could be overcome with careful planning including bribery and blackmail. If successful, he would be treated as a hero. His future, now so uncertain, would be filled with acclaim and financial rewards beyond his wildest dreams.

He took a deep breath, put the glass down on the table, and turned to Mr. Allen. "Interesting news, sir. An unexpected event. I shall look forward to meeting the famous general—and enjoying a round of fine parties in his honor."

★★★

CHAPTER TWENTY-FIVE

December 14, 1778

Winter had arrived with a heavy fall of freezing snow. The icy streets became treacherous. The branches of trees were bare and only a few birds called out. People wore layers of thick wool and huddled in their cold houses. To add to the misery, a severe form of influenza was rapidly spreading.

At the Loring's, the front parlor was closed, but the dining room was close to the kitchen where an iron stove attached to a fireplace radiated heat

This morning Louisa was doing her daily chores in her father's room. His pain could be relieved by doses of laudanum from a bottle, but he still needed constant nursing. Three weeks ago she had felt compelled to ask Cousin Molly if Will could stay on. She missed Will, but it would be far better for him to be playing with Robby and doing his lessons there. She had admitted that her father's leg was not broken, that the Loring's were in serious trouble, but that this was all she could safely say. Cousin Molly had accepted the mystifying situation with her usual kindness and good sense and asked no questions.

Louisa finished changing the pillow under her father's head and began to refresh the essence of lavender. She was going to more parties, listening and looking at every man with a sharp eye. So far no one had asked inappropriate questions, but Cox had made it clear that there was still fear that an assailant might try to silence her father, that they must continue to take every precaution—and Nat said the same. His daily visits were the brightest moments of the day. Over cups of tea their talks ranged from unrest in the city to classic books—he was far better educated than she. They would laugh about his little sister's conversations with her dolls. They shared the same fondness for their families. It was hard to remember that six months ago she had barely noticed him.

The fire in the small bedroom was keeping it warm and now her father was sleeping. She folded the soiled linen, put another log on the fire, and went down through the cold house to the warm kitchen. Yesterday Peggy Shippen had called and asked if she would come over and cut greens to decorate the house for her sister Betsy's wedding. Lately she hadn't seen much of Peggy except in passing at parties. Peggy was always with General Arnold and Major Franks—and now it was clear to Louisa that David Franks had lost all interest in her, as if when the outings ended it was no longer necessary to be attentive. It was humiliating to remember how she had longed to be with him, how she had planned their future together, but at least she had managed to hide her feelings. At parties she made a point of showing high spirits. His rejection was hurtful, but no one must guess that she had been so foolish.

Jessie was making bread, flour up to her elbows. Louisa threw the linen into the scullery washtub, then reached for her coat. "Miss Peggy asked me to help her cut greens for the wedding, so I might as well go now."

"Dress warmly. I hear there's ice on the river."

A few minutes later, armed with shears, she and Peggy were standing in the Shippen garden. Today Peggy was wearing a fur hat that framed her pretty face. She threw a bunch of holly into a basket and rolled her big gray eyes.

"You won't believe this."

"Believe what?"

"Sarah Champion is back in town, but she isn't Sarah Champion anymore."

"Isn't Sarah Champion? What *can* you mean?"

"My dear, she married Charles Colborne, the British officer she went to parties with last winter. They did it *secretly* before he left for New York. She was going off to England to live forever, why she asked my father to sell the house on Third Street. Then the dashing Charles was killed at Monmouth and she rushed off to that obscure little village."

"Good heavens. I remember you told me she was dreadfully upset about something. I thought it might be a death in her family."

"Well, now she's back, out of mourning, and she's opening the big house. Receiving callers and planning to give parties. It would be a huge scandal except that Sarah is so beguiling—and so rich that she can get away with *anything.* Anyhow, you'll see her putting on airs at the wedding."

Louisa hesitated. Peggy did not appreciate having been kept in the dark about this secret marriage, but Sarah had suffered a sad loss.

"Well, strange things happen during a war," she said "We're all looking forward to Betsy's wedding. Only three days, now."

Peggy rolled her eyes again. "The wedding—I just want it to be over. The house is upside down and Betsy acts as if she was the only person in the world who ever got married. We're all running around like servants at her beck and call. What's worse is that everyone approves of Neddy Burd because he worked with my father. No one wants me to marry General Arnold—and right now the poor man is working flat out on this imperial visit."

Louisa hesitated again. This was not a good sign. When crossed, Peggy had tantrums that resonated through the house and lasted for several days. "I can see why you're upset," she said quickly.

"I *am* upset. Horrid people are accusing him of petty things like buying and then selling for a profit which is only what many others are doing. Besides, he's owed money from former campaigns. Outrageous, when he served his country so well and was badly wounded." She paused for breath. "It's so unfair, but there's a ray of hope. My dear Benedict has been offered a chance to become a big landowner in upstate New York. If he doesn't receive the recognition and payment that is owed, he is seriously thinking of leaving the military."

Louisa opened her mouth, then decided to be silent. It was hard, extremely hard, to understand Peggy's intense devotion to the tainted general. Her passionate wish to further his prospects, whatever they might be.

Peggy tore angrily at a branch. "I hate winter and being cold. Life was far more fun when it was warm." She glanced at Louisa. "I think you should make eyes at David Franks. He fancied you, my dear, but then you got on your high horse and refused to go out with us. I forgave you, but it was heartless of you to desert me like that. Anyhow, I think we could go back to all doing things together again, that is, if you're willing to make a little effort over David."

Louisa winced. This was like pressing down on an aching tooth. The last thing in the world she wanted was to be reminded of her dashed hopes.

"That's over, completely over," she said quickly. "When we meet he's polite but nothing more. He hasn't even come to call."

"And I can assure you he would, if you gave him the least little push." She clapped her hands together. "I know! I'll arrange for you to get together at the wedding. Plan for another meeting."

Louisa swallowed hard. This was too much. What was going on in Peggy's manipulative mind? Why the sudden need to push back the clock? She must leave before a surge of anger flared out of control.

"You're wrong about David Franks," she snapped. "Totally wrong. Nothing will change and that's all I will say. Take this." She thrust the basket at Peggy, turned, and ran toward her house.

The marriage ceremony of Betsy Shippen to her cousin Neddy Burd was held in beautiful Georgian-style Christ Church with fifteen bridesmaids in attendance.

Louisa joined the Morrises in the White family pew, exactly where she used to sit with Mamma. As a child, she had learned that the building of an Anglican church was a condition in William Penn's original charter. It was now an historic landmark, with a steeple two hundred feet high. The ornate silver vessels had been sent over by Queen Anne. A far cry from the sparse Congregational church where the New England Lorings had worshipped. She sat there, glad of a chance to think about her life. To pray for guidance and for resolution.

A reception followed at the Shippen house. The parsimonious judge had opened his wallet, so food and drink was lavish. Few newcomers had been invited, and the elite of the city had done their best to relive the halcyon days before the war. The gentlemen had fine lace at their throats. The ladies were dressed in their best silks and satins worn over wool petticoats.

Louisa had chosen a red brocade dress that had belonged to her mother and she knew she looked well. People greeted her warmly and asked about her father's health. She thanked them and said that he soon would be out and about, an answer that was becoming a little thin with use.

Soon the sound of raised voices was almost deafening; the conversation centered on Mrs. Washington, who had arrived in Philadelphia that very morning. She had come from Mount Vernon some days before her husband, and the plans for their entertainments had been finalized, causing extreme pleasure for some and acute disappointment for others.

There was a little stir as Sarah Colborne entered the room. Instead of a heavily laced and beribboned gown, she was wearing a simple lavender silk dress and a string of pearls, an heiress who had the sense not to show off her money. She saw Louisa, then made her way through the throng.

"Louisa Loring," she said, smiling. "I've only seen you at a distance at parties It seems an age since Peggy and Becky brought you to see me. How is your little brother?"

"He's very well, thank you," Louisa said, pleased that Sarah had remembered the visit.

"I'm glad. I've wanted to call on you, but I know that your father is ill. Perhaps you'll come and have tea with *me*."

"I should like to very much," she managed to say before they were interrupted by portly Mrs. Chambers. She listened for a moment, then turned and smoothed her skirt. It was now or never to summon up resolve and find Peggy. End her devious conniving once and for all.

After a short search through the crowd, she found her sitting in the dining room with the General. David Franks was standing nearby.

"Good evening, Major," Louisa said with a flirtatious smile. "How very nice to see you. I hope you are well."

He made a formal little bow. "Good evening, Miss Loring. This is a fine occasion," he said, then moved away to speak to Mrs. Thompson. Louisa took a deep breath, then leaned down and spoke into Peggy's ear.

"You saw that? I was right, you were wrong—and *never* try to use me again for your own purposes." She straightened, then turned on her heel and walked away, head held high. Her hands were shaking but she'd done it. The demeaning relationship with Peggy was over.

The reception was ending; the Morrises had left some time ago. She found her coat, thanked Mrs. Shippen, and slipped out of the house.

The cold air was reviving as she ran through the gardens and unlocked the back door. The kitchen was deserted. Jessie must be upstairs with her father.

She sat down at the pine board table and rubbed her flushed cheeks, glad to be alone with a chance to think. Breaking with Peggy was sure to make significant changes in her social life. Peggy might decide to say nothing, or she might retaliate with anger. People might take sides, and it would be interesting to see who among them were *her* true friends. After all, she wasn't the first girl to be taken in by a man's looks and charm—and she would learn from her mistake.

She lowered her hands and folded them on the table. It was important to move forward and concentrate on the old-fashioned virtues. Honesty. Hard work. Patient and loving care for her father and Will. In time she might find lasting love with someone she could trust and respect. A man like Nat Haddam.

Footsteps sounded on the stairs. She straightened and smoothed her hair.

"I'm back," she said as Jessie came in. "How is he?"

"He was restless earlier but now he's sleeping." Jessie poured water into the kettle. "I'll make you a cup of chamomile tea. The wedding must have been very fine. Did you enjoy yourself?"

Louisa hesitated, then she smiled. "Did I enjoy myself? Well, I can say this. It was a night to remember. For a very long time."

★★★

CHAPTER TWENTY-SIX

December 18, 1778

It was several weeks before a frustrated Andrew Warren could organize his New York network and leave for Philadelphia. The man who was to replace him came down with the dreaded dysentery. Then a young recruit went missing and was found knifed to death in an alley.

But at last he was able to cross the river and meet Tallmadge's aide, Captain Boykin, a southerner who proved to be competent and helpful.

Once back in the city, he had wasted no time. His first move was to rent a small house in Norris Alley. The owner, a Mrs. Foster, was away in Boston. Through Cox, he found and hired Aaron Shanks, a gruff and grizzled former sergeant in the Pennsylvania militia. Aaron was well able to cook, deal with minor problems, and carry messages. Important contacts were being renewed and plans made for late night meetings in various locations.

After four days of intense preparations, he felt ready to report to Tallmadge. The new intelligence headquarters was located on Chestnut Street, a large house on loan from William Talbot. It was a bitterly cold afternoon. Needing to revert to detested disguises, he put on shabby clothes and set out, pulling a grubby cart filled with used clothes. Spies were everywhere and he couldn't chance drawing attention to himself and being followed.

A light covering of snow had turned into treacherous ice, and people were going carefully on the walkways. Halfway down Market Street, a carriage had skidded and overturned. A crowd of men was trying to help the driver right it. Many were drunk, a common sight these days as people struggled to warm themselves with hard liquor. He could sense a growing anger that would likely break out in violence against the rich; it was the cold and hungry poor who suffered and were being struck down by the deadly influenza.

When he finally reached the impressive Talbot house, he pushed the cart against a side wall and knocked on the back door. An aide named Livens opened it and shook his head.

"Be off with you," he began.

"Captain Warren to see Major Tallmadge," Andrew said to him.

Livens stared, then laughed. "Good Lord, Captain. I didn't recognize you. This way, if you please."

Tallmadge was seated behind a desk in a gentleman's library; shelves of books smelling of fine leather rose to the ceiling, He looked up, frowned, looked again, and nodded. "One of your better disguises, Warren. Come in. Take a seat. I had a message you had arrived but I expected you far sooner. What kept you?"

Andrew pulled off his wool cap. To avoid dirtying the upholstery, he sat down on a straight wood chair. "I couldn't leave without getting a competent replacement. Andre at British headquarters would have been happy to pick off a recruit, torture him, then take down the rest."

"Any progress on your search?"

"Plans are underway. I'm working with a man I used last winter. A large group is fanning out across the city, watching and listening in streets, coffee shops, bars, any place where people gather. Anything suspicious is reported to me. There's a rabble rouser who wants to set himself up as a dictator. We're keeping an eye on him."

Tallmadge frowned. "It's not just rogues who can cause trouble. Far harder to locate the wealthy loyalists who fear change and too many are out to gain power. You were still in New York so you may not have heard that certain loyalists organized a march on the State House to take over Congress."

"What happened?"

"A number of citizens saw sense and stopped it, but the threat is still there." He pushed back his chair. "Back to security for the General. The Life Guards will be with him whenever he goes outside, but we need far more of them. All the aides have been alerted to stay close to him inside the buildings, even if he's dancing at a party. We'll do our best, but it's going to take weeks for him to achieve his goals with Congress."

Andrew was silent. The phrase—too little and too late—resonated in his head. Voices sounded in the hall as aides went back and forth. Tallmadge shook his head. "There's more bad news. Last fall you warned me about troop movements in New York. Word has come that when Colonel Campbell and his troops left the city they headed for the Savannah River in Georgia. After a brief battle they took Savannah. A severe blow that gives comfort to our enemies—"

"—and more doubts to our allies," Andrew added.

"Precisely." Tallmadge shook his head again. "I'm late to a meeting at the Laurens's house. Mrs. Washington arrived there yesterday and her kindness and affability is much appreciated. Before I go, is there anything you need from me today?"

Andrew stood up. "Not today. I'll try to recruit more watchers and simplify the way they report to me. In any case, I'll keep you posted. Now, I'll be off," he said, then picked up his woolly hat and left. Outside the temperature was dropping. It might even snow again. Six days until Washington arrived; by now it was still like playing a deadly game of chess. Trying to match wits with his opponents and remove their pieces before they removed his.

He collected his pushcart and started toward Christ Church. Messages were left in the cemetery behind a certain grave. He would check, follow up if necessary, then head back to Norris Alley. Aaron, his trusty aide, would cook him a hot meal. Then he would change into another disguise and slip out into the cold again.

His first call would be to the Lorings on Fourth Street. They had received a message to expect him, and Cox had given him useful information. Eben Loring might never fully recover from the poison he had swallowed at the City Tavern. His young apprentice, Nat Haddam, was now in charge of the law practice. Haddam had managed to find the poisoner and locate the killer who had provided the poison. He needed a full account from Haddam.

Cox had also warned him that Miss Loring felt that if he had come back sooner, he could have prevented the attack. That feeling was understandable and would require adept handling. At their meeting in August, at first she had treated him with head tossing hostility but when he finally persuaded her to help her father she had shown that she could be forgiving.

A gust of wind sent the branches of the trees crackling and swaying. He bent over and pushed the cart faster. He was bone tired and his first priority was security for the General. He would make this call as brief as possible. Apply his limited diplomatic skills to adding protection and mending fences, then move on.

★★★

CHAPTER TWENTY-SEVEN

December 18, 1778 *Later that day*

There were no lights in the front of the Loring house when Andrew arrived dressed as an elderly Quaker gentleman. He knocked on the back door. It was opened by the tall black servant. "Please come in, sir," she said and closed it quickly.

"Thank you." He took off his broad-brimmed Quaker hat and handed her his heavy coat. "Your name is Jessie, if I remember." He paused. "This has been a hard time for you, Jessie."

She nodded. "Yes, sir, very hard. Mr. Loring, we gave him up for dead and he's still in pain. Miss Louisa and Mr. Nat, they waiting for you in the dining room. We don't use the front room now on account of the cold," she added, and opened a door.

The room was large, with chairs pulled up to the long table. Louisa Loring and Nat Haddam were standing in front of the fire. She was thinner and the strain showed in her face.

"Good evening, Captain," she said coldly. "It's been a long time since you were here. Since then we've had great trouble."

Forewarned was forearmed. "Miss Loring," he said, bowing. "I deeply regret what has happened to your father. I tried to lay on enough protection for him.

It failed and for that I take full responsibility. I'm here now, in one of my disguises, to discuss how that can be improved."

"There's no way to undo the harm to my father. Too late for that, but now it's important to find out what more can be done. Please sit down, Captain."

Nat pulled out a chair for her and seated himself beside her. Andrew joined them. At least this was a start. He adjusted his simple neckcloth and cleared his throat. "Cox the apothecary tells me you both have shown great fortitude, Miss Loring in nursing her father, Mr. Haddam in carrying on with his practice." He turned to Nat. "I also understand that you acted quickly and located the man behind the poisoner. I've found that these attacks often have a pattern. It would be helpful to know exactly what happened. Leave nothing out."

At their first meeting in August, Nat sat off to one side and said little. Now, in carefully worded sentences, he described how he had found Dan the waiter in his miserable shack. Learned from Dan that a person known as Killer Man met deserters once a week and paid them a few shillings for watching and following victims. Questioning Dan had led him to the Bunch of Grapes Tavern. He had bribed a young servant boy to get more information.

"Go on," he said as Nat paused. "What exactly did this boy tell you?"

"Told me the killer pays a hefty sum for a cellar room. Said he's a surly bloke, always wears a hat pulled down over his face and has one shoulder lower than the other. Calls himself Mr. Brown. He had one visitor, a young well-built fellow. A real toff, according to the boy."

"In other words, a gentleman."

"The boy was scrubbing the floor, he couldn't hear what was said, but he saw this toff—er, gentleman—give the killer money."

"He gave him money? Interesting—very,, but

unfortunately it would be extremely difficult to find this gentleman and bring evidence against him."

Nat nodded. "Very difficult," he said. "Miss Loring knows that it may not produce results, but she's going to more parties. She's a good observer. She hopes that one of the gentlemen she meets might give himself away by asking too many questions about her father."

Andrew frowned. This was disconcerting, but he had learned the hard way that any chance, however small, was worth taking. The girl was determined, and it was possible that an agent might be mingling with the elite. "Very well," he said, "but I should point out that while chances of finding an enemy agent are minimal, by asking questions you may be putting yourself at risk, Miss Loring. These people, if threatened, are ruthless."

She raised her chin. "I know that. Nat has persuaded me to just listen but believe me, Captain, I will do anything I can to find the man who did this to my father."

He nodded. "Very well," he said again. "The decision has been made. Now we should start to work out more plans to keep you safe. Unfortunately we are still up against some wily and relentless adversaries."

A number of plans were considered and accepted. Finally he glanced at his watch. "I must go," he said. "I won't come here again but Cox can send and receive messages. More watchers will be in place, but Miss Loring should not go out on the streets alone."

"I'll see to that," Nat said with vehemence and looked at her. It was obvious, watching them, to see that adversity was bringing these two together.

"Right." He pushed back his chair and stood up. "One last piece of advice. If an urgent problem arises, go straight to our intelligence headquarters in the Talbot house on Chestnut Street. You can't miss it, a large brick house with four pillars. Ask for Major Tallmadge or one of his aides. They have resources and will help you."

"Chestnut Street. A large brick house with four white pillars," Nat said. "We'll remember."

"Good man. You've done well. If you weren't needed here, I'd try to enlist you for our intelligence."

Nat looked pleased. "Thank you, Captain."

As they talked, the room had grown cold. Louisa put her hands on the table then got to her feet. She took a deep breath. "Captain Warren, I have to admit I was—upset—when it took you so long to come. No doubt there were reasons, but now I want to thank you for what you are doing for us now."

"That's generous of you, Miss Loring," he said. "This has been a trying time for you, a time of fear and sadness. You and Nat have handled it well. My best wishes for your father." He made a small bow, and went quickly to the door.

Jessie was in the kitchen, standing at the table and kneading dough. She wiped her floury hands on her apron and turned to fetch his coat and hat. As he waited, another idea rose to the surface of his tired mind. Black servants in the city knew a great deal about their masters' lives, and this competent woman would be respected in her community. He should be making use of those sharp eyes and ears.

"Jessie," he began. "I know how much you've done to help this household."

She shook her head. "I do what I can. Miss Louisa, she's a fine young lady."

"She is, but we live in a difficult time." He paused. "You'll have heard that General Washington is coming for a long visit. It's important to make sure that no one tries to harm him."

"Yes, sir. It surely is."

"Which brings me to a request. I believe that much of what takes place in this city, good *and* bad, is known to you and your friends."

Jessie's calm face grew wary. "I don't understand, sir."

"What I mean is this. I'm working hard to prevent a possible attack on the General. I would like you to spread the word to keep an eye out for anything, anything at all, that looks unusual or suspicious. If that happens, the person should come straight to my house next to the cemetery on Norris Alley. If I act on the information, there'll be a generous reward. Very generous." He paused. "If this request doesn't seem right to you, we'll say no more about it."

Jessie hesitated. "Let me think on it, sir," she said and went to the table. She stood there, staring at the unleavened lump of dough. After a moment she turned.

"It seems right to me, sir. I'll speak to the ones who can be trusted. The General, he'll be bringing Billy Lee, his personal servant. Billy should hear about this. Told how to reach you." She paused and smoothed her apron. "We'll do whatever we can for the General, sir."

"I understand, and I appreciate your willingness to help." He put on his Quaker coat, settled his hat, and turned toward the door. "Good night, Jessie, and thank you."

"Good night, sir."

He stepped out, bracing himself against a blast of cold air. On the whole, the meeting had gone well, and fences were mended. Now he could only hope that the right decisions had been made, ones that would ward off yet another devastating blow to the valiant but vulnerable Loring family.

★★★

CHAPTER TWENTY-EIGHT

December 18, 1778 *Later the same evening*

Andrew's second call was to Sarah Colborne. Because she had volunteered to gather information and pass it on to Cox, this was an official visit, but for him it was far more than a duty.

As he turned the corner onto Third Street, he did another quick summing up of their long and rocky relationship. It had ended badly a year ago in wintery Valley Forge when she helped to foil an attack on Washington. Then, last October, events had forced him to support her in New York as she tried to find ex-Captain Ian Jamieson, the spy behind the murder of her husband in Monmouth. The perceptions they had formed about each other altered when they rode through the night to capture him. It was a hazardous journey, a severe test of her fortitude, and it finally brought them together.

Two days later, sitting in a house across from Washington's headquarters in Westchester, they had been open about their changed feelings. She had talked about her short, secret marriage to a British captain: "It was the war ... I loved Charles very much ... I was devasted when he died, but I could never have lived in England ... in the end, we both would have been unhappy."

He had summoned up the courage to tell her how much he cared for her. He hadn't asked for a commitment, but her response had given him hope. It seemed then that she might want to be part of his life.

But now it was time to face reality. Those moments of hope could have been a delayed reaction to the harrowing night ride together. Nothing more. Now she was in Philadelphia, a sought-after rich widow. She might have met someone who could give her a different life, so any talk of the future must come from her. All the same, he wished he was in uniform, not looking like a shaky old Quaker.

The front windows of the big house were covered to block out the cold. He went to a door at the rear and knocked. The bolts slid back and Sarah stood there holding a candle. She let him in, looked at him and burst out laughing.

"Good heavens, Andrew. Have you come to scold me for missing a Quaker Friends meeting?"

"Don't scoff." He grimaced and pulled off the hat and the wispy white wig. "I could have been the peddler in his dirtiest clothes. You once rode in his wagon."

"I remember that revolting wagon. All too well. We'll go up to the withdrawing room. I sent the servants to bed early and there's a fire."

The withdrawing room on the second floor was the most informal room in the house; there was a round mahogany table in the center, several upholstered chairs, and a small sofa under the bookshelves. He had never been here before, always meeting in the formal front parlor.

Sarah set the candle on the table. As he sat down, he took a closer look. Slender and lovely as ever, auburn hair falling loosely under a frilly cap. The blue dress was warm but fashionable. Last winter, at the British parties, her dresses were always the finest, but she had looked like a grubby boy when he took her to Valley Forge.

She arranged her skirt, then folded her hands on the table. "Andrew, I know you're here to get information from me, but I'm afraid you'll be disappointed."

"Remains to be seen. Start at the beginning. How were you received when you reappeared as the widowed Mrs. Colborne?"

"As you can imagine, there was much shock and shaking of heads, but people can't resist my money. I opened the house right away. I go to parties and meet old friends and newcomers. Many are foreigners here for various reasons. I listen, but it's mostly gossip and talk about politics."

"Tell me what might be useful."

"Well, Silas Deane, the former envoy to France, is being vilified in Congress by the influential Lee brothers of Virginia. John Jay has replaced Henry Laurens as head of Congress. His son, John Laurens, Washington's aide, fought a duel with disgraced general Charles Lee over Lee's insults against Washington. Major Hamilton was Laurens's second and no one was seriously hurt. A number of the original delegates have been replaced. I wish I could give you something of real value but that's all." She was talking in an easy way, but he could sense strain.

"Don't feel badly. We're all in the same situation. We know our adversaries are out there, operating under our noses. Some are killing off members of my old network. I've just come from the Loring house. Eben Loring was poisoned in the City Tavern. He's alive, but he may never completely recover."

"Cox told me and I'm sorry. I like Louisa. When asked, she always pretends that it's just a minor illness but that's no longer credible."

"Which is another reason why I'm here. It's a long story, but the young man who took over her father's law practice discovered that Loring's attacker may be paid by a gentleman who is accepted socially. Miss Loring—Louisa—told me she's trying to identify him at parties."

"She's looking for him at our parties? Heavens, that doesn't seem in the least likely."

"Sarah, you go to the same parties. Two heads are better than one and you are both very observant."

She raised an eyebrow. "Are you asking me to join forces with Louisa and look for a gentleman who leads two lives? I'm willing, of course I am, but it's an exercise in futility as you well know."

"Perhaps, but at this point anything is worth trying. I say this because Washington will be here in a few days and his enemies think killing him is still the best way to win the war. It was hard enough to protect him when he was contained in camp. Here he'll be going from place to place. I met with Major Tallmadge this afternoon. I've never seen him so worried. What's more, I'm to lead the search to uncover any attempt at an assassination. Every man I can muster will be out on the streets watching and listening. I'm doing all I can but it may not be enough."

Sarah gave him a worried look. "He's laid it all on you? But that's not fair. One person shouldn't be made responsible—"

"No excuses." He struck his knee with his fist. "Christ, Sarah, if something happens to the General, it means I've failed—" he stopped and rubbed his hand. "Sorry, but you know what's at stake. You ran through a storm and risked your life to save him last winter."

"Yes, but that was different." Sarah bent her head. "Andrew, I—I'd help you, do whatever I could, but right now I feel —I feel so *useless*."

He frowned. "You? Useless? Why do you say that?"

She swallowed. "It's hard to explain, but I'm not sure—I'm simply not *sure* of who I really am. I mean, once I was just a pastor's daughter who worked on a farm. Aunt Sage made me into a belle and a spy. Now I'm a rich widow, living the high life on the money she left me. Not carrying out her wishes to spend every day fighting for freedom and independence." She swallowed again as if holding back tears.

He sat still, taken aback. This startling outburst, this vulnerability—it seemed that being open about his anguish had unleashed hers. He must reach out and reassure her, but do it with great care. He leaned forward. "Sarah, you're not useless. You've helped the cause for independence You've proved your worth many times and you are greatly valued. Believe this, because it's true." He sat back and waited.

She blinked hard. Tears were filling her eyes. She fumbled in the pocket of her blue dress, pulled out a handkerchief, and wiped them. "Sorry," she said in a choked voice.

He shook his head. "Don't be sorry. I'm glad you told me. I understand because I 've felt the same way. Uncertain. I was a student at Harvard College until my patriot cousin Joseph Warren was killed in the battle at Breed's Hill. I wanted to be a soldier and avenge him. Be a fighter, not an undercover spy." Again, he waited .For a moment she didn't speak. She seemed to be collecting herself. Then she took a deep breath. "Thank you for sharing your story. It helped, and I'll try to stop being foolish." She clasped her hands tightly, hesitated and looked at him. "Andrew, there's something—it's hard to say this, but before you leave there's something I ought to tell you."

"What?" He braced himself for bad news. If it was another man he must accept her decision with good grace. Not let her see his pain.

"It's about what you said to me in October, sitting in that parlor. Since then so much has happened. You may have changed your mind about wanting me in your life. If so, I understand, but I hope we will always be friends. Good friends."

Not want her in his life? For a second he couldn't move, not sure what he was hearing. He leaned forward and grasped her hands.

"Good God, Sarah. My feelings for you haven't changed. They're stronger than ever, but on my way here I told myself on no account to bring up the future, that any talk about it must come from you."

"But—"

"Sarah, I could never love another woman as I love you. All I want is to care for you. Make you happy. Be with you for the rest of our lives." His hands tightened. "Am I asking too much?"

"Too much? No, Andrew. You're not—asking too much—" her voice faltered. Tears streamed down her face.

It was here, the moment he had longed for with little hope. He pulled her to her feet, bent his head and kissed her forehead, her cheeks and then her lips. At last he let her go. Her body was trembling.

"Come," he said and led her to the little sofa. He put his arms around her and kissed her again, the first step to ultimate fulfillment, then pulled off her frilly cap and drew her head to his shoulder. For a moment they were silent. Then she stirred and took his hand.

"I can't believe this is happening—not after all this time. Not after so many mistakes. First the sad tears, now the happy ones—so many ups and downs to get to this place so many surprises. How did it start?"

He smiled and wrapped his fingers around hers. "Not well, as you know: 'I hate you, Captain Warren. I will never speak to you again.' But I couldn't get you out of my mind."

She gave a shaky little laugh. "It took me quite a lot longer. My aunt was furious when you refused to let us send information to General Washington."

"She was right and I was wrong. But in the end, few people have been through as much together as we have. We already know each other well. So many obstacles overcome, so many lie ahead, but now we will face them together."

"Yes." She touched his cheek. "But what happens now? There's still so much we don't know about each other. After the war, what do you want to do? Where do you want to live?" She was talking very fast as if to hide emotion.

He stroked her hair. If she wanted to talk about the future, he would do his best to answer. "It depends. Once it might have been Boston. Now I think it must be Philadelphia. We need to form a new government. It won't be easy, but you could play an important part."

"I'll try, if only to please my aunt. Do you have family in Boston?"

"Two sisters and parents who will welcome you."

"Mine will welcome you and I know you're not marrying me for my money. Abigail, the girl you recruited to be my maid in New York, told me your family is one of the richest in Boston."

"That's true, but the army has a way of making one's background irrelevant. I haven't seen my family for years."

"But you loved them? Respected them?"

"Yes. I did—I do."

The candle was flickering. He gazed around the room, a place he would never forget, wanting to draw out the precious moment, then studied her face as if wanting to engrave it on his heart before leaving. There was still a late night meeting behind the church.

She looked at him as if sensing his thought. "Oh Andrew, when will I see you again?"

"Not for a while. I'll be working day and night for the next few weeks. You'll never be out of my thoughts, but I can't risk another visit, not even in disguise. Not until Washington returns to Middletown."

She nodded, then drew away. "Andrew, be careful."

"I will, and now I have good reason to watch my back," he said and stood up.

"Do you promise?" She put her arms around his waist.

"Sarah. My precious Sarah." Gently, he loosened her hold, unwilling to make a promise he might not be able to keep. The clock was running and events were closing in. To survive and return to Sarah, he would have to prevail against a determined and merciless opponent. Fight and defeat him with more information, more skill—and more luck.

The following morning began with a disagreeable drizzle of rain that melted the dirty snow left from the last storm. Finder stood close to the Farmers Market. There was no sign of Pottle. He turned up the collar of his coat and fixed his mind on how best to make a tricky request.

Washington would be here in several days. There was no time to waste, and he was determined to go down in history as the man who had killed him. Without Washington, the army would collapse and the colonies were far too divided to survive. No doubt the General's guards would lay on heavy protection. It was a David and Goliath situation, but if successful, the rewards would enable him to give up spying, an existence he was beginning to despise. He would start a new life, maybe in France. A life that continued to include a wife and children. Horses and dogs.

As a church bell rang the hour of ten, Pottle appeared at the meat counter. Finder studied him. The man had the will and the ability to execute a quick kill. All the same, asking him to murder a general required a combination of arm-twisting persuasion and a temptingly baited hook.

Shaking the rain from his coat, he walked toward him. "This way," he said under his breath. "That sharp-eyed farmer is looking at us." Keeping his distance, Pottle followed him to the last stall where a counter of cooking pots was on display. The owner was at the back, drinking from a bottle to warm himself.

Finder straightened, then spoke in a low voice. "Pay attention. I was going to end work on that useless network and leave for New York. Now there's a reason to stay." He leaned close. "General Washington arrives on Friday. He'll be going back and forth to parties and meetings for several weeks. He'll be vulnerable to an attack, and I've figured out how it can be done."

Pottle was silent.

He leaned closer. "When I was in New York with ex-Governor Tryon, he had me infiltrate into a number of Washington's badly underpaid Life Guards. Most are loyal, but I bribed a few for information. I aim to find one who can tell me ahead of time where the General will be." No need to add that two Guards in New York had been caught and hanged.

Pottle shifted his feet, looking surly. "Sounds risky to me," he muttered.

"Risky, but possible. Whoever succeeds in killing the General will be well rewarded by the British. Paid in gold and plenty of it." He gave Pottle a hard look, then lowered his voice to a whisper. "This attack on the General. You've got the skills and you've never been caught. You are well able to do it."

Again, Pottle was silent.

The drizzle had turned to heavy rain. Shoppers were raising umbrellas, hurrying away. The owner of the stall came back to the counter. "Best pots you'll ever see, gentlemen," he touted. "Cheap at a shilling a pot."

Finder coughed. "Too dear," he said to the man and turned away. "See here," he muttered to Pottle. "I can give you gold in advance, but I need your answer now."

Pottle stared at the ground and said nothing.

Hiding his anger, Finder wiped the rain from his

neck and began to walk down Market Street. But after a moment, there were footsteps behind him.

"I'm in," Pottle growled. "Got nothing to keep me here. What happens now?"

"I'll work out the details. That'll take time." He paused, aware that another word was needed. "You're in now and don't forget it," he snapped, then gave Pottle a slap on the shoulder. "We can do it, man," he said in a voice meant to convey assurance. "This will be your only chance to be rich and to better yourself, so fix your mind on that and leave the rest to me."

★★★

CHAPTER TWENTY-NINE

January 15, 1779

It was now mid-January. General Washington had been in Philadelphia for over three weeks, and Intelligence headquarters was experiencing acute tension. There was a sense that if an attack was planned, it would have to take place soon. There was a need for intense watchfulness, and the endless stream of lavish entertainments was becoming hard to endure.

In a letter to his stepson, Jack Curtis, the General expressed profound frustration. "It appears to me that idleness and dissipation seems to have taken such fast hold of everybody that I shall not be at all surprised if there should be a general wreck of everything ..."

His entourage echoed the same dismay. General Nathanael Greene wrote that in order to perform his duties he was "obliged to rise early and go to bed late. In the morning a round of visiting came on. Then you had to prepare for dinner after which the evening balls would engage your time until one or two in the morning ...."

Tonight's ball to honor Washington was being held at the City Tavern, hosted by Joseph Reed, president of the powerful Pennsylvania Supreme Council. Yesterday, in his efforts to impress the General, Reed had announced, with great fanfare, that the Council had commissioned renowned artist Charles Willson Peale to paint a full-length portrait of the General.

The Long Room was already crowded when Louisa arrived with the Morrises. Her father was slightly better, and she was looking forward to a few hours of music and dancing.

"Another of these frightful crushes," Cousin Molly said as they stood in the doorway. "Such a strain when different factions are forced to be polite to each other night after night." She looked around. "Well, the Washingtons are here. I see Martha sitting over there with her friend from Boston, Mrs. Hancock. Amazing how Martha always manages to keep a smile on her face."

"That's true. She does," Louisa said. When they first met, she had observed with great interest the small portly lady who was able to convey such gracious dignity. According to Cousin Molly, Mrs. Washington was born a Dandridge of Virginia. Her first husband was a Daniel Custis. There were several Custis children but none with General Washington to whom she had been married for twenty years—she called his officers and troops "my family." They loved her and called her Lady Washington.

The General was standing at the far end of the room, a tall commanding figure. His hair was powdered and his expression was grave and reserved. Nearby, Sarah Colborne, lovely in pale blue silk, was holding court surrounded by hopeful suitors. She saw Louisa, waved, and gave her a speaking look.

Louisa smiled and waved back. Last week she had gone to Sarah's house for tea. At first, as they began to sip, Sarah had talked about feeding people at her back door and that she was starting a sewing circle to make clothes for the soldiers. Perhaps Louisa would like to join.

"I'm not sure," Louisa had said. "My father still is unwell and I spend a lot of time with him. "

Sarah had leaned forward. "No need to give me that farce about dyspepsia and a broken leg. I think you'll be surprised to hear that Captain Warren and I have worked in Washington's intelligence for over a year. Here and in New York. He told me you're looking for a gentleman who goes to our parties, a man who could be a double agent. He doesn't hold out much hope, but he thinks that we should join forces, that two heads have a better chance than one."

For Louisa, this was startling news. She could never have guessed that Sarah was so deceptive, but so was she when she told these lies about her father. It completely changed her perception of Sarah and it was a relief that she no longer had to rely on her own judgment. They had discussed the loose talk of Mrs. Gurney's nephew and decided that the boy was simply young and indiscreet. They agreed that finding an agent was unlikely but worth a try.

By now the Long Room was filled with people. The musicians on the little platform were picking up their instruments, a sign that another dance was about to begin. One of her favorite partners, a Major Newsom, appeared, an officer who had fought at Monmouth. "Miss Loring," he said with a bow. "May I have the pleasure?"

"Yes, you may," she said, smiling.

As the lively polka began, Louisa saw that General Washington and pretty Mrs. Greene, the popular wife of General Nathanael Greene, had joined a set. The General was a tireless dancer who took great pleasure in the steps, but she found it easier to see him as the commander-in-chief, galloping into battle on Blueskin, his famous gray horse. Holding his tattered army together at Valley Forge.

Next came a country dance with Lieutenant Clark. People and seasons might change, but the dance steps remained the same. By now the Long Room was very warm and there was a large gathering around the punch bowl. After the dance ended, the lieutenant went to get her a cooling drink.

Louisa waited, fanning herself, and looked

around. Peggy was sitting with General Arnold and she was wearing her tallest wig. The two girls avoided each other as much as possible but apparently Peggy had decided not to provoke a spate of interested gossip. As for David Franks, he was Becky's clever older cousin. Nothing more.

But as she finished the glass of punch, she was dismayed to see Mrs. Talbot's conceited nephew prancing toward her—and was relieved when Mason Ross cut in front of him. Mason was a good dancer with equally good manners.

"May I have the pleasure?" he asked, bowing.

"You may," she said. Before callers were discouraged, he had come to the house bringing toys for Will. He said that he missed his little brother. As a stately gavotte began, the steps were so slow that they were able to talk.

"By the way," he said, "I've found two books for Will. How is he? May I bring them tomorrow?"

She hesitated. Will was still at the Morrises. "Tomorrow? How kind, but I'm afraid that won't be convenient."

"Then perhaps the day after tomorrow?"

Again, she hesitated. This was becoming difficult, too hard to explain. "Oh, I'm sorry but I don't think that will be possible."

The dance parted them, but when it brought them together again he cleared his throat. "Miss Loring, I'm sorry because there was another reason for that call. I hear your father is still ill. I hope it's not serious because I was hoping to come and consult him about a pressing legal problem. I understand that he's a fine lawyer. May I?"

She stiffened and almost missed a step. Nat had told her to watch for someone who asked questions. Someone who had no reason to be inquisitive. First the pressure to see Will. Now he was asking if her father was seriously ill because he wanted to see him about a legal problem. Was this a way of trying to get information about his condition?

Once again the dance drew them apart, giving her time to think. Mason Ross had a trusted position with John Holker, a respected trader and now the French Consul here. Surely Holker would have carefully checked Ross's credentials before hiring him. All the same, this was suspicious behavior. She must keep her head and be composed.

"I understand," she said, keeping her voice light. "I'll see what can be arranged."

The dance ended with a flourish on the drums. He bowed. "A pleasure. Would you care for more punch?" he asked.

"Thank you, but I must look for my cousin, Mrs. Morris. She wanted to leave early and I must go with her." She smiled. "Enjoy the rest of the evening, Mr. Ross."

"Thank you, Miss Loring. I shall." He bowed again and walked away.

A set was forming for the next dance, a polka. She stood still, her heart beating fast. She must keep a smile on her face and find Nat. Fanning herself rapidly, she looked around for him. After receiving an invitation from a rich client, he said that he knew most of the dances, but finding the right outfit was both expensive and tiresome. They had laughed and she had promised him at least one dance—but where was he now? Had he decided not to come? She felt almost faint with relief when she saw him making his way toward her, looking unfamiliar in evening clothes.

"Until now you were always with a partner," he said. "When the music begins again, may I have the next dance?"

"No, no, you can't—that is, it just happened—we have to talk." Her voice was shaking.

He took her arm. "What happened? What's wrong?"

She swallowed. It was hard to be heard above the noise. "That man. Over there. The one talking to Joseph Reed. His name is Mason Ross. He works for the French Consul, everyone likes him, but just now, while we were dancing, he asked me—he asked me *questions.* Questions about my father's illness. He kept wanting to come and call."

"This way," he said and led her to a less crowded wall. "Slowly, now. What exactly did he say?"

She took a deep breath. "It was during the last dance. He wanted to call tomorrow with presents for Will. I told him it wouldn't be convenient. Then he suggested the next day. I thought he was too insistent. But then he said he'd heard my father was ill and he hoped it wasn't serious because he wanted to come and see him about a legal problem. He was determined to find out how he is. I pretended nothing was wrong." Her voice faded as she ran out of breath.

His hand tightened on her arm. "Wait. If he *is* the agent, he himself wouldn't attack. He would want to find out if your father is well enough to cause trouble, but more evidence is needed."

She shook her head. "Nat, believe me, it wasn't just the words. It was the *way* he said them, as if little Louisa Loring would never have the wits to see anything odd about his questions."

"Then he underestimated Louisa Loring." He paused. "Tomorrow I'll find Captain Warren. Give him the facts. He'll know how to proceed—" He stopped as Mr. Allen and elderly Mr. Gurney came up to them.

"Good evening to you, Miss Loring, and to you, Mr. Haddam," Mr. Allen said. He turned to Mr. Gurney. "John, you should know that this young man has the makings of a very fine attorney."

"So I've heard," Mr. Gurney said. He nodded to Louisa. "A pleasant evening, Miss Loring. Please give my regards to your father."

"I will. Thank you, sir."

A stir in the room indicated that General and Mrs. Washington and their entourage were preparing to leave. The General took his wife's arm. A few words were exchanged with bowing Joseph Reed, and the party left the Long Room. As she watched, a shiver ran down Louisa's spine. She knew from her own experience how tragedy could strike without warning. Tonight the General had cut a lively figure on the dance floor. Tomorrow he might be lying in a coffin.

The Morrises were standing near the front door. Cousin Molly waved. "There you are. I was about to send Robert to find you."

Louisa stepped forward. "Cousin Molly, I don't know if you've met Nat Haddam. He's taken over my father's practice."

Cousin Molly smiled. "I have. Once when I came to call. I'm delighted to see you again, Mr. Haddam. You've been such a help to the Loring family and Will is very fond of you."

Nat bowed. "Thank you, ma'am. Will is a fine boy."

The big Morris coach was waiting outside. Louisa looked at Nat. "You'll come tomorrow as usual? With any news?"

"You can count on it. Good night, Mrs. Morris, good night, sir." The liveried footman lowered the coach's steps, Louisa and the Morrises got in and the coach moved on.

The air always felt cold after hours in the overheated Long Room. Louisa pressed her hands together under the fur rug, Her mind was spinning wildly. She had wanted to find the gentleman responsible for harming her father, but it was hard to believe that she had succeeded. Even harder to believe that Mr. Ross was a cold-blooded agent deceiving his many friends. Somehow she had managed to stay calm, and he hadn't seemed suspicious.

It would be humiliating if she was wrong about him, but Captain Warren could investigate. It was all out of her hands.

As they passed the Friends Almshouse, Cousin Molly stirred. "It was nice to meet Mr. Haddam again. I was quite impressed with his looks and manners."

"I agree, my dear," her husband said. "It's good to see that young man making a mark for himself. I hear the law practice is doing very well."

Louisa nodded. "Yes, it *is* doing well, thank goodness, and he comes every day to see my father and make a report."

She lifted her hands from the rug and thought about Nat. Until tonight she had always seen him at home or in the office. She relied on him and just now he had helped her again in a precarious situation. Taken charge quickly with authority. As well, she was beginning to realize the extent of his acceptance by prominent members of society. Praised by men like Mr. Allen and Mr. Gurney, by Cousin Molly and Cousin Robert—and he had looked so handsome in his formal evening clothes.

They were reaching Fourth Street, breath from the horses rising like steam. Cousin Molly broke the long silence with a heavy sigh. "No one admires Washington more than I do, but I wish to high heaven he would finish his business here. Go back to New Jersey and leave us to recuperate in peace."

Her husband grunted. "Well, you're not alone in that. I took refuge in the Map Room and two of his aides were fast asleep in a corner. I hear the General still has considerable work to do here. He seems tireless, but I suppose life in the military instills endurance."

Molly tossed her head. "Perhaps, but most of us lack that training. Robert, tomorrow you must spread the word that I have come down with a highly contagious fever. For the rest of his visit, I shall spend the evenings lying in my bed, sipping hot chocolate, and reading the latest novels."

Her husband laughed. "You know very well I'll do no such thing."

"A pity. Louisa, what about you?"

"Well, except for my father, I would do exactly the same. Keep Jessie running up and down the stairs with delicious little treats. Lie in my room with the fire blazing and pretend that I was a child again, that Mamma was alive, and that war was only a word in a dictionary."

Molly sighed again. "A word in a dictionary. If only that was true. It's a worry, this waiting to see what will happen next."

Louisa, returning to her new perception of Nat, was silent.

★★★

CHAPTER THIRTY

January 16, 1779

It was mid-morning two days later when Andrew knocked loudly on the front door of the Chestnut Street headquarters. Today he was wearing a plain brown coat, a gray wig, and he was carrying the type of case used for containing papers—the very picture of a minor official.

"Yes sir! He's at a meeting but I'll tell him it's urgent,"the orderly said on opening the door."

He was shown into the library, a room he knew well. He waited, trying to contain his impatience, and looked around. It was generous of Mr. Talbot to turn his fine house over to the military. There was a large globe on a stand in the corner. He was giving it a quick spin when Tallmadge came in.

"Sorry to keep you waiting. I'm told you have urgent news."

Andrew straightened up. "It's this. We may have a suspect, but there's a problem. The courier who brings gold from New York usually arrives about now. This time I had watchers at the bridge, so my men were there when a rider came to pick it up. He was followed to a boarding house on Elfreth's Alley."

"Good news indeed. The problem?"

"They never saw a face. A way to identify him. Earlier this morning, I went there acting like a city official needing information. I questioned the landlady, a Mrs. Coulter, about her boarders. She was quite affronted. Assured me that she had three and all were extremely respectable. Clifford Ford is an aide to Congressman Perry. Mason Ross works as an accountant for John Holker, the French Consul. Matthew Downton is an agent in one of Robert Morris's shipping companies. I'm trying to find out more about them without drawing attention to myself. In the meantime, they're being followed by my best people, but I need advice.

Tallmadge went to his desk, sat down and folded his hands. "Tricky, Three suspects and all are working for high-ranking men. A false arrest would stir up a hornet's nest of trouble."

"It would," Andrew said. "Following them is key, but I'm looking into other ways. The landlady has a black servant who cleans rooms and does laundry. After talking to her I had a word with him. Gave him a few shillings and told him if he saw anything unusual he must come at once to Norris Alley and there would be a reward for useful information." He paused. "If one of them is working for the British, he'll be competent—and we may have to move fast."

Tallmadge nodded. "Right. I'll lay on extra protection for the General around the clock." He studied a paper. "Tomorrow's schedule. A morning meeting with foot-dragging Congressmen, then lunch at the Laurens's house for several merchants with deep pockets. At two-thirty, he leaves and goes to painter Peale to arrange sittings for his portrait. It's a gift he never wanted and he's not pleased. Then we have another of those damned parties that last until after midnight."

"So he's protected until he goes out at two-thirty. Where does this painter live?"

"At the corner of Third and Lombard Streets."

"Who'll be with the General?"

"Ordinarily he'd go with two Life Guards and an

aide, but that can be changed."

"By tomorrow I should be able to narrow the field from three to one. Those background checks may turn up something useful, but getting them will be difficult."

"Understood. Let me know as soon as you have any information."

Once back on the street, he began to limp, a trick to add to the disguise. As he reached the corner of Second Street, he looked around. No one was following, but he walked faster, breathing hard. How long before one of those three respected men acted in a suspicious way? It was going to happen—but when? And how?

Tonight the Bunch of Grapes Tavern was enjoying a full house. The tables were filled with loud customers consuming quantities of rum and beer. The air was heavy with acrid smoke.

Finder seated himself on a bench with a noisy group. He ordered a tankard of ale, then paid the harassed waiter to fetch Pottle from his room in the cellar. It had been a long day, but he felt calm and confident. Now he must instill the same confidence in Pottle.

It was more important than ever to make sure that he wasn't being followed. He had checked often, saw no one, but decided to be cautious. He had worked long hours in his office, dined with a group of congressmen at the City Tavern, then gone back to his lodging. When it was dark, he had changed clothes and slipped here through back streets and alleys.

A moment later Pottle swung his legs over the bench and sat down beside him. "What's up?" he muttered.

Finder raised his tankard and sipped. Without turning his head, he spoke under his breath. "A bribed Life Guard gave me Washington's schedule for tomorrow.

He'll be at a house on the corner of Lombard and Third at two-thirty. A small house, only a few servants. It belongs to Peale, the painter. I checked the front and back entrances."

Pottle coughed. "Washington will have guards."

"He will, but here's my plan. I've hired a chaise. It'll be on Pine Street, one up from Lombard. At two o'clock sharp, we meet there. We go off to the back of Peale's house and wait until the General comes. There'll be guards at the front door, but if there's one below, you'll take him out and I'll go back to the chaise."

Pottle said nothing.

The men around them were competing to see who could tell the bawdiest joke. There were roars of laughter. Finder raised his tankard again, then put it down.

"Surprise is key," he muttered. "Figure on two guards in front. You're dressed as a courier in muddy riding clothes—there's a bundle under the bench. You're bringing the General an important message from Middletown. Urgent. For his eyes only. Your only problem is to get past the guards. The General should be in a front room. You'll hear voices. Shoot for his head, shoot others if you must, then run to the chaise. We'll get to the ferry and be off to New York before a chase can be organized." He paused. "Is that clear?"

Pottle shifted in his seat. "Easy enough for you to say, but this is—"

"No time to show weakness. I thought you had balls, man. Looks like I was wrong. Anyhow, I'm out of here tomorrow. You'll be on your own with no money, hiding from a bunch of deserters who are hell bent to find you, cut your throat, and throw you in the river." He wrapped his hands around the tankard. "I said it before and I'll say it again. You have the experience. You've done this many times and have never been caught."

The men beside them were still exchanging

obscene jokes. The waiter brought more drinks. Pottle coughed again and lowered his head. "Meet you two o'clock, chaise on Pine," he grunted. "Go in the front dressed like a bloody courier. Shoot, get out through the back, then run for the chaise. What about money?"

"I'll have gold, but there'll be a fortune at the other end. We can do it. Take heart, man, and think about rewards." He paused. "Now get some sleep and for God's sake don't drink."

Coins were thrown on the table as men on the bench got up to go. Ignoring Pottle, Finder joined the group as they made for the door.

The cold air was reviving after inhaling thick clouds of smoke. He sauntered along as if he was enjoying a night out with a rowdy bunch of friends. By this time tomorrow the great George Washington might be dead, a useless corpse, and the country would fall apart.

The men were peeling off, shouting good night. He walked faster. This was a daring act, a test of his skills, a gamble he had to win. Blood would be shed, but before long the world would know that Mason Ross had the courage and the wits to succeed where so many others had failed.

★★★

CHAPTER THIRTY-ONE

January 18, 1779

The temperature rose slightly during the night, but the change did not reflect Andrew's mood as he sat in his small sitting room. Failure was now a stark reality, clutching him by the throat. Yesterday the three suspects were followed around the clock. No results, and he had been forced to stop and give his men a rest. Successful following required stamina, and he had no reliable replacements.

With a groan, he kicked the leg of the table. His assistant, Aaron, was clashing around in the kitchen, making sure his overworked young captain had enough to eat; he could tell by the smell that Aaron was frying grits. After some thought he had given up the idea of making background checks. Too difficult to know where to start, and he could risk revealing his own identity.

This was now a waiting game. Until one of the three suspects could be outed, there was no hope of a breakthrough. All the same, he couldn't just sit here mulling over failure. He must eat the grits, put on a disguise, and go out to do his routine checks.

He gave the table leg a parting kick and stood up. But as he headed for the kitchen, he heard heavy pounding on the front door. He turned and went to open it. Jethro, the black servant at Mrs. Coulter's boarding house, was standing there, breathless from running.

"Seems as if it's Mister Ross you want, sir," the boy panted. "He's packing all his clothes like he's leaving for good."

"What?" He reached out and pulled the boy into the hall. "Mister Ross is packing his clothes?"

"Yessir, and there's a lot of 'em. Mister Ross, he goes to parties most every night. A lot of washing shirts and neckpieces—"

"Never mind that. Did you see anything else?"

The boy scratched his head. "He told me to get out of the room, but there's more, sir. He paid Pokey in the kitchen to go to Johnson's Livery with a message. Pokey showed it to me. Mr. Ross—he's hiring a horse and chaise. Wants them ready early this afternoon."

Andrew winced as every muscle in his neck tightened. Clothes packed. A chaise hired for this afternoon. He turned to Jethro. "You've done well, Jethro. Very well," he said, keeping his voice steady. "There'll be a reward for bringing me this news. Say nothing and keep your eyes open. If anything more happens, come back."

"Yessir, I'll do that."

"Hurry now, before you're missed."

He let Jethro out, then returned to the sitting room, sat down and ran his fingers through his hair. His decision to use Jethro had paid off. A breakthrough, but this was a moment when experience counted. Facts lined up and put in the right sequence. Mason Ross appeared to be planning an attack. In a few hours the General would be at the Peale house. An offensive must be organized without delay. He ran upstairs, put on his peddler's dirty clothes, then raced down to the kitchen.

Aaron was filling a kettle. "You ready to eat, Cap'n?"

"No time. I'm off to headquarters." He paused. "A boy just came with important news about a suspect. If there are messages, get them to headquarters fast as you can."

"Will do. Dress up warm, it's still colder than a witch's tit."

Even with no hampering push cart, the streets seemed endless. At headquarters, an aide he had never met opened the back door. With great firmness he told the shabby peddler that Major Tallmadge was in a meeting and could not be disturbed. Andrew looked him in the eye. "Tell the Major that Captain Warren is here with news of the utmost importance. Now *go*."

In a moment, Tallmadge appeared. "We can talk down here," he said motioning to an alcove at the end of the hall. "Which one?"

Andrew squared his shoulders. "Mason Ross. The young boy who works at his boarding house just came to me. Ross is packing as if he's leaving the city. He's hired a chaise from a nearby livery to be ready early this afternoon. He must have had word that Washington is going to painter Peale's."

Tallmadge struck the palm of his hand with his fist. "Good God. How—but that investigation can wait. Should we cancel the meeting?"

"We could, but if Ross makes another move, we might not be warned in time. This way we have an advantage."

"Point made. What do you know about Ross?"

"Mustn't underestimate him. Devilish clever to link himself to Holker, respected trader and French Consul. By becoming his aide, he was able to mingle with the most influential people in the city. Well positioned to infiltrate and spread lies."

"Accomplices?"

"If Ross is the bastard who ordered the attacks on my old network, he hired a killer who does his dirty work and leaves no traces. It's happened several times."

Tallmadge frowned. "But today the killer would have to get past well-trained Life Guards."

"Difficult, but not impossible. He might try to get in through the back, so we should have a guard down there. Trickier at the front door. He could pretend to be a trades person with a valid reason to enter, but if the guards send him away then we end up with no evidence."

Tallmadge shook his head. "So what are our options, if any?"

Andrew stared down at the patterned carpet. He thought for a moment then cleared his throat. "There's one solution. I could go to Peale's house a little before two o'clock. Tell Peale I'm an advance aide, then take a position near the front door. Be ready to confront anyone who comes in and shows signs of aggression."

Tallmadge's lips tightened. He shook his head again. "I don't like it. You'd be taking a serious risk. Don't want that, but it seems we have no time to work out alternatives. What do you need from me?"

"Three of your most trustworthy Life Guards. Two for the front door, one for the back in case that's used. Give them orders to let anyone in, whatever the pretext, then be quick to help me subdue him."

"Done." He paused. "What about Ross himself? I assume he'll watch the house or stay in the chaise. That chaise mustn't leave the city."

"Which means it will have to be guarded, but not by soldiers. That would be a tip off and Ross will be armed."

"I'll organize three of my best people dressed like ordinary citizens. Which street?"

"Probably not Lombard. Too close. Maybe Pine, the one just above, or Spruce, the one above Pine. They would see him waiting in the chaise."

An aide carrying papers passed by the alcove. Tallmadge pulled out his watch. His face was grim. "It's a little after eleven. Three hours to organize. Come back at half past twelve to regroup." No need for further discussion. There was solid trust on both sides.

The streets were filled with people going in and out of shops. As Andrew went by, he thought about impending danger. He had never actually fought in a battle, so how did men prepare to face the enemy? Religious ones would pray. He'd seen British soldiers shining brass and singing songs like "The Girl I Left Behind Me."

Many would be reminded of loved ones like Sarah. He avoided her house on Third Street but they might meet elsewhere. Even in disguise, she would recognize him and they would have to pass without speaking. Every night before falling into exhausted sleep, he thought of her, held her in his arms, and wondered if she was thinking of him. If he died, she would mourn, but after a while she would find solace with someone else.

A fire wagon rushed by, horn blaring. Men began to run after it, carrying their waterproof leather buckets. Andrew hurried on. When he reached his house, he would ask Aaron to cook him a good meal. Then he would polish his boots and the buttons on his uniform.

Thrusting his hands into his pockets, he breathed deeply. If he had to lose his life, let it be quick, not a festering wound. In any case, he must overcome all feelings of fear. Remember Cousin Joseph Warren's courage at Breed's Hill, a dedicated man who was willing to stand up to tyrants and die for a great cause.

The Christ Church bells rang out the noon hour. He took another deep breath. Earlier today he was filled with despair over his failing operation. Then Jethro had come with life- changing news. The plans were in place, his part was set, and he must be ready to face the next few hours with a clear and confident mind.

★★★

CHAPTER THIRTY-TWO

January 18, 1779 *The same day*

At a little after two-thirty, passersby on the corner of Lombard Street watched as General Washington's large carriage drew up in front of the unpretentious Peale house. The General was accompanied by three Life Guards and an aide. He was greeted warmly by Peale and soon was drinking Madeira wine in the front parlor.

Andrew, now in his captain's uniform, stood in the narrow front hall lined with the artist's paintings. He had sent one guard to the back yard and alerted the two at the front door.

"We're setting a trap. Whoever comes, no matter what he looks like or what he says, let him through. I'll confront him inside, but leave the door open and rush in if I call." They assured him that they understood and were prepared to act quickly.

There was a murmur of talk in the front parlor. Andrew waited, squaring his shoulders. One pocket contained a loaded pistol, the other held three short lengths of rope. A pretty young maid carrying a bottle came by. She smiled at him.

"Can I fetch you a drink, sir?"

"Nothing, thank you. I'm here in case I'm needed."

A church bell struck the hour of three. He flexed his hands to ease the growing tension. It was now or never for the attacker to make his move, and the waiting was becoming intolerable. The trap had been set, but it might never snap shut. Ross might not be involved—or he might have changed his mind.

A group of children were on the walkway, chattering in shrill little voices, but as they passed by, heavy feet pounded up the front steps. A man spoke to the guards. His voice was hoarse and breathless. "Courier from Middlebrook … urgent message for the General … his eyes only."

Andrew braced himself. The door opened. The man who came in was short and solidly built. His hat almost covered his face and his riding clothes were muddy. He looked at Andrew and snapped out his words. "Message from Middlebrook for the General, his eyes only. Servant at the Lauren house said he's here."

Andrew nodded. "Right, but my orders are to see that no one disturbs the General during this meeting. You can give the message to me. I'll see that he gets it." He held out his hand.

The man didn't blink. "Has to be now. Could be important news for the General and I was delayed on the road."

The convincing tactic would have fooled any unprepared aide. Andrew shook his head. "Sorry," he said firmly. "Nobody sees the General. Give me the message, then go to our headquarters on Market Street. They'll look after you."

Voices sounded from the parlor. Andrew placed himself in front of the door. The man stood still. Andrew could see that he was trying to decide whether to shoot him and then the General, or whether to hand over a false message and leave.

"Market Street. Obliged," he muttered. His right hand inched toward a pocket.

Andrew knocked it to one side, The man grunted. He raised his other hand to strike but Andrew deflected the blow. "Guards," he shouted.

In seconds they were there, seizing the man's arms. He fought like an animal, kicking and clawing. It took three of them to pin him down and extract a pistol from his pocket.

"Tie him up," Andrew panted and pulled out his ropes. "We'll have to get him—" He stopped as the parlor door opened and John Laurens, Washington's aide, appeared.

"Heard a noise," he said, staring. "What's going on?"

Andrew got to his feet. "An incident, Laurens. Say nothing."

Laurens, no fool, nodded. "Right," he said. The door closed.

The man was still fighting, thrashing back and forth. It was a struggle to propel him along the hall and down a flight of stairs that led to the kitchen. A thin white-haired woman wearing an apron was stirring a pot on the stove. She dropped the spoon and looked around as they burst in. The man was still fighting, cursing loudly.

Andrew released an arm and stepped forward. "Captain Warren, ma'am. Don't be alarmed. General Washington's Life Guards caught this man as he came into the house. As you can see, he's resisting and he's violent. Is there a place at the back where we can hold him until help comes?"

The woman looked startled. "Heavens to Betsy, such language and in front of a young girl. The sooner he's gone the better." She wiped her hands on her apron and turned to the pretty maid who was standing nearby, mouth wide open. "Show them to the storeroom, Mary, and take a candle. It's dark in there."

"Obliged, ma'am," Andrew said and stepped back.

The storeroom was musty, lined with bins for coal and wood. The man was dumped against a wall. He stopped trying to loosen the ropes and lay still. Only his slits of eyes moved, as if he was sizing up his captors. The hat had slipped, revealing a vivid red scar across his upper face.

A door led to the back yard where the third guard had been stationed. Andrew crossed the room, went out, and looked around. No guard. No sign of him. He swore under his breath and looked harder. The guard was lying under a frost-covered bush, bleeding from the head. Andrew leaned down and touched his face. He was unconscious, but alive.

He ran back to the storeroom. "One of you. Come quick," he snapped. The taller guard followed him out to the bushes.

"Oh Jesus, Tim's down," he whispered.

"He's breathing and the blow didn't crush his skull. Have to get him inside. You take his legs and I'll try to steady his head." They lifted him, staggered into the store room and laid him on the dirt floor. The blood stopped flowing and he began to moan.

Andrew straightened. The attempt to kill the General had failed but Ross would be waiting in the chaise and must be stopped. He motioned to the Life Guards. "I'm off to Pine Street to keep the man behind the attack from escaping in a chaise. I'm leaving you in charge," he said in a low voice. "One of you go back to the front door. The other stays here. Ask the cook to fetch blankets for Tim and make sure that bastard doesn't loosen the ropes. The General will be leaving soon. He'll notice there's only one guard and want an explanation. Say that there was an incident, now under control. The aide who came out of the parlor can confirm. Is that clear?"

"It's clear," the taller one said, looking grim.

On Lombard Street, people were out, going about their business. He headed toward Pine Street, walking fast. Ross's well-planned attempt at assassination had failed, his hireling was now a prisoner, but it could have gone the other way and Ross was still a threat. By now he might have decided that something had gone wrong and it was time to cut his losses and run. If so, Tallmadge's soldiers dressed as civilians would have taken action and stopped him. He'd have to be removed to headquarters and a doctor sent Peale's house.

He had almost reached Pine Street when two shots rang out, a blood-chilling sound. People paused and looked around. He sprinted ahead, almost knocking an old lady down.

"Oh Christ," he muttered as he reached the corner. There was no sign of the chaise. A small crowd had gathered on one side of the street. A child was screaming. A woman sobbed. Several men stood looking down at the man who lay sprawled on the cobbles. The pool of blood was spreading, already congealing. Another man sat huddled on the curb, holding his arm.

The situation called for authority. He pushed forward. "Captain Warren from General Washington's headquarters," he shouted. "Madam, take that child away. Then one of you tell me what happened here."

The lady picked up the screaming child. As she disappeared, the story poured out in a garbled stream of voices. "He was in a chaise tied up to the post over there … it had red wheels … those two tried to hold the horse … he had a pistol … he shot them … he whipped the horse and went off lickety-split …"

Andrew stood still, assessing the situation. The two soldiers hadn't been quick enough. Now one lay bleeding in the street, maybe dying. Headquarters must get the bad news but he had no way to get there. Who could help? He was staring at the motley bunch of bystanders when a heavyset older man detached himself and came forward. "Howard Farnham, local magistrate. I was across the street in my gig, about to leave my house. Can I be of assistance, Captain?"

A magistrate with a cool head—and transport. Andrew drew him aside. "Sir, this is the situation. The man who escaped in the chaise is a spy paid by the British. Headquarters must be informed and the wounded here need care."

The magistrate nodded. "The chaps here can carry them into my house. My wife and daughter will look after them. As for headquarters, I'll take you in my gig."

"Much obliged, sir. Very much obliged." Later he would make sure the magistrate's service was recognized, but at this point help was all that mattered.

It was now half-past four and headquarters on Chestnut Street was in full crisis mode. A doctor was sent to painter Peale's house, another to the magistrate's home.

An emergency meeting of all aides was underway in the library as Andrew made his report. How the attacker dressed as a courier had gained entrance to the house. How he and two Life Guards had subdued him, then found the third guard lying unconscious in the back yard. How he had been on his way to Ross's chaise when he heard the shots. Two soldiers had been wounded, one badly, and Ross had managed to escape. He blamed himself for not requesting more guards or soldiers.

"The attack on Washington was averted due to Captain Warren's actions," Tallmadge said as he finished. "Now we have to move fast. We have the hired killer locked up in one of our back rooms. Nasty bloke, all lies. Says he was a respectable citizen until Ross hired him and applied threats unless he killed General Washington. Distancing himself from Ross as fast as he can. Pretends he has no idea where Ross could be going."

Decisions had to be made, but confusion was inevitable. Tallmadge rapped on his desk. "Captain Warren, you've been dealing with Mason Ross. What do you think he'll do now?"

Andrew shook his head. "Hard to say. He's wily and he's armed. He could hide in the city, but if he crosses into Jersey, he's got two choices. The Camden Road is the shortest to New York, but he might take the Old York Road just to fool us." He hesitated. "Traffic on the river will stop when it gets dark. My advice is to send soldiers with supervising officers to all the ferries with orders to search every vehicle. Look for a man alone in a chaise with red wheels."

There was a murmur of agreement. After receiving a nod from Tallmadge, Lieutenant Carstairs hurried from the library. An agitated discussion followed; talk of sending out a general alarm was rejected. After several minutes Tallmadge cleared his throat.

"Gentlemen, your attention, please." He paused and looked at the silent group. "Ross's attempt at assassination failed and he's now a wanted man." His voice was grim. He raised a hand and struck a palm with his fist. "It's a bad situation but one thing is clear. We are determined—and we are going to do our damndest to make sure that bastard never reaches New York."

★★★

CHAPTER THIRTY-THREE

January 18, 1779 *The same day*

The afternoon sun was shining through the kitchen windows when Louisa turned from the stove and sat down at the scrubbed table. Jessie was away on her annual visit to her son in Baltimore. Until she came back, Louisa was alone in the house.

She smiled, then hugged herself tightly. Last night Nat had asked her to marry him. There had been signs that he cared for her, but his success at the General's ball had finally convinced him that he would be accepted in her world. He had grasped her hands, saying that there were no words to express how much he admired and honored her. That his greatest wish was to make her happy. With no hesitation she had accepted him. They were so *right* together. The intense longing to be with him had grown stronger and stronger along with the desire to care for him, sleep with him, and have his children. And it wasn't just that she was happiest when they were together. She was filled with admiration for what he had accomplished in such a short time.

At first there would be gossip about her marrying a farmer's son, but that wouldn't last long. This was a new country where intelligence mattered more than birth. Those close to her would be delighted. Mamma, still a presence, would be pleased, "At last my headstrong daughter has come to her senses. She has chosen well and is ready to begin a new life." Still, before proposing, Nat had made sure that she fully understood the differences in their backgrounds. He took her to visit his family in their simple house. She met his parents and his talkative little sister. What she saw was a family that valued hard work. Kindness. Pride in Nat's achievements. The connection might be awkward at first, but she left feeling that they would gladly receive her as his wife.

The clock in the parlor was striking the half hour. It was time to stop musing and feed her father again. She got to her feet and went back to the stove. She was heating a nourishing chicken broth when the unmistakable sound of gunfire reverberated through the air. Two loud shots, coming from the vicinity of Pine Street, only a few blocks away.

She frowned and put the spoon down. There was often violence at the docks, but not in this part of town. Not in broad daylight. This was disturbing but Peter was in the barn. Perhaps he should come over in case there was trouble.

Quickly, she lifted the heavy pot and put it to one side. Pulled on her red cloak, opened the door, and stopped. Mason Ross was coming from the barn leading their horse. She clutched at the handle and stared. Why on earth was he here, on foot, taking their horse and gig? Where was Peter?

She ran out. "Good afternoon, Mr. Ross," she said. "This is rather a surprise. I hadn't expected to see you today."

He looked startled, then he smiled. "Good afternoon, Miss Loring. My horse has gone lame down the road and I have an important meeting, why I'm borrowing yours. It's quite all right, no need to trouble yourself."

She stiffened. First the suspicious questions at the ball, now this unconvincing story—no, taking their gig was *not* all right.

"Wait," she said. "I'm sorry but our horse is needed here. The groom has to go to the apothecary and fetch medicine for my father."

The pleasant smile disappeared. "It's only for a short time, Miss Loring. If you don't mind—"

"But I *do* mind." She stepped forward and grasped the reins. He reached out and tried to loosen them. For a few seconds she held on, but he was far stronger. Rather than fight, she should let him go, then run to the Shippens and sound an alarm. Judge Shippen would know how to do this.

"Oh, very well," she said, tossing her head. "If it's so important, this meeting, be on your way but for goodness sake, hurry back. My father needs his medicine." She tossed her head again and pulled her cloak tighter. "It's cold out here. I'm going in—"

"No." He seized her arm. "I know what you're thinking: Let him go, then get help to catch him. That's not going to happen." With his free hand he pulled out a heavy pistol and held it to her head. "I just shot two men. I silenced your groom. I need to cross the river and get to New York. To stay safe, I have to take you with me."

"What?"

"You heard me. Get in," he grunted and pushed her into the gig. Took off his muffler, tied her wrists together with it, pulled the ends around her waist and knotted them to a door handle. Shoved the pistol back into his pocket, and jumped in. The old horse snorted and walked on.

At the end of the drive, he turned left onto Fourth Street. A horse and chaise had been tied to a maple tree nearby. He leaped out and pulled a canvas bag from under the seat. Placed it under his feet, then gave the horse a sharp slap with the reins.

A moment later they were bowling along familiar streets. People were going about their business, unaware that a girl in the passing gig was being abducted. Louisa's heart was beating as though it would crack her ribs. This couldn't be happening. A few minutes ago she was sitting in her warm kitchen thinking about Nat … he would see that she wasn't in the house … her red cloak was missing … he would find Peter alive or dead … the search would begin but no one would know where she had gone … no one would know how to find her. She sat still, numb with cold and fear.

They were reaching the river. A busy wharf led to the long flat ferry. Several vehicles ahead of them waited in line to cross. Soldiers were checking them, overseen by a mounted officer.

"Silence," Mason Ross muttered, touching his pocket. "Good afternoon," he said to the young soldier who looked in. "We're going to visit my wife's cousin in Turnersville. We'll be back tomorrow." The soldier nodded and went on. Their horse and gig was loaded and the ferry began to move.

The rope creaked, the horse in the farmer's cart ahead of them stamped. They were now in the middle of the river. Louisa sat still. He shifted in his seat and loosened the reins, as if now he was beginning to feel safe, and looked at her.

"Almost there," he said. "They were looking for a chaise with red wheels driven by a man alone. Unfortunate that you came out of the house when you did."

She said nothing. Her mouth was too dry to speak.

"Yes, most unfortunate. I liked you and your little brother. Violence is against my nature and I regret being forced to use it on you."

She shuddered and closed her eyes. He didn't need her any longer. He was getting ready to kill her. Leave her body by the road or hidden in bushes where it wouldn't be found until spring. It was about to happen—dear God, let it be quick.

The waves were flattening as they arrived at the wharf. There was a short wait as the vehicles ahead of them were unloaded. The farmer's cart clattered off, then they too moved forward.

By now it was dark except for the light of a small half-moon emerging from under heavy clouds. The empty road ahead was wide and straight. After a short distance he pulled to one side. Untied her hands and retrieved his muffler. Leaned over and handed her down. "I kept my word, Miss Loring, but I doubt anyone will come along now. Again, my most sincere regrets." He sat back on the seat and gave the horse a slap with the reins. The gig began to move. In seconds he was out of sight.

★★★

CHAPTER THIRTY-FOUR

January 18, 1779 *Evening the same day*

Louisa stumbled to her feet and stood there, shivering from head to toe in her thin red cloak. She was alive, but if no one came along she would surely die of cold, the blood slowly freezing in her veins.

She rubbed her arms and pulled the cloak tighter. Standing still would be fatal. To survive, her only hope was to walk until she came to a house. There was just enough moonlight to show her the way. Without it, he might as well have killed her back by her kitchen door.

There were dark woods on either side. An owl hooted, a loud cry. She jumped as a small animal emerged from the bushes and ran across her path. In the distance a coyote howled. But as she went, her dazed mind wandered. Jessie was coming home tomorrow … she would look after her father … Nat would go to headquarters to report her missing … but if she died, who would tell little Will?

One foot forward then the other, step by painful step with no sense of how far she had gone. She was reaching the limit of her strength when at last she saw it—the outline of a building. She limped toward it. Slowly, the outline became a farmhouse with barns. No lights shone from the windows. Farmers went to bed early and no one welcomed strangers after dark.

Her legs were giving way, the blister on her heel was agonizing, but she kept on until she reached the large house. Unlatched the picket gate, staggered to the front door, and began to bang the knocker down and waited. Dear God, there *must* be someone here.

Finally bolts shot back. The door opened a few inches. An old man peered out. He was wearing a night cap and was holding a candle. He stared at her, then turned away.

"Mattie," he called in a quavering voice. "Mattie. Come!"

An equally old woman appeared. She too was wearing a night cap. She pushed him aside. "Merciful heavens, it's a young girl. What do you want, miss? Why are you out alone on a cold night?"

Louisa swallowed. "Ma'am, I beg p-pardon for t-troubling you. I live in the city, but I was t-taken by force from my house and l-left on this road near the ferry—" Her chattering teeth made it hard to speak.

The old lady reached out and pulled her in. "Good gracious, child, you walked here from the ferry? Your hand is like ice. Ezra, shut the door and go light a lamp." Still holding Louisa's hand, she propelled her across a little hall and into a large kitchen.

Louisa collapsed into a chair by the table. She closed her eyes as the old lady pulled off her cloak. "Let's get you warm or you'll catch your death. Quick, wrap yourself in this blanket and I'll heat up some soup. It gave me a real bad turn to see you standing there," she said, and began to bustle about.

Louisa pulled the blanket around her shoulders, lay back and kept her eyes closed. She was no longer walking down an endless road. Somehow she had reached this warm room. The old woman was kind and she was going to live.

Slowly, painfully, feeling began to return to her hands and feet. After a while, she opened her eyes and looked around. The fireplace was hung with kettles, baking ovens bordered the sides, and glowing embers were banked on the wide hearth.

The old man was dozing in a corner, the nightcap drooping off his bald head. His wife went and spoke to him. "Ezra, you want some soup? No? Then get yourself off to bed." She hurried back, lifted a pot from a hook in the big fireplace, and filled a bowl.

"There, my dearie. Wrap yourself around that, and here's a bit of bread just baked today. I've put a kettle on for tea—those thin little shoes—I'll throw them in the fire and here's a pair of Ezra's old boots—good gracious, what a blister. I've a salve for the men's hands after they've been digging potatoes, it's our biggest crop."

A dog was lying in a corner. He lifted his head, sniffed, and got up. A large brown dog with a white muzzle.

"Leo," the old lady said. "Old like us, used to be a good watch dog." She broke off a chunk of bread and gave it to him. "Here, you beggar. Now go and lie down."

The soup was thick with winter vegetables. She ate a few spoonsful. The woman sat down at the table and folded her hands. White hair showed under her nightcap and her thin old face was furrowed with wrinkles. "That will do you good, dearie. What is your name?"

"Louisa. Louisa Loring."

"Mine is Corning—Mistress Corning and I'm eighty-one. Now tell me how you got yourself into such a fix."

Louisa hesitated. She took another mouthful, not wanting to talk, but kind Mistress Corning deserved an answer. "It's—it's like I said, ma'am. A man abducted me from my house. He had a gun. He made me cross the river with him. Left me on the road and drove off."

Mistress Corning shook her head. "Terrible. What a terrible thing to do. There must be a way to catch him. Make sure he's severely punished. Yes, he should be caught and punished for what he did to you. But you're safe from him now. I'll make up a bed in the spare room and put a warming pan in the bed—no, that room will be too cold. My son John lives over the barn. He'll bring the mattress down here. Yes, that would be best, but first the tea." She stood up and went to the hearth.

Louisa didn't move but her dazed mind sharpened. Mason Ross—those morning calls with presents for Will, the lively dances. The terrible moments when he had forced her into the gig and then later left her to die on the road—

Louisa drank more soup. Mistress Corning was right. Mason Ross should be caught and severely punished for what he had done to her and to others.

Mistress Corning handed her a cup of tea. "Drink up, my dearie, and then I'll settle you for the night."

Louisa grasped the cup, as hot as the anger that was clearing her dazed mind. If only headquarters knew which road Ross had taken there might be a way to stop him. The horse was old and it was a long way to New York.

"Do you not like your tea, dearie?" Mrs. Corning asked.

Louisa hesitated. There *was* a way if she could summon up the strength to take it—and any hope must start with Mistress Corning. Difficult, but any hope must start with Mistress Corning. She swallowed and sat straight. "Ma'am, I thank you for your trouble, indeed I do, but I can't stay. I have to find a boat and a man who will row me to the other side."

The old lady looked startled. "What's this? Go out again? Nonsense, my dearie. You need to sleep. You can go back on the ferry tomorrow." A soothing voice, as if calming a fractious child.

"No, ma'am, I truly need to cross. I truly do. Is there a neighbor, someone who has a boat? Later I can pay him, pay him well."

"Please, child, no more of this foolishness. My son has a boat, he takes our vegetables across, but he never goes out at night."

A son with a boat—but she would have to be convincing.

"*No.*" She hit the table with her fist. "I *must* go and I *must* go *tonight.*"

Mistress Corning looked alarmed. She picked up the candle. "No need to carry on like this. I'll go to the barn and wake John. Maybe he can talk sense into you,' she said, and hurried from the room.

Several minutes passed before Mistress Corning returned with her son, a large man with the weathered face of a farmer. He looked at her warily; no doubt his mother had warned him that he would be dealing with a distraught female. He seated himself at the other end of the table.

"Well, young lady," he began." Seems you're in a bit of trouble."

She folded her hands. All depended now on presenting the need. "Sir," she said, keeping her voice steady. "Did your mother tell you that I was abducted from my home and left to die on this road?"

"Aye, she did, and now you want to go home." He paused. "You're tired, missie. You had a bad scare. Sleep the night here. I'll see you to the first ferry that comes over in the morning." The dog, hearing his voice, got up and went over to him. He leaned down and stroked its head.

This was not going well. She leaned forward. "Sir, I beg of you, please believe me. It's not about going home. Not that at all. I have to cross because the man who left me in a ditch to die is a spy for the British. He shot people, he stole our horse and gig, and now he's escaping to New York." She pressed her hands to her cheeks. "Sir, no one else knows he's on the Camden Road. I *have* to get to headquarters. Tell them so they can organize a chase before it's too late."

John Corning looked dubious. He scratched his chin "A spy, you say. Are you sure?"

"I'm sure. His name is Mason Ross and he's done great harm. I know because he was behind the attack that poisoned my father and maybe killed others. You would be doing a real service for your country—and I'll pay you well for your trouble."

A log in the huge fireplace sparked loudly. John Corning scratched his chin again. "Spies—we've had a few around here. They're a pesky lot, I've no liking for them, but you shouldn't go out in the cold again. I'm willing to take the message meself. Mebbe you could write it down—what you want me to tell them at headquarters, wherever that may be."

A kind offer. She thought for a moment, then shook her head. "There would be too many questions. They'd want to know exactly what happened—and they don't know you."

"Aye, there's that." He frowned. "Happens it's a calm night, no wind, otherwise no chance. We have two workers here, strong boys at the oars. The boat is small and leaky. You'd have to double up on the floor."

"I can do that, of course I can, but please hurry."

"Patience, missie. Me mother won't be best pleased, but I'll calm her."

In a moment ,Mistress Corning was back. She looked distressed "I don't like to let you out again, indeed I don't, but John says the man is a British spy and has to be caught. Finish the soup and mind you eat the bread. That'll perk you up a bit."

Louisa nodded. Her throat was growing sore. She picked up a piece of bread. Tried to swallow, but it stuck in her mouth. To go out and be numb with cold again—the thought was agonizing, but she must fix her mind on getting to headquarters. Every hour that passed meant less chance of organizing a capture.

At last there were voices in the hall. John Corning appeared. "Ready, missie. No more walking. We'll take you in a cart."

She stood up and looked around a room that she would never forget, nor would she forget such kindness. She grasped Mistress Corning's thin hands. "You've done so much for me—I would have died if you hadn't let me in," she whispered. "When this is over, I'll be back to thank you."

Mistress Corning blinked. "It was little enough. God bless you, my dearie."

The small farm boat was pulled up to a dock. The moon continued bright, no need for a lantern. She was helped to a little space in the bow and the three men picked up the oars. As they moved forward, oars creaking, she curled up and then lay still. Her legs were aching painfully, but a few minutes more and the ordeal would be over, her mission achieved. She would give her story to the officer she'd seen checking the vehicles earlier. He would take charge, rush her message to headquarters, and arrange for her to go home. By now Nat must be thinking that she was dead, that they would never have a life together.

As they reached the wharf, the men shipped their oars, breathing heavily. John Corning fastened the rope to a stanchion and lifted her out. "What now, missie?"

She looked around, then looked again, appalled. The wharf was deserted except for a man who was scrubbing boards. No soldiers, no officer. They must have left after searching the last boat.

"There were soldiers here before," she whispered. "They were searching for him—there's no one here at all, no one who can help. I should have known they wouldn't stay all night—Oh God, oh God, what can we do?" Her voice was rising. Her legs were giving way.

John Corning caught her as she fell. "Hold on, missie. I'll find someone. There's a light in the shed over there. We'll go and see what can be done." With an arm around her waist, he supported her to the shed and knocked loudly on the door.

After a moment it opened. A small man stood there, holding a bunch of papers. He didn't seem pleased to see them. "What's wanted?" he said in a gruff voice.

John Corning pulled off his wool cap. "I'll cut to the chase, sir. This young lady was abducted by a British spy. She was taken across the river and left on the road near our house. I brought her here in my boat. She's tuckered from walking and now she needs a way to get to our headquarters and let them know the spy is on the Camden Road heading for New York."

The small man frowned. "A British spy? There were soldiers at the wharf earlier, searching vehicles, but they never found him." He rubbed his hands together. "I do the ferry schedules here. Never been to headquarters but they'll want to hear about this. The sooner the better." He stopped rubbing his hands. "I was about to leave for the night but now—well, follow me," he said and led them to the rear of the shed where a small horse and gig were tied to a post. "I trust you won't be long," he added.

"Not long. My boys are waiting in the boat. Thankee, sir," John said and lifted her into the little gig. As they left the shed and started toward the road, he turned. "Headquarters. Which street, missie?"

She stiffened. "It's—it's—I can't—I can't—I don't *know.*"

"Too bad, missie. We'll go back. Mebbe that little fellow can think of a way."

"No. Wait." She dug her fingers into her scalp. Her eyes blurred as panic set in, but slowly a picture began to form in her mind. She could see Captain Warren standing in front of the fireplace giving them final instructions. If the matter is urgent, he was saying, you should go to intelligence headquarters on Chestnut Street. Brick with white pillars.

"Chestnut Street," she whispered. "Brick. Pillars."

"Right, missie," he said, and they started off.

There were still people in the lighted streets, some walking, some riding in carriages. She clutched the side of the gig and closed her eyes. She ought to thank this kind man but she had come to the limit of her strength. Her legs were useless, her head felt as if it was separating from her body, but she must endure for a few moments more. Find enough voice to utter five words: "Ross. New York. Camden Road."

The horse slowed and stopped. "Seems they're working late at headquarters," John Corning muttered. She opened her eyes and stared. He was right. Lights shone from every window. He tied the horse to a hitching post and lifted her down. "I'll carry you to the door and make sure you're let in. Then I'll be off." Holding her carefully, he knocked on the door. It was opened by a young officer. He looked at them, a burly man in workman's clothes and a disheveled girl covered with a grimy blanket.

"Good evening," he said. "May I—er—be of assistance?"

"Yes, sir," Corning said. "This lady has news of an escaped British spy. She wants to speak to the person in charge here."

The officer looked startled. "She has news of—" he opened the door wider. "Come in, please."

"Just the young lady. I brought her across the river. She's had a real bad night, can't walk. Good luck, missie," he said and disappeared.

The young officer wasted no time. He picked her up and carried her down a long hall. Opened a door. "Major," he said. "This young lady just arrived. She says she has news of Mason Ross."

The room was filled with officers, now on their feet and staring at her. "Good God, it's Louisa Loring," one of them said. "I know her, she's the girl Haddam reported missing." He took her from the young officer and lowered her into a chair. "Major, quick. The brandy." A glass was placed in her shaking hand.

The fiery liquid burned her throat but it revived her enough to speak. "Mason Ross … forced me to cross with him … Camden Road … our horse is old …" Her voice failed.

For a few seconds, no one spoke. Then the tall man who had given her brandy raised his hand.

"Attention, everyone. If we act fast, we have a chance to catch him. Carstairs, you go to the barracks and organize a dozen armed troopers. Hanson will see to the horses." He stopped as a man she knew, Captain Warren, stepped forward.

"Major, I want to lead the chase. Ross will be armed. He'll tell convincing lies. From what I know of him he won't give in without a fight."

The tall man nodded. "Request granted. We'll regroup in the front hall." As the room emptied, he turned to her. "Mason Ross was escaping after an unsuccessful attempt to kill General Washington. You've given us a way to stop him. Well done, Miss Loring. We'll talk more tomorrow. I'll have a carriage take you home." Then he too was gone.

She grasped the arms of the chair and lay back. Ross might have left the road and hidden himself in a village. There might be a confrontation with more blood shed. As yet, nothing was certain.

She let go of the chair arms and closed her eyes. It was hard to believe that she had managed to stay alive, do her part, and was now safe in this warm room. It was too much of an effort to move, but her mind wandered back to the hot July afternoon when a shy untested girl arrived at a ruined city and house. Six months of adversity had changed her, had given her the resilience to survive a terrifying experience.

A log fell in the fireplace. The room was growing

cool. Soon the carriage would come to take her home. She took a deep breath. The ordeal was over, but it seemed that being so close to death had given her a sense that from now on each day should be lived to the full, that God had spared her for a purpose. Looking ahead, there would be more dangers in a country torn apart by divisions, but Nat would be with her. He was strong and resourceful. Together they could face an unpredictable future with renewed confidence and with courage.

★ ★ ★

CHAPTER THIRTY-FIVE

January 18, 1779 *Late the same night*

At nine o'clock there were few travelers on the Camden Road and they were easily identified. As the horse plodded forward, Mason Ross loosened the reins and began to assess his failed operation. Killing Washington had always been a gamble, but all his careful planning had gone wrong. It was galling to realize that someone had outed him and set a trap. Pottle had never appeared, and the two men he shot by the chaise had clearly been given orders to prevent him from escaping.

Dangerous situations required dangerous measures, why he had made the hasty decision to go to the Lorings and switch to their gig. Pretty Miss Loring had been his favorite among the girls, but to be safe he had no choice but to take her with him. It was unlikely that she would be picked up before the cold killed her. Until now, Ross had always been able to separate himself from actual violence. Her death was regrettable, but he must put it behind him. Banish it from his mind.

As he passed through a darkened hamlet, he tried to look ahead. This could be a serious setback to his career, but he was well able to justify the sudden departure. Convince headquarters that he had accomplished a great deal. It was their unwarranted orders to eliminate a useless network that had caused him this frustration, but all was not lost. He had escaped capture. A small fortune in gold was tucked under his feet. He had valuable skills. He could start over.

Open fields were changing to a dense stretch of woods. In the distance, a wolf howled and was answered by others in the pack. An eerie sound. He frowned and tightened the reins. After several hours on the road, the old horse was slowing. When they reached the next tavern, he would stop and sell the animal. Pay for a room and stay out of sight until the next stage to New York came along. To avoid notice, he would travel under a false name. Develop a severe cough to discourage conversation.

Ross was working out his options when he heard horses coming up behind him. A number of horses, hooves pounding heavily on the hard road. An ominous sound. He straightened, every sense alert. Seconds later the riders swept by and surrounded the gig. Not a bunch of ragtag highwaymen. These men wore military uniforms and carried muskets.

"Hell and damnation," Ross muttered. This shouldn't be happening, but he had been in tight places before. The pistol was useless, so a strong verbal attack would be his best weapon. He kicked the bag of gold farther under the seat and leaned out.

"Halting private citizens on this highway is against the law," Ross called in a firm voice. "I must proceed without delay to Bordentown. My father is ill and I must see him before he dies."

A trooper answered. "Get out. If you reach for a weapon, you'll be shot."

The voice had authority but he didn't move. "You have no right to give me orders," he snapped. "My name is Henry Farwell and I have no weapons. For my father's sake, I must be on my way—"

"Lieutenant, pull him out and search the gig."

There was no way to escape. Cursing silently,

Ross climbed down. Threw his pistol into a pile of dirty snow and stood to one side as a trooper dismounted and got into the gig, dragged out the heavy bag from under the seat and opened it.

"He's carrying gold, Captain. It's him for sure."

A trooper moved forward. His horse was stamping, flanks steaming. He raised his hand. "Mason Ross, my orders are to return you to Philadelphia where you will be charged with criminal activities against General Washington and the Continental Army. You will be interrogated and then tried in a court of law."

"What's this?" He shook his head. "Arrest me? This is an outrage. Save your unwarranted threats for Mason Ross, whoever he may be—"

"Enough lies. Lieutenant, you'll be driving the gig. Say nothing if Ross tries to get information from you."

"Understood, Captain." Roughly, the young lieutenant tied his hands together and pushed him onto the seat. The gig turned and the cavalcade started back to the city. Ross gritted his teeth to hold back a surge of rage. With a faster horse, he might have reached the next tavern. Reached safety while the troopers pounded down the road in a futile chase. But hindsight was not productive. He must keep a cool head. Focus on the best way to extricate himself from trouble. "Lieutenant," he began. "Surely you can see you have no right to treat a respectable citizen like a criminal. It is reprehensible. What's more, it is my legal right to know where you are taking me. To be given information."

The young officer was silent.

After a moment, Ross turned onto his side; it was difficult to be comfortable with hands tied behind his back. By now Pottle must have been caught and grilled. The little weasel would try to save his own skin by shifting blame. He could denounce Pottle as a demented rogue who had organized the attack on General Washington and tried without success to involve him in the plot. Tricky, but after a few hours of sleep he would be ready to take on whatever charges were thrown at him.

It was growing colder outside and he stamped his legs to warm them. According to the trooper, he was to be tried in a court of law. If so, he could assert his rights. Hire a lawyer.

The moon was casting a pattern of shadows over the highway. Ross stared out at the troopers riding beside him. This was only a temporary setback. He would not be facing a British court with a seasoned judge and jury. No doubt his accusers would be untrained colonels who would find it hard to produce creditable evidence and even more difficult to match wits with him. Then, with no grounds to hold him, he would hire another chaise, retrieve his gold, and set out once more for New York.

★★★

CHAPTER THIRTY-SIX

January 19, 1779

It was after midnight when the posse of troopers clattered through the streets and arrived back at headquarters. The front door opened and orderlies ran out to hold the steaming horses. Lieutenant Carstairs and another trooper escorted a protesting Ross into the house. Andrew dismounted and followed them into the hall.

Tallmadge was there, waiting. As they came in, his worried face lightened. "You're back. Carstairs, take the prisoner up to the back rooms. See that he is given bread and water and is well guarded." He turned to Andrew. "Come," he said and marched him down the hall to the library. Went to a cupboard and pulled out the half-empty bottle of brandy. "Drink up. You deserve it."

Andrew sat down and emptied the glass in a gulp. He was cold and stiff but the brandy began to warm him. He handed Tallmadge a canvas bag.

"Ross's gold."

"Heavy. He must have been doing valuable work for the British. This can be used as evidence against him." He went to the big desk, opened a drawer, locked up the bag, then sat down. The expression on his face was one of deep relief. "You caught up with him, but what took you so long?"

"Ross's horse, that is, the Loring horse, was tired and slow."

"How far had they gone?"

"Just past Jenkintown."

"Did he put up any resistance?"

"No fighting, but he spun a convincing tale of a respectable citizen going to his dying father in Bordentown. Outraged at being stopped on the highway. I gave him a speech about committing crimes and had him tied up. He's still ranting about how badly he's being treated."

"That tune may change if one of the men he wounded dies. The doctors say the Life Guard and two of the soldiers are doing well. The third is in a bad way. The doctors are doing their best to save him." He leaned back and sighed. "It's late. We'll meet tomorrow and decide what to do with Ross, whether to interrogate him ourselves first or arrange for a court martial."

Andrew poured himself more brandy and shook his head to clear it. "I'm not sure we should wait," he said slowly, feeling his way. "We should never underestimate Ross's ability to lie himself out of trouble. Except for Louisa Loring, he'd be on his way to New York. Now he's acting like a wrongfully detained citizen, but he has influential friends. People will find it hard to believe he has deceived them. He'll likely hire a lawyer who could drag the process out for weeks, maybe months." He shook his head again. "I think we should confront him tonight. Try to get a full confession before he has time to act and we're caught in a long legal battle."

Tallmadge said nothing. He seemed to be assessing this request. After a moment he nodded. "You have a point, Let me consider," he said and began to drum his fingers on the desk. "Worth a try," he said at last. "There's a drawing room we seldom use. Impressive, with fine furniture and mirrors. I can round up several aides and have them put on dress uniforms. Show Ross he's not dealing with lesser ranks who might be fooled by his eloquence."

Andrew narrowed his eyes. "That might work. He

won't be expecting an interrogation so soon. You can accuse him of plotting to kill Washington. Then you could ask him about his orders to kill off everyone in my old network. Two were murdered and one was poisoned."

Tallmadge stopped drumming and folded his hands. He looked at Andrew. "If this was the usual situation, I would lead off, but this is unusual. What's more, you have the facts needed to make a valid case against him. You've had no legal training, true, but you've proved that you have ability. I think you should go first. If that fails, I'll take over."

Andrew was silent. This was not what he was expecting, but he had persuaded Tallmadge to act tonight. It would be difficult to refuse this request—and he had another incentive. For months Ross had hurt his people and remained in hiding. At last there would be a chance to confront him face to face. Try to deflect his lies.

Tallmadge was waiting. Andrew drew in his breath and raised his right hand. "Major, I'm no lawyer. but when I think of what Mason Ross has done—believe me, I'll do my damndest to take him down."

"Right. Decision made." Tallmadge looked at his watch and stood up. "It's one o'clock. I'll need an hour to organize. There's a room upstairs where you can eat and rest. At two o'clock, I'll issue orders to have Ross waked if he's sleeping and brought to the drawing room."

Orders were issued and carried out. A fire was lit in the drawing room, tall wax candles were placed, and by two o'clock in the morning, the scene was set. Four aides in full dress uniforms were lined up in front of the marble fireplace. Andrew stood with them, still wearing the uniform he had put on that morning. His neck muscles were tight, his breathing was shallow, and he had a sinking feeling that Tallmadge would have been able to act with far more authority than he could.

The atmosphere in the room was tense as they waited. At last the door to the hall opened and Ross appeared, flanked by two soldiers. His clothes were rumpled but his hands were loose. He looked around, raised his eyebrows, then cleared his throat.

"I trust that someone will tell me why a respected citizen was illegally stopped on the highway, returned to the city, and subjected to extremely harsh treatment. There must be a reason, but no one has extended me the courtesy of an explanation." His voice was calm and steady. He was reverting to his wronged and innocent victim tactic.

Tallmadge moved forward. "Major Tallmadge of General Washington's intelligence service," he said curtly. "I have requested that Captain Warren start this investigation."

Andrew placed himself squarely in front of Ross. Seen up close under the glow from the candles, Ross was a good-looking young man, Nothing villainous about him. It was easy to see how he had infiltrated society and was a trusted employee.

The two men stared, sizing the other up. Andrew kept his face impassive. "Mason Ross," he began, choosing his words carefully. "On the tenth of August last, your hireling Ralph Pottle, also known as Mr. Brown, broke into Jonathan Merrill's house on Elfreth's Alley. Pottle strangled Merrill in his bed and stole a list naming members of a patriot network. Since then, he has killed two others in this network and poisoned a third. What have you to say?"

Ross's annoyed expression changed to one of exasperation. "Nonsense. Who is this Pottle person? I know nothing of him."

"We have evidence to the contrary. Ralph Pottle is now our prisoner. He has given us precise details of your efforts to eliminate the network."

"Again, this man sounds like a rogue out to cover

his own misdeeds. We know how misleading that can be. I repeat, I know nothing of him."

"Denial noted." He raised his voice. "Mason Ross, at three o'clock yesterday afternoon, you and Raph Pottle attempted to assassinate General George Washington when he met with painter Charles Peale on Lombard Street. The attempt failed. You abandoned Pottle and tried to escape to New York."

Ross shook his head. "Assassinate General Washington? Lies. All lies. This Pottle, whoever he is, has concocted another vicious story to hide his own actions. The man is certifiably mad. I insist that you produce reliable evidence and end this highly illegal interrogation."

Andrew hesitated. His effort to crack the other's defense using Pottle wasn't effective. He must do better. He narrowed his eyes.

"To continue, large amounts of gold were brought to you by courier from New York at the end of every month. It was packed with tins of tea and placed under a bridge outside the city. Late Tuesday night, you rode out and collected it. You were followed to your boarding house. Yesterday morning a servant there saw you packing. He learned that you had hired a chaise from Johnson's Livery and would pick it up at two o'clock, Which, in fact, you did."

Ross's exasperated expression didn't change. No tell-tale vein throbbed in his forehead. No eyelid twitched. He shrugged his shoulders. "I'm not aware of any law that forbids me to receive gold. Or makes it a crime to hire a chaise and leave town. I've heard that William White is a competent lawyer. If you persist in making false accusations, I will ask him to represent me in court."

An officer behind them coughed. Andrew could sense mounting anxiety. Like the parry and thrust of sword play, he had attempted to draw blood, but Mason Ross was all too convincing. The man had better verbal skills and was fighting for his life.

Taking a deep breath, Andrew thrust his hands into his pockets. "Sir, why were you sitting in a chaise on Pine Street? For what reason? I can understand your need to avoid arrest, but when you tried to escape you shot two soldiers. A magistrate and others on the street witnessed the shooting and can identify you. Let me be clear. If one of those soldiers dies, you will be charged with murder."

Ross looked surprised. "Those men were soldiers? They weren't in uniform. They attempted to hold my horse and I assumed they were attacking me. I acted in self-defense which a fair judge would take into account."

He adjusted his crumpled neckcloth, then folded his hands. "I don't ask for an apology. Return my gold and I will leave the city." He looked around as if to enlist support, the confident expression of a man who had done no wrong.

It was a brazen attempt to intimidate his captors. Andrew clenched his fists. He was facing defeat, but before Tallmadge stepped in he had one final chance. One last card he could play. He stiffened his shoulders and spoke slowly.

"After shooting two soldiers, you went to the Loring house on Fourth Street. You exchanged your chaise for their horse and gig. You abducted Miss Loring and took her across the river. Abduction is a serious crime with severe consequences."

Ross lifted his eyebrows again. "Abduct Miss Loring? This is becoming a farce as dramatic as any at the Apollo Theater. I'm acquainted with Miss Loring, but I haven't seen her for days."

At last, the lie that could bring him down. Andrew crossed his arms over his chest. He looked Ross in the eye. "Not a farce, sir. You left Miss Loring by the side of the road where she might have died of cold. A cruel and heartless act. It may surprise you to hear that she was able to walk to the nearest house, cross back, and get herself to headquarters. She is safe, and she is prepared to testify against you. Tonight, if necessary."

It was a damning piece of evidence. Ross opened his mouth. He started to speak, then stopped.

Andrew drew himself up. He raised his hand. "Mason Ross, you have done your best to avoid conviction, but you cannot undo the blunder you made when you abducted Miss Loring. You will be tried as a British spy in an established court of law. I think you know what happens to spies when they are finally caught and pronounced guilty."

The room was silent. Andrew waited, every sense alert to counter a new strategy, but Ross said nothing. He appeared to be deep in thought. Finally he spoke. His mouth was set in a tight little smile. "Captain, I am not a hardened criminal and I detest violence. I received orders from Sir Henry Clinton to come to Philadelphia, but some time ago I decided that when that mandate was finished, I would no longer be part of the unsavory spying game." He paused and shook his head. "I started life with nothing and I wished to become respected and rich. I let ambition cloud my judgment. I deeply regret any harm I may have done, deeply regret it, and now I ask for your understanding."

Andrew didn't move. An emotional plea for mercy, but if events had gone the other way, his body would be lying in a ditch or floating down the river. This talk of regrets was just another lie, and Mason Ross had finally been exposed as an arrogant and conniving rogue.

"I understand this, Ross," he said in a low voice. "You came into this room a common prisoner. You leave a prisoner. That's all." He turned and went back to the others. Ross, head bowed, was taken by his guards to the door.

For a moment no one moved. Then Tallmadge spoke to his aides. "A successful interrogation. Your presence was appreciated. Stand down and get some sleep."

It was now a little before three and once again Tallmadge and Andrew sat facing each other in the library. Tallmadge looked at Andrew. "You won in the end, but the fellow was extremely convincing. It was the threat of sending for Miss Loring that finally broke his nerve."

"At last. I was running out of ammunition."

"Well, most spies are clever actors. That's why they are so dangerous. Speaking of Miss Loring, she is a brave girl who did us a great service."

Andrew nodded. "She did. Without her help, Ross would be closer to New York by now, not locked in a room upstairs. What will happen to him now?"

"Hard to say, but he's no longer an asset to the British. There may be a prisoner exchange. All the same, it was too close a call. I've said it before and I'll say it again, lose our general and we lose the war. That means we must be better prepared for the next episode. Hard when our internal politics is more dangerous than the British.

Andrew said nothing. Exhaustion was setting in and he wanted to go home.

Tallmadge cleared his throat. "It's late, but before you leave there's something else I want to discuss with you."

Andrew suppressed a groan. Tallmadge leaned forward. "It's this, my friend. It turns out that my decision to give you heavy responsibilities was well justified. Good intelligence is crucial and you've done well. With that in mind, I'm planning to add to my staff in Middletown, where your experience in the undercover world would be extremely useful." He paused. "If this offer suits you, it would mean leaving New York and joining us as soon as possible. I hope you will consider making the change."

Andrew's head jerked back. He could hardly believe what he was hearing. Leave his detested undercover work? Move to Middletown and be with men he deeply respected? He let out his breath and tried to steady his voice.

"No need to consider," he said quickly. "None at all. There's nothing I'd like better."

"Good," Tallmadge said. He got to his feet. "We'll meet tomorrow and settle details. Now I should go up and check on our prisoners. A carriage will take you home." He paused at the door. "A long day and night, Warren. A time neither of us will ever forget," he said softly and went out.

Andrew stayed seated in the chair; it was hard to wrap his mind around the unexpected change in his life. This morning, before Jethro arrived to say that Ross was packing, failure had seemed inevitable. Now there were new opportunities. A chance to improve networks. Allocate resources. And at last it would be safe to contact his family. Let them know he was alive.

He closed his eyes and thought about Sarah, lovely Sarah. He would go home and sleep for a few hours. Then he would get up and go to her. Hold her close, kiss her and stroke her hair. Tell her how much he loved her and that they need not wait any longer to be married. The wives of officers often stayed with their husbands, even at Valley Forge. The General and Mrs. Washington would welcome the arrival of Sarah in Middletown. The General might even try to make use of her. Marriage to strong-willed Sarah would be challenging, but he couldn't imagine life without her.

He opened his eyes and stretched his cramped and aching legs. Last July, he had gone to Tallmadge determined to end undercover work and rejoin his regiment. That hadn't happened. Events had tested his ability nearly to the breaking point, but survival had given him confidence. Now he was ready to move forward and, with Sarah, play a part in winning the war and then help to form the thirteen stand-alone states into a new and productive "we stand together" nation.

★★★

CHAPTER THIRTY-SEVEN

January 26, 1779 *A week later*

The city was once again enduring bitter cold and snow. Months would pass before there would be signs of spring and warmth in the sun. But the Loring household on Fourth Street was experiencing profound elation and relief. Mason Ross and his hired killer had been caught and were no longer a threat.

For Louisa, it was as if she had emerged from a dark cave and could lift her face to the light. Her love for Nat gave her great joy. Her father was showing some improvement—he could eat solid food and hold a book. Will might soon come home, and at last she was able to be open with Cousin Molly with thanks for her endless and unquestioning kindness.

To celebrate their new freedom, Louisa had invited three guests for tea. Now, at four o'clock in the afternoon, she sat in the dining room wearing a favorite blue dress that matched her eyes. After spending three days in bed following her ordeal, she was well again except for a nasty little cough.

Feeling pleased, she looked around the room. Earlier, she had gone out and cut bits of greenery to decorate the mantlepiece. A cake and cookies were arranged on the best plates. Mamma would have approved of her efforts.

Nat was a few minutes early. He walked in and gave her a loving hug. "A new client came in today." He glanced at the table. "A feast. You and Jessie have been busy."

She returned his hug. "We used the last of the flour and butter. We'll be on rations for a while. Go on up. Father will be glad to see you."

Sarah was the next to arrive, buoyant and pretty in a green dress that set off her auburn hair. She blew Louisa a kiss. "A real party! I gave Andrew the message. I hope he won't be delayed."

But as Nat returned, Andrew walked in. "Sorry if I'm late, Miss Louisa."

"Welcome. You're not late."

"Good, and before we sit down, I'd like to make a short presentation."

"A presentation?"

"You'll see. Come in, Jessie," he called.

The door to the kitchen opened and Jessie appeared. She was leading young Jethro, neatly dressed in a suit.

Andrew stepped forward. "Jessie, we owe you and your community thanks for helping to prevent an attack on General Washington. Jethro, last week you performed a notable service. As a token of our appreciation, I am pleased to give you this reward."

Jessie gave Jethro a little push and Andrew handed him a gold coin. Jethro grinned. "Thank you, sir. I thank you very much." Everyone clapped. He ducked back to Jessie and they returned to the kitchen.

Louisa smiled. "A happy boy. Now, if you'll all sit down, I'll pour the tea."

Chairs scraped as they settled themselves. Andrew took a seat next to Sarah. Nat handed cups, and Sarah passed a plate after helping herself to a small cookie.

"Oh my goodness," she said. "I've just come from a sewing bee at Mrs. Thompson's. All the talk was about

Mason Ross. His employer John Holker is in shock. No one can understand how on earth the man managed to deceive us all for so long. Mrs. Gurney said she will never trust her judgment again." She paused. "Andrew, you've been questioning him. What can you tell us?"

Andrew put down his cup. "Well, it's hard to see into another person's mind, but I gather he started life in an English back street with nothing. He had a good brain, he acquired accounting skills, and was also skillful at spinning convincing lies. Now he's saying that he wants to leave spying and lead a different life. He's blaming others for his downfall, but it's clear that he has always been motivated by wanting to make money. Big money, like a reward for killing General Washington. He might have escaped except for you, Louisa. In any case, he now has to pay the price for his crimes. In the end, it may be up to General Washington to decide on a sentence."

For a moment no one spoke. Then Louisa coughed. "We're here to enjoy ourselves, so no more talk about Mason Ross." She took another sip of tea and looked at Andrew. "Last July, when we came back from Braintree, I'd never met you or Sarah or Nat. The night you came to tell us that my father was in trouble, I thought you were the most arrogant, unpleasant man I'd ever met. You barked out orders like a drill sergeant."

Andrew grinned. "Well, I wasn't impressed by you. Flighty and spoiled—"

Sarah broke in. "Louisa, you didn't dislike him half as much as I did. For a long time, I couldn't stand him. Now I don't want to let him out of my sight, but that's about to change. A wedding will take place. He'll go back to New York to find a replacement, then he's to join Major Tallmadge's staff in Middletown."

"Oh, Andrew," Louisa said. "You'll be with Major Tallmadge and General Washington in Middletown? I'm delighted."

"Congratulations," Nat added. "A well-deserved

promotion."

"Better than going around dressed like a dirty peddler. Speaking of weddings, I hear you and Miss Louisa are to be married."

"We are." Nat smiled. "When we first met I thought she was like a princess in a fairy tale. I never imagined that we could be good friends, let alone marry."

Louisa touched his hand. "Like you two, our feelings finally changed. We're so happy, and Nat has been asked by a committee in Congress to help establish a workable court system. Rewrite laws when necessary."

Sarah clapped her hands. "What an achievement! Louisa, have you set a date for the wedding?"

"Not yet. What about you?"

"I want to be married by my father at the farm, and now we don't have to wait until the end of the war." She rolled her eyes. "You may not have heard, but there's a rumor going around that Andrew is marrying me for my money, that he would never feel comfortable living in my big house. The truth is that he comes from a well-off Boston family and grew up with far more wealth than I ever had."

Louisa shook her head. "I hadn't heard, but how truly ridiculous. It's amazing what some people will say and others will believe." She lifted the teapot. "More tea, anyone? Sarah, I understand about the farm, but people will be expecting a big event in Christ Church with bridesmaids and a large reception to follow. Like Betsy Shippen's."

"They can expect all they like. I'm sure that's what Peggy wants, but her father is still against the marriage and as we all know General Arnold is facing a court martial. He's in serious trouble and there will be days of tantrums and tears."

"I know, and I feel sorry for Peggy. We had our differences, big ones, but it's hard to be so pretty, so intelligent—and she's so set on having her own way."

Sarah rolled her eyes again. "You're being kind, but she and General Arnold are a strange pair. Frankly, I don't predict a good future for them."

Louisa shook her head again. "It's difficult to predict the future for any of us, but we are friends who will help each other whatever comes. What's more, all four of us have found love—and we've all been involved with spies."

"Lovers *and* spies," Sarah echoed. "How true. You and I—we have Nat and Andrew and we've both received letters of thanks from General Washington for helping to catch spies."

The two men looked at each other. "Watch out for these formidable ladies," Andrew said. "Who knows what they'll do next?"

Louisa smiled. "Yes, watch out for us, but on a more serious note I'm beginning to wonder if coming generations will wonder what it was like to live the way we do—that is, to exist in such constant fear and uncertainty."

Sarah shrugged her shoulders. "They'd probably laugh at our clothes and think we were very quaint.

Andrew frowned. "Perhaps, but if we gain independence, we must hope that those generations will value it and fight to keep it. Forming a government means creating a solid foundation. Electing capable men to office. Preventing attacks from foreign powers. Lessening the deep divisions among us."

Nat nodded. "And making laws that cannot be broken by an ambitious tyrant. There will always be that threat. We have to establish ways to remove such a person from power. It won't be easy."

For a moment no one spoke. Then Louisa coughed. "You're right. It won't be easy, but we want people to remember that we were the daring ones, the ones who faced great hardship and fears about the future."

Andrew looked at her. "The daring ones. Well

said, Louisa. I think this calls for a toast. It ought to be champagne but tea will have to do."

The four looked at each other. Sarah spoke first. "To winning the war and gaining peace."

Nat was next. "To liberty and to those who value it."

Andrew followed. "To those who lost their lives in battle so that others might live. Like my cousin Joseph Warren."

Louisa hesitated. Then she picked up her cup and took a deep breath. "With God's help and with hope in my heart, I drink to a new nation that will prosper and endure forever."

The four got to their feet. They raised their teacups. "To a new nation," they said in unison. "To a new nation that will prosper and endure forever."

THE END

ACKNOWLEDGMENTS

It takes the proverbial village to move a book from a gleam in the author's eye to completion. This is especially true after the author turns 100. As always, many people helped me along the way with advice, support, and encouragement. A special shoutout to my supportive children and Richard Buel, emeritus professor of American History at Wesleyan University. Much appreciation to Mary Guitar and Justina Everett for technical aid, and thanks to all the staff at Essex Meadows for their fine ongoing care.

ABOUT THE AUTHOR

Eugenia Lovett West (known as Jeannie) was born in Boston in 1923. She grew up in New Haven, where her father, the Reverend Sidney Lovett, was the much loved former chaplain at Yale. After attending Sarah Lawrence College, she worked for *Harper's Bazaar* and the American Red Cross. Then came marriage, four children, volunteer work, and freelancing for local newspapers. Her first novel, *The Ancestors Cry Out,* was published by Doubleday; it was followed by two mysteries, *Without Warning* and *Overkill,* published by St. Martin's Press, and a third, *Firewall,* published by SparkPress. An interest in history led to *Sarah's War* set in the American revolution, and then to *Lovers and Spies.* West lives in Essex, Connecticut and in Holderness, New Hampshire with her large extended family. Visit her website: www.eugenialovettwest.com

www.ingramcontent.com/pod-product-compliance
Lightning Source LLC
LaVergne TN
LVHW100520110826
845146LV00002B/719

* 9 7 9 8 2 1 8 4 4 6 9 5 6 *